BY DEATH POSSESSED

BY DEATH POSSESSED

Roger Ormerod

CHIVERS LARGE PRINT
BATH

British Library Cataloguing in Publication Data available

This Large Print edition published by Chivers Press, Bath, 2001.

Published by arrangement with the author.

U.K. Hardcover ISBN 0 7540 4613 3

Copyright © by Roger Ormerod 1988

Printed and bound in Great Britain by
BOOKCRAFT, Midsomer Norton, Somerset

CHAPTER ONE

I might have known he would be there, peering disdainfully over shoulders and strolling around with that rolling gait of his, as though to claim as much space as possible. My son. You wouldn't guess it, I hope, with that up-tilted little nose and the sneer he'd been experimenting with. Tatty, disorganized, contempt oozing from him; my son, Aleric: nineteen years of solid and inflexible loutishness. This was exactly the setting in which he excelled—an Antiques Road Show. There he could treat the excited throng to one undiluted dose of his practised disdain. Their precious possessions, which they'd brought to display to the experts, were nothing more than out-dated rubbish to him.

I tried not to catch his eye, but it never works. He spotted me before the door swung shut behind me, and pushed his way through.

'Hiya, Pop!' His little eyes fell on the package under my arm. 'You ain't brought The Picture! Never! You've got a cheek.'

The noise was appalling. The hall was large and echoing, and the swirling crowds made my head swim. For a moment I felt lost. Aleric always did that to me, denigrating everything I ever did. I didn't answer. Suddenly I felt ashamed at having brought

1

along The Picture.

It had possessed capitals ever since my marriage, my fault I suppose for having given it too much importance. But it was important to me. My father had passed it on, with the implied suggestion that his mother had painted it, though he hadn't seemed certain about that. It was twenty by sixteen inches, on canvas on stretchers, and in a rather poor frame. I hadn't even been certain whether to be proud of it. Certainly I liked to look at it, but was it really Grannie's work? The subject was a country cottage, early morning, the sun dappling the walls through the leaves of a tree. You could feel that sun on your cheek, and see the dapples moving to a slight breeze through the leaves. And it was mine, you see. The initials, an A and an F superimposed, could well have been my grandmother's. It was dated 1910, and she had been Angelina Foote at that time. I knew that, but not much more about it.

I stood there like a fool, suddenly convinced that I should turn about and retreat. But I was trapped. A man, dapper and placid in the chaos, touched my arm.

'A painting, is it? You want Dr Dennis, over there on the right.'

As Aleric at the same time told me his mother would be mad, me bringing The Painting, I was caught between the two speeches, not really registering either.

2

'Come on!' he said, grabbing my arm. 'This is gonna be great. Wait till you get an eyeful of this picture expert.'

I don't know why crowds part to allow his progress, but they always do. It's probably because he exudes the certainty that they will. There were protests and nasty remarks, aimed at me of course, and suddenly I was in a short queue, well towards the head of it, and when I looked round in apology all I saw were tentative smiles and nods. Already there was an air of expectancy, that here was a man of importance bearing, in now-torn newspaper, something special.

Aleric was no longer with me. Then I spotted him, large ears and tip-tilted nose reaching over a shoulder in the spectator group. (Where *had* he got that nose from?) I looked away quickly, and it was only then that my eyes fell on Dr Dennis. Dr Margaret Dennis, I learned later. I don't know what she was a doctor of, but the title clearly merited a suit: straight skirt, large-lapelled jacket with the shoulders cut wide, and the white shirt and stringy black tie of the almost obligatory uniform. But none of this hid the fact that she was a woman, every inch of her, out where she should go out, in where she should go in, every contour shouting out that there was a female body inside all that, yearning to get out. There was a feeling stirring inside me that I hadn't felt for years, and I realized she was enthralling me with an exposition on the various imitators of John Sell Cotman. Art is not a subject that has ever seized me with enthusiasm. As a professional photographer, my concern has always been for how things look. Was the photograph balanced, appealing, and did it make its point? There appeared to be rather more than that to art.

She was working at a small table with a couple of easels at her shoulder. To one side a TV camera was spying on the proceedings. I assumed they were recording everything for later editing and, suddenly seized by a fit of stage fright, I prayed that my bit would be cut.

Then I was into it before I was emotionally prepared, tearing at the wrapping, determined not to waste one second of the precious time of this splendid doctor of whatever it was. Numbly, I handed it over. The camera eye leered at me. It's strange that photographers so rarely experience the frightening side of the lens. I wondered how I would manage to register the correct amount of delight—or disappointment as appropriate—when the fatal decision was made on the value of The Painting.

'Well!' she said. 'What have we here?'

She placed it on one of the easels. Her voice, close to, had been a soft and liquid burr. Now I was hearing nothing of the

4

background din. There had been a momentary relaxation of her on-camera smile as her hazel eyes fell on my offering, a pucker of her delicately moulded lips, a blink, a nod. Then she'd recovered, standing back from the easel with one finger to her lips, and taking what seemed to me a devil of a time on the scrutiny.

'It's very dirty,' she observed at last. She swivelled her head at me. 'I bet it's been hanging in a living-room—and you smoke . . .'

I inclined my head, patting the pipe in my pocket. My mouth had gone dry, my teeth felt sore, and I didn't think my lips would unseal again. She nodded severely, and turned back to it.

'Of course, since he's become famous there have been dozens of copiers. Only six have survived, you know, so, from a rarity value alone, the prices have rocketed. He sold six before he died. That would be in 1917. He enlisted in the French army, a *poilu*, and was killed in the trenches. This is really a very good fake, though. Where did you get it?'

I coughed to clear my throat. 'Who?' I croaked.

'Pardon?'

'Who are you talking about?' I asked, shaking the hair out of my eyes.

'Frederick Ashe, of course: 1887 to 1917. British. Really post-Impressionist, but the

5

style is pure French Impressionism. This is remarkably good, I must say. The brush strokes have all the power and confidence of Frederick Ashe. Where did you get it?'

'My father,' I whispered. The way she was talking, I was beginning to feel like a crook. Fake indeed! 'From his mother.'

She turned and considered me with some severity. I realized she was only an inch short of me, which would make her five feet nine. Her make-up was subdued and perfect. Well, it would be, wouldn't it, she being an art expert. Behind her eyes she was making calculations, assessing my age, probably within a month of my true forty-one. They're good at ages, these people. She wouldn't need to carbon-date me.

'But that would make it . . .' Her voice faded away.

I could appreciate her difficulty. She had already hinted that this Frederick Ashe, of whom I'd never heard, had become collectable, and therefore worth forging, only in recent years, and here was I claiming it had been painted in my grandmother's days.

Abruptly she turned away, and snatched the canvas from the easel, turning it over, examining the deterioration to the back of the picture, fingering the wooden stretchers. What she discovered seemed to upset her.

'But of course,' she said to herself in exoneration, 'it's always possible to obtain a

6

canvas of the correct period. Your grandmother?' she threw at me.

I nodded. There seemed nothing to say.

She turned the canvas back, licked her finger, and wiped it across the lower right-hand corner. The superimposed initials and date appeared.

Ā 1910

'Not just a fake,' she said fiercely. 'A forgery. It's even got his signature. An F and an A overlapping. Nineteen-ten,' she said. 'He went to France in 1910.'

'So he painted it in England,' I suggested, helping her out.

'I can't believe that.'

'It's always looked very English to me.' I was feeling more relaxed, probably encouraged by her uncertainty. 'The cottage, I mean.'

'It must be a forgery. Well worth the effort—the last genuine Ashe fetched eighteen thousand at auction.'

At that I gulped. Then recovered. After all, it wasn't a Frederick Ashe, it was a Grannie Angelina.

'It's not F.A.,' I ventured, before she took it too far. 'And it can't be a forgery.'

'Why not?' she demanded.

'If the existing six genuine Frederick Ashes

7

were sold in Paris, and he didn't go there till 1910, it'd be a bit stupid to forge one and date it before he sold any abroad. You'd at least have the sense to date it around 1913, I'd have thought.'

She considered me again. I might look stupid, but I do like logic, and that seemed logical to me. Her eyebrows lifted delicately, not disturbing the smooth, high forehead. 'Very well.' She was brisk, turning back to the painting and attacking it with her licked thumb, her tongue flicking out vigorously. Portions of the original colours began to appear, and indeed it *had* become dirty. I resolved to treat it to a toothbrush and washing-up liquid when I got it home.

'They're his colours,' she declared. 'This yellow. Surely it's his yellow! You'd never be able to match . . . And the chairoscuro! This play of light on the wall! The shadows in the doorway—the luminosity! But it *must* be a Frederick Ashe. Oh dear Lord, a seventh! They'll go wild at Christie's.'

'It's not,' I said quietly, 'a Frederick Ashe.'

'What?' She didn't turn.

'It's not F.A. It's A.F.'

Then she swung round. 'What are you saying?'

I twisted my head and looked into the camera, making it a statement for posterity. 'I said it's not F.A., it's A.F. My grandmother. Angelina Foote.'

8

'Nonsense.'

I shrugged. I think I smiled. 'My father gave it to me. He was under the impression that his mother painted it.'

'Under the impression?'

'That's what he said.'

She took a deep breath. 'Have you got it insured?'

'No.'

'Then I'd advise you to do so. To a value of around twenty thousand pounds.'

It was at this point I was supposed to register shocked delight. I regret to say that I laughed. 'Gerraway,' I said. 'It's my grannie's.'

'It's a pity, then, you can't ask her,' she said, her voice acid. Who could blame her, being laughed at in front of the camera? 'I'll stake my reputation on the fact that it's a genuine Frederick Ashe.' She mentally added a number of years to my age. 'If she was alive, your grandmother would agree, though how she got hold of it . . .'

'Oh, but she is. Alive, I mean. Around ninety-five, but alive. Maybe I'll take your advice, and go and ask her.'

'You do that, Mr . . .'

'Hine,' I said. 'Tony Hine.'

'Very well, Mr Hine.' She reached into a shoulder bag, which had been sitting on the floor between the easels, and produced a small wallet, extracted a business card, and handed it to me. 'And when you've discovered the facts—the provenance, we call it—I'd be very pleased if you'd contact me again. Any time.'

I took it, and slid it into my jacket breast pocket, producing one of my own with the same two fingers.

'Thank you,' she said. 'A photographer? Hmm!' Was there disapproval there? She leaned closer. This was for my ear alone. 'Guard it with your life,' she whispered.

Then she was all teeth and encouragement for an old dear behind me, who was presenting a tightly-rolled canvas I could hear crackling as it was forcibly straightened out.

I looked round for Aleric. When I wanted him—pretty rarely, I must admit—he was never on hand. Now I did, but he'd gone. Dr Dennis had impressed me. Guard it with my life? She must have been certain that I was carrying a seventh, and unknown, Frederick Ashe. No doubt he'd painted dozens in his life, short as it had been, and apart from the known six the rest had been assumed to be lost. So perhaps I really was carrying something very valuable. Nah! It was Grannie's. How else could she have given it to my father? The art lady was mistaken, put it like that.

Nevertheless, I would have felt more comfortable with Aleric at my shoulder. All right, so he was moronic, obstinate and unpredictable, but he was six feet of bone and muscle and heavy boots and hard fists. You have to exploit what you have available, and heaven help us, my wife and I had been presented with this. So I would have liked to encourage him in a little exploitation of his abilities. Trust him to disappear.

Hugging the canvas close, now without wrapping because I'd been too confused to collect it up, I sidled towards the door. I'm usually inconspicuous. I vanish into backgrounds, an ability that can be useful to a photographer. It didn't help me then. A hand touched my shoulder and a hoarse voice said: 'Got a minute?'

I turned. He was a weasel of a man, smelling strongly of tobacco and something else less pleasant, draped in tattered cast-offs and with a battered cap over one ear.

'Not really,' I said.

'Five thousand,' he said. 'On the nail. Used fifties.'

I had never met anyone who spoke in terms of fifties, plural. And *used* fifties suggested a close acquaintance with such wonders.

'No,' I said.

'Six.'

'Sod off,' I said.

He shrugged, and melted into the crowds.

But he'd done something for me. Probably he was a man who followed these Antiques Road Shows around, pockets packed with

11

used fifties, in search of quick bargains. His offer indicated confidence in the abilities of Dr Dennis. He, to the tune of six thousand, was prepared to back her judgement. This disconcerted me.

A woman held open the door for me. Fresh evening air brushed my face. I smiled my thanks. She slid a card into my breast pocket, her fingers like claws, her eyes meeting mine with obdurate impersonality. 'Insurance,' she whispered hoarsely. 'Give me a ring. Any time.' She smelt of violets.

I nodded, and headed for my Mini, hoping it would start reasonably quickly. I wanted to get away from there, to think, to decide on my attitude. The impulse to take The Painting along for appraisal had been urgent. Somewhere in the back of my mind must have been lurking an uncertainty about the history of it, and the opportunity had presented itself. So why, you ask, hadn't I thought of going to ask my grandmother? Well, to tell you the truth, I hadn't visited her for over twenty years—not since, just before I married Evelyn, I drove her to Wiltshire to show her off to Grannie, and for some reason the two women had hated each other on sight. Grannie Angelina had at that time been over seventy, an age when the restraining of one's opinions had become an effort not worth making. She had expressed herself on my choice of a wife in precise terms, as though

Evelyn had not been in the same room. The journey back had been strained. The fact that Grannie turned out to be pretty accurate in her assessment didn't help at all. So I'd refrained from visiting her only from a sense of loyalty to Evelyn, but I'd refrained for too long. Now it would be embarrassing to visit, particularly if I used the painting as an excuse, thus indicating self-interest. Yet clearly such a visit had now become urgent and imperative.

All these things I intended to consider on the way home, but the time for that had disappeared when my car finally started. The garage had spoken about a new starter motor, but I really had to get a zoom lens for my Olympus, so . . . I'd discovered that I could get action by first striking the starter with a spanner, which entailed lying on my back in a dark car park—it *always* didn't start in the dark—and bashing away blindly.

When I got to my feet there was a tweedy gentleman with a tweedy moustache watching me with interest, his business card already in his fingers.

'Security,' he said. 'Give me a ring. Doors and windows. Direct alarm to the nearest cop-shop. Satisfaction guaranteed.' He nodded, and stood back as I climbed into the car. It started. He waved me goodbye.

Heavens, I thought, I couldn't *afford* to own a valuable painting. It was like winning a

13

Rolls-Royce in a raffle; you'd have to sell it in order to have enough money to run it. But I didn't own a valuable painting, did I! I owned the same old picture I always had, an Angelina Foote, worth nothing more than its sentimental value to me. But unfortunately . . . ah, there was the snag . . . unfortunately, the clever Dr Margaret Dennis had broadcast the general idea that I was the owner of a unique and previously unknown Frederick Ashe. If that hall had contained insurance touts, tatters and security buffs, then there was a good chance it had also had its share of crooks and ruffians, eyes and ears well open for the useful snatch.

I peered into the rearview mirror. Nothing was following me.

The canvas sat on the passenger's seat. It hadn't changed. All that had changed was my life, and that by the strange coincidence of the initials: F.A. and A.F. No, more than that . . . the coincidence of the matching style, if Grannie Angelina *had* painted the picture. Two coincidences were too much to accept. It had to be a Frederick Ashe. My scalp tingled. Around twenty thousand pounds sat on the seat beside me.

Then why wasn't I delighted, excited, panting to get home and share the joy of it?

Two reasons. The first was that I felt robbed, in a strange way. I would have to part with it. And if it was not Grannie's work, I'd

14

lost that too, the proper pride of family worth. The painting had been a visual indication that there had been, if only in the past, some small artistic ability lurking in my blood. Don't laugh. I was a photographer. What's artistic in that? you say. I'll think about it and let you know.

The second reason for my lack of enthusiasm was that I was uncertain of my reception when I got home. With Evelyn, you could never be sure.

My wife is a solicitor. She had just qualified when I first met her, and I admired her for the intellectual accomplishment which had brought it about. She was certainly not a beauty, but I saw something attractive in her puckered, mobile features, her huge blue eyes, and the flaming, hectic red hair she insisted was auburn. She laughed a lot in those days. Her face at such times achieved the most adorable shapes. I thought she had a sense of humour, but it was apparently only a reflection. I made a joke; she laughed. After a while I discovered she had no sense of humour at all. Or she deliberately acquired no sense of humour. After all, a solicitor is expected to be reasonably solemn. If a client said she wanted a divorce because her husband wore his jeans in bed, it would not be politic to burst into roars of laughter.

So now, Evelyn finds nothing to laugh at. She has also become a little pedantic. The law doesn't allow much freedom of deviation from specific meanings. Or tries not to. Evelyn began by allowing me no use of an incorrect word. Syntax was her god. After a while the area covered by the lack of freedom extended upwards and sideways, so that she came to expect no deviation from anything. Life was a pattern. A perfect and precise pattern. I was an extending stain that obliterated its complex line.

Naturally, she earned good money, the sort that had an overflow allowing it to grow and mature. I earned very little. A professional photographer these days has to specialize. With the modern automatic cameras, anybody can run off a spool of perfect wedding photos. So I have to look for something with less facility involved, and for the past two years I've had to look deeper and further.

This disparity in earning capacity, and thus in the provider stakes, has never been mentioned. But it has hung like a cloud around the house. I try to ignore it, laugh it away. But, as I've explained, my laughing is done alone.

When I got home, Aleric's motorcycle—her present to him on his last birthday—was propped in the drive. Its engine was bigger than the one in my Mini. I parked behind it. The house had no distinction: a detached residence in which we resided, with three bedrooms, living-room, dining-room, kitchen, and Evelyn's study. She worked evenings. Loved it. Aleric had the front door open before I reached the porch. He gave a mock little bow to the man bearing a fortune, and a lop-sided smile that was ruined by the tail-end of a sneer. I marched on through. She was in the living-room, as I guessed she would be. I stood in the doorway.

What impressed me was that she had nothing on her lap or in her hands. Always, she was reading something. Now I had her full attention. On the wall behind her there was a lighter patch on the Regency striped wallpaper where The Painting had lived. This was now under my arm.

'Darling,' she said, smiling her crumpled, encouraging smile, 'you own a Frederick Ashe! How splendid for you.'

I stood there. Aleric edged past me and went to stand by his mother's chair. He was all attention.

'It's not a Frederick Ashe,' I said. 'It's an Angelina Foote. There's just a wild coincidence in the initials.'

'Nonsense,' she said briskly, reminding me of Margaret Dennis for one second, before I clamped down on the memory. 'You've always been stupidly romantic. Your grandmother . . . didn't you tell me she came from a wealthy family? She was probably in Paris, you know the way they used to tour the

17

Continent. Around 1912. She'd be about nineteen. I'll bet she bought it somewhere along the left bank, for a hundred francs or so, precisely because of the initials. You have to be logical in these things, Tony.'

'You seem to know all the details.' I was playing for time.

'Of course I do. Aleric's told me every detail. Clever boy.'

Did I say she has no sense of humour? It's just that she doesn't recognize a joke when she makes one.

'We'll put it up for auction,' she decided. 'Sotheby's, I think.' She had never taken any interest in it, but it had become 'we' when it was a question of parting with it. 'Twenty thousand, possibly. You can get yourself a new car, and we'll have the room re-papered. Some decent clothes for you. How you can hope to impress . . .'

I didn't really take in the rest. My mind, prompted by that blank patch on the wall, was roaming the house. Now that there *was* a blank patch, it drew my attention to all the other things of mine that weren't within those walls. The answer came back: pretty well everything wasn't. Apart from a few clothes in the wash and a paperback or two, all I personally owned was either at my photo-lab in town or in the Mini. I'd been away for a few days at a factory in Maidstone, getting colour shots for a set of twenty-by-sixteens in

18

the boardroom, to remind the board members that work was performed beyond those four walls. So the floppy bag containing a few spare items of clothing, and my camera equipment, were still in the car. Nothing of note was in that house. The house itself was Evelyn's, in her name, bought with her own money. Considering the sneer on Aleric's face and that weird nose, I began to wonder whether in fact he was mine. Why else had Evelyn married me? And why in such a hurry? Perhaps that was what she'd found worth laughing at in those days.

Then suddenly my ambivalent thoughts about the painting flowed together and became one warm glow. It was mine. It was under my arm. It didn't matter who had painted it, nor whether it was worth a lot of money. I derived pleasure from looking at it. That pleasure would not be enhanced by the thought that it was valuable, nor reduced if Grannie had painted it. Rather the reverse. So I wanted no discussion about what was to be done with it. I would keep it. But not there, on that barren wall, where unfeeling eyes would rob it of its worth to me, and unspoken thoughts blame me for not realizing its possible worth in spending-money.

It was mine.

I didn't know whether she had finished her exposition on how the sale would be handled, and probably on the legal aspects of ownership. Perhaps I cut in without consideration. Certainly, I recall very clearly her startled expression and how very ugly it made her seem.

'Well,' I said. 'I'll be off, then.'

And I walked out of there.

CHAPTER TWO

It said a lot for our marriage that Evelyn didn't run after me and ask what the hell I thought I was doing. She knew very well, and she was not prepared to do anything about it. For too long we had been separate people living under the same roof.

I was aware that she stood at the dining-room window to watch me drive out of her life. Probably she would be wondering whether I might claim alimony from her, and what legal gambits she could toss beneath my flying feet. But that was where my artistic heritage came into play. I told you I'd think of something. My exit had a certain balanced pattern to it: it stated the truth in simple lines, it had design, it had composition. Until I reached the Mini, it also had dignity. Then once more the car let me down.

Nothing. Not a whimper from the starter motor. I saw her pale, expressionless face at the window. Even at that moment she failed to smile. Then something happened that added the final touch to the picture, produced the colour and the tone, the chiaroscuro. A Volvo Estate drew up at the drive entrance, Dr Margaret Dennis got out, and she called: 'Want any help?'

I think she must have guessed exactly what had happened. The Mini's door was open and the painting (now it was outside Evelyn's house it did not need the support of capitals) was clearly visible. I had brought it home; I was taking it away again.

'Want a lift?' she asked.

Clearly I could not sink to the indignity of crawling under the Mini with my magic spanner. I had only one choice.

'I'd be much obliged, if you'd give me time to unload.'

She not only gave it to me, she filled it in by helping. To Evelyn, the picture she was staring at must have changed. It crackled now, and sparkled with naked colour. I'd returned home to 5 Laurel Grove with the express intention of leaving again—and with a woman. At the window she made no move. She would be preparing the legal tangle with which she would bind me.

We stripped the Mini of all my possessions, and loaded them into the back of the Volvo, where they assumed a shameful insignificance. We went round and climbed in the front.

'Where to?' she asked.

'I've got a little place in town.' Did my voice sound right? 'A display window and my working lab. I thought I'd rig up a bed of sorts . . .'

'Sounds terrible.'

'I can't afford a hotel.'

'Of course not.'

Her conversation was colourless. She was allowing me to take the lead. I was the custodian of a Frederick Ashe, and she had to keep an eye on me. Commission loomed. It was necessary to remain in touch. And yet . . . there was something in her attitude that hadn't been there at the Road Show, something more than the casting off of an official cloak. She was relaxed with me. There was a light intimacy in her voice.

'I can do better than that,' she said. 'There's a place . . . it belongs to my firm. It's used for entertaining wealthy clients. A cottage. You'd like it. You'll be safe there.'

Safe? There it was again, the implication of danger.

'I can't let you go to any trouble.'

'I'm not allowing you out of my sight. I've got a proprietorial interest in you, my friend.' Then she laughed, a free and unforced liquid sound. 'There's the smell of money around. It always makes me slightly hysterical.'

'And practical.'

'I'm extremely practical. The appreciation

22

and assessment of art isn't an art in itself. It's a science. Very down-to-earth, I can assure you. We use scientific methods. It's very depressing. Contrast the artist's attitude to his work with ours! They'd weep if they knew. Sometimes I long to do wild things—forge a masterpiece, something like that. Wild, impulsive things.'

I'd just done a wild and impulsive thing myself, and at that moment I couldn't find anything in its favour. There was an emptiness, a choking feeling of irrevocable error. I couldn't see any distance into the future, not with optimism.

'Such as driving to Laurel Drive . . .'

'That! Exactly! It was an impulse. I wanted to see where the Frederick Ashe had hung.'

'Whether the house justified the honour?'

'Now you're being sarcastic.'

'This isn't the way into town.'

'Isn't it? Where does your grandmother live?'

I glanced at her, only then aware that she'd found time to change, and was now in jeans and a denim jacket. 'Wiltshire.'

'Excellent. It's on the way.'

'What is?'

'The cottage I mentioned. Where we're going. You said you intended to take the painting to your grandmother, and ask her about it. Now you haven't even got transport. So I'll have to take you. The cottage is in

23

Worcestershire. As I said, on the way.'

'Got it all worked out, haven't you?'

'I told you, I'm practical. I can even put it all down as business expenses.'

'Hmm!'

I was beginning to realize that leaving the Mini behind had been a mistake. Cranky and difficult though it was, it had given me independence. Now I was trapped. Talk about frying pans and fires! I'd become lumbered with another female of my wife's species: dogmatic, efficient, autocratic. Professional women! It would have been better if I'd asked her to stop the car, got out, and started walking into the night.

She was moving too fast for that to be a possibility. Her driving was a reflection of her personality, practical in that she pressed the correct things and turned the right ones, but there was an over-confidence in her expectations. Other vehicles were expected to do exactly what suited her. It seemed to work, though. We sliced the night apart, in the general direction of Worcestershire.

'Keep your eyes open for a sign saying Kidderminster,' she called out, racing through a crossroads.

'If you slowed a bit, I might have time.'

'So much to do. You can't imagine.'

Which was true; I had no idea of her intentions. All I wanted to do was settle somewhere, get something to eat, get some sleep, and think of some way I could find myself another car. I wasn't wildly happy about visiting Grannie with Margaret Dennis in tow. The odds were she'd have *me* in tow by the time we got there.

We took a corner too fast. She said: 'You missed it. This is the way. Only a couple more miles.' I sighed.

I had expected something remote and desolate. Hadn't she called it a cottage? Isolated it certainly was, but we drew up in front of a modern, semi-bungalow that later proved to be on two levels. When she'd parked, and we'd entered the building through a side door, we were on a wide balcony with an open stairway down to a large room that occupied the full width. She must have operated a switch inside the garage, because all the lights were on. A whole bank of curtains ran across the far wall, and I had to guess they covered a row of full-length windows.

She led the way down. 'Unload your stuff later,' she said. 'I'll get some coffee going, then we'll see what's in the deep-freeze.'

I was on edge, my nerves jumpy. For the whole of that evening I'd been in no position to control my own life. Even now there was uncertainty. I roamed the room. Paintings covered all available space on the three walls downstairs, and along the head of the stairs. Genuine oils and watercolours, I could see

25

that, and even I was able to detect they were copies. The original Constables, Turners and Monets, etc., were in National art galleries.

Above the clattering in the kitchen, I called through the open door: 'The paintings? Fakes, are they?'

'Copies. All of them.'

'Who did them?'

'Me.'

'The lot?'

She came in smiling, carrying a tray. 'I've put something in the oven. It'll keep us going. Yes, they're all mine.'

I sat on a padded stool, facing the low table. 'White, please,' I said. 'It's not a company house, is it? It's yours.'

'True.' Her eyes were dark with amusement. 'There isn't any company. I work on my own.'

'You lied to me.' I don't know why I'd assumed I could trust her, but the remark emerged with a tone of disappointment.

'Sorry about that.' She glanced away. 'I had to get you here.'

'The painting, not me.'

'You.'

'They come together,' I told her. 'One package.'

'I wanted both.'

We sipped her coffee. I produced my pipe, and gestured around. 'From what you said . . . I suppose you'd rather I didn't . . .' I indicated the paintings.

'Oh, those! Smoke by all means. They're rubbish. It's all I was ever capable of, when I was at art school. Copying. Any fool can copy.'

To me, that seemed to be a somewhat sweeping statement. I'd had enough time to realize the copies were excellent work. But I'm no expert, and felt I had no right to offer praise. I shrugged, which seemed to annoy her.

'Not fakes,' she said intensely, 'not forgeries. Copies.'

'It matters?'

She banged down her empty cup and got to her feet. 'Of course it damn well matters, Mr Tony Hine. You're not *that* blasted ignorant, I hope.'

But I was. Beyond her, where she stood with her feet straddled, her jet hair untidy and her high cheeks flushed, there was a copy of Monet's *Cart In The Snow*, which I recognized. I would have loved to own it, and it wouldn't have mattered to me that the brush had not been held in Monet's fingers. It would simply have been a constant pleasure to look at.

'I am, you know. Dead ignorant.' Then I lit my pipe. There's a time when you know you've touched flame to a fuse, and I sat and waited for the explosion. I needed information, you must have realized. There

27

was a question of whether my painting was a Frederick Ashe or an Angelina Foote. I needed to understand why it ought to matter to me, and why its value could fluctuate from around £20,000 to nil on the answer.

She began quietly enough, after a long stare at me to decide whether I was serious.

'Tony,' she said at last, 'I'm calling you Tony because this is going to be personal. I've never told anybody this before, because in the art world I've never met anyone so ignorant. But of course, you're a photographer.' She jutted her lower lip. It was a challenge.

'Take me to the original with my camera . . .' I was pointing at the Monet.

'It's in the Jeu de Paume in Paris.'

'. . . and I'll produce a colour print, same size, that's as good as that one on the wall.'

'Yes?' she demanded. 'Yes? Then listen to me, friend Tony. I've been involved with painting for thirty years. Yes, since I was eight. My father . . . well, never mind that. I started with copying. Every student does, and of course I went to art school. Three art schools: London, Paris and Prague. We copied. Until of course we progressed to our own work in our own styles. All except me. I went on copying. Don't think I haven't thought about this, over and over. Maybe I started copying too young. But the basic fact was that I couldn't paint for myself. There

28

wasn't anything I didn't know about colours, techniques, composition . . . but I couldn't *do* it. No artistic ability, you see. No flair and no imagination. I'd copied for too long. I had to look at a fixed picture, not at a scene or a model or a still life. As an artist I was a failure. Every art school rejected me.'

I got up and walked round the room, just in order not to look into her eyes. She continued as though I was still sitting there. I doubt she could see.

'There'd never been anything but art in my life, Tony. It was as though the world had cast me out. My father fetched me from Munich, where I'd drifted to, took me home, and treated me like a baby. He got me to understand in the end, hammered it into me, that it didn't have to be a door that'd slammed in my face, it could be a door that had opened. He persuaded me to study art as an academic subject—the history, the techniques. And that was what I did.'

There she stopped. I didn't believe she had finished, only that she'd paused for some intimation that she had my interest. Standing in front of a Renoir, I said: 'You certainly succeeded in that; you got a doctorate.'

'Yes. You could say I succeeded. Because I had to, or there was nothing. For my doctorate, I specialized in forgeries and in the detection and exposure of forgeries. I became an expert on the composition of pigments used for the past few centuries, on techniques, brush strokes even, and the mediums used. And at that stage I realized something else. Can you guess what that was, Tony?'

I had drawn back a curtain and was looking out into the darkness. It was after midnight, but a few lights still sparkled in the distance, below my level. I was staring over an invisible valley. She was a career woman. There'd been no time for emotional interruptions. Sexual incidents, perhaps, but nothing that might have diverted her from her purpose. She was now going to tell me about accomplishment and involvement, about fulfilment. I swept the curtain shut and turned, not knowing what I could say. I smiled.

'I wouldn't care to guess.'

'I realized I was in an ideal situation and had all the abilities and knowledge to paint real forgeries, undetectable ones. Not quite copies of known works. Slight changes. A tree moved, or a colour change in a hat. That sort of thing. And d'you know what?'

'Tell me.'

'I couldn't do that, either. Just couldn't. Not because I wasn't capable of doing it. I knew I was. But because I knew I'd be degrading myself, and the original artist. Now wasn't that ridiculous, Tony? I'd at last found something I could do . . .'

'You'd already done—'

'. . . and I couldn't put a brush to the canvas. The laugh was . . .' Her voice faltered, but she hadn't tripped over laughter. 'The joke was on me. All my learning and studying and . . . and understanding, I suppose, stopped me. I knew how that artist had striven to develop his technique, how he'd starved to provide himself with materials, how he'd perfected his choice of colours . . . and there I was, prepared to pick up his whole‚ life of endeavour, and make some tawdry use of what had been his basic reason for living. And for what? Not for money.' She waved an arm blindly. 'I had what I needed. Not for fame or to fool the establishment. I was part of the establishment. So can you see why I couldn't do it? Can you, Tony?'

And there I was, caught, expected to produce a few words that in some way indicated an empathy with her point of view. She'd said she hadn't told this before. Did it matter to her that a virtual stranger, a philistine in her art world, should express an opinion? Perhaps it was because I was a stranger, and yet enough of a friend for it to matter.

'I can see that it had to be *his* hand holding the brush,' I ventured. 'Renoir's, Degas', Constable's. His. The first stroke of the brush and your hand would wither.'

'Superstition?' She pouted her disappointment.

'Not superstition. Sympathy and understanding.'

I waited. She stared at me with moist eyes, swallowing. I watched the smooth line of her throat moving.

'Didn't you put something in the oven?' I asked, and went to check.

I was alone, peering into her oven. She had put in a lasagne, and it was ready. Crisply ready. I looked round for oven gloves, and somewhere to put it down, and she was at my shoulder.

'Let me.'

She put it on a plate, and we started at it. Then she laughed.

'I'm starving,' she said. 'Let's try it.'

We sat facing each other across the kitchen table. She had put a bottle of hock in the fridge. The lasagne was too hot, the wine too cold. We ate, and between bites and swallows we chatted. Nothing important. My life, and my gradually escalating failure to achieve; hers and her growing prominence in the art world. World was the correct word. She travelled world-wide as an expert on forgeries. Her fees had bought this house and a small flat in London. She was already in sight of the culmination of a dream.

She was not a tidy person. She dumped the crockery and glassware in the sink for future attention, and said: 'Let's get our stuff out of the car, and I'll show you where you can sleep.'

This we did. As we returned from the garage and moved along the landing, she flung open a door. 'This is my room.' Flung open the next door. 'You can sleep here. Or in the other room, as you wish.'

I made no comment, simply walked into the second room, dumped my floppy bag and the camera holdall, and looked round. It was luxurious. She stood just inside the door. 'Bathroom over there. You can take a shower if you like, while I get to work on your canvas.'

It was under my left arm. I turned and looked at her. She raised her eyebrows delicately.

'Get to work?' I asked.

'You don't think I could sleep until I've at least cleaned it and taken some colour readings? Come on, Tony, I know what I'm doing. I'm not going to do it any harm.'

I handed it over. 'Where shall I find you?'

'Through the kitchen, the far door. Come down when you're ready.'

I had my shower, and felt much fresher, but my brain refused to respond. I couldn't take in the events of the day, analyse them, and produce a clear decision about my attitude. If it turned out that I was a fairly wealthy man, I still wouldn't be able to bear the thought of parting with my painting. So

33

I'd gained nothing, except perhaps a cleaner canvas. Certainly, I thought, as I dug out a nearly-clean shirt and a clean pair of Y-fronts, and covered them with my disreputable working clothes, it would be pleasant to buy a couple of new outfits, in order not to soil the seats of a new car. What I couldn't balance in my mind was the loss of the painting against a transient gain in affluence.

Her workroom was a brightly illuminated and windowless laboratory, all shadow-free light, as near white as I've ever seen produced artifically. She had microscopes and magnifiers, a chemical bench, spectroscopes and viewers. On the side bench lay my painting. It was clean. I couldn't remember it like that. It glowed. Colours I had never realized as being there were now revealed in their naked glory, and new detail set my eyes roving across it.

She straightened. 'What d'you think?'

'I'd intended to do it up with a toothbrush and washing-up liquid.'

She flinched. 'I was certain before. Now I'm dead certain. It's a Frederick Ashe, painted before he left this country. It could even be a painting of his own cottage. He was late to be using this style, you know. The French Impressionist movement lasted until the end of the century, but there he was, using the same fragmented colour techniques, the pure colours, the use of light, just as

34

they'd done. He sold only six in his life. He must have painted many more, and this is one of them. It'll cause great excitement . . .'

She stopped, probably aware of my reaction. Her implication had been that I would let it out of my hands to be gloated over by the pundits.

'I've never seen it looking so wonderful,' I compromised.

'I've analysed the yellow—'

'If what you say is true,' I cut in, 'that the Impressionists over there had had their day, then there must have been no end of painters, over in Britain too, who were picking up on the style. Hundreds. So apart from the initials, which I still say could be A.F. for my gran, there's nothing to tie it down to Frederick Ashe.'

This thought, more or less, had been tracking through my mind for some time, and I was determined to get it out. It seemed I'd insulted her.

'Nothing!' she cried. 'There's a dozen points. His impasto—that's the thickness and build-up of the paint. I've *seen* it, Tony, on his other known works. His use of the palette knife. Here and there, his use of a finger. The choice of colour. The yellow—I've had time to analyse that, not chemically, but with the spectroscope. It's cobalt yellow. Hardly known in England in 1910, but the French were using it. He was known to have

35

corresponded with Monet, who could have sent him pigment. When he went to Paris, Maurice Bellarmé was a close friend. *He* could have sent him pigment. And there's viridian green. Another pointer—'

Clearly, she was going to take some stopping. 'All right,' I said. 'Pax. You know your job. Other works, you said. Six, you've mentioned. Where're those?'

She stared blankly at me for a moment, then suddenly grinned. 'The great disbeliever! No, you can't very well go and see them, to compare. Two are in a private collection in this country. I haven't seen those. I *have* seen, and examined, the other four. In detail. It's my job, Tony. One in the Musée des Beaux-Arts in Rouen, one in the Lecomte Collection in Paris, one in the Staatsgalerie in Munich, one in the Metropolitan in New York. Quite a round trip, that would be.'

I grimaced. 'Look,' I said, 'I can understand your enthusiasm, but I've never been one for speculation. Tomorrow, if you're still prepared to do it, we can go and ask my grandmother. She'll know. She'd have been about seventeen when this was painted. She'll certainly know where it came from.'

'I can't wait to meet her.'

'So . . . if you don't mind . . . I'm very tired and I'd like to get some sleep.'

'If that's what you want,' she said

solemnly.

I nodded, the lock of hair flopping forward. 'Sorry—it is.'

'No need to apologize.'

'There might well have been.'

She turned away. 'I'll be here for some time. Might as well do a chemical analysis on that yellow.'

'And the green,' I suggested. 'Good night.'

But she was already absorbed with the painting.

CHAPTER THREE

In the back of my mind there was the vague recollection of a scandal involving my grandmother. My father told me about it, but at that time I was very young, and probably didn't understand. There had been, now I came to probe my memory, never any mention of my grandfather, though I had the impression his father was the reason Dad had left home. Why else had my own family been living in the Midlands, when my father's original home had been in Wiltshire?

These memories were returning to me whilst we were on the journey there. Margaret was not the sort of driver who encouraged conversation when she was behind the wheel of a car, and I'd decided she needed all her concentration to keep us on the road. Perhaps she had her own thoughts. She seemed tense and expectant, eager to get there. Certainly, she wasn't wasting any time.

'The ring-road's coming up,' she said suddenly. 'Do we take it, or straight on into town?'

It had been twenty years. There hadn't been a ring road last time. I had been hoping that my memory would pilot me to the house, but it was doing nothing. Too much had changed.

'Surely you know an address,' she said irritably, pulling into a lay-by. 'The name of a street, even.'

'It wasn't a street. Nothing towny like that. My impression is of isolation. Countrified. A large house. She was living with a companion. Grace or Gloria.'

'But the name was Hine?'

'Of course.'

'Of some importance?'

'They were grocers.' Not 'we' were. The 'they' had been automatic. 'My father's grandfather was the mayor.'

'Oh . . . lovely. Let's find a post office.'

She drove into town, parked with difficulty, found a post office, and we consulted a phone book. There it was: Hine A., Mandalay, Forster Grove.

'Mandalay?'

'Great grandfather was an officer in the Indian Army.'

'What an artistic background you do have, Tony.' Impatience was peeking the corners of her mouth.

'Let's go and find Forster Grove,' I said with dignity.

I recognized the Grove at once. The trees were thicker and taller than I recalled, and the roadway more narrow. The drive entrance-columns seemed closer together, and surely they had possessed gates. The drive was short, and the overhanging beeches dripped from morning rain, which we hadn't encountered on the journey.

'Looks a bit gloomy,' she commented.

'My memory's of dark rooms and depression. Silence. The companion looming like a ghost in the background. It wasn't a place I yearned to return to.'

'You're completely out of touch. Admit it. Your grandmother might have died, and you wouldn't know.'

So what did I say when the companion opened the door? 'Is my grandmother still alive?'

We were standing in the porch, staring at the stained-glass panel in the heavy front door. I had pressed the button in the frame, but we'd heard no sound. I pressed it again, and silently the door opened.

I recognized her at once, and with the

recognition there came the certainty of her name.

'Hello, Grace,' I said, trying to smile. 'It's me. Tony.'

'No need to keep on ringing. I'm not deaf, you know.'

My smile was difficult to hold, she'd changed so much. She had always been large and bulky, but now she was simply ungainly, distorting the shape of clothes that she'd probably possessed when I was last there. Her puckered face was coursed with lines, her cheeks sagging in wobbling dewlaps, her eyes sunken deeply into hollowed, dark sockets. All that was left was her resilience. She could be . . . how old? She had been their maid—a young and pretty girl—when my grandfather, Arthur Hine, had died. Heavens, that had been all of fifty years ago. It would make Grace at least seventy-five. How the time marched on! But for her it would have crawled leadenly. For all those years she'dhad no life except as a companion, and later almost a nurse, for my grandmother. Every bitter, lost year had carved its passing in her face.

I risked a social disaster. 'I wanted to see Grandmother.'

She sniffed. Her red nose indicated it was habitual. 'You'd better come in. A lot of good it'll do you, though. If she'll see you, she probably won't recognize you, and they've pretty well stripped the house.'

40

This last I didn't understand. We moved into the hall, with its patterned quarry tiles and its ancient hallstand. No, no hallstand, and the black old chest wasn't there either. The hall was wide and chilly, and smelt slightly damp. The staircase to the left was uncarpeted, though I couldn't remember whether it had been before. There had been changes. Surely Grannie Angelina hadn't had to resort to selling her antiques! The stair carpet had probably been priceless. I had always understood that Grandfather Arthur had died a wealthy man.

'I'll go and tell her,' said Grace, flinging open a door into what I recalled as a drawing-room. 'You'd better wait.'

Then she closed the door on us, and we were left alone to stare at each other.

'Stripped the place?' asked Margaret. 'She couldn't mean the bailiffs, surely?'

I shook my head. Certainly not. But this room, too, was more bare than I recalled it. I would have described it then as oppressively over-furnished, but now you could have played basketball in it.

'It wasn't so empty,' I admitted. 'And the ivy should have been cut back from the windows, that's why it's so dark. Grannie Angelina used to say it was better not to have direct sunlight on the furniture.'

'No sunlight, and not much furniture now.'
'True.'

41

We waited. Eventually the door opened. Grace, still a heavy woman, moved with silence. She now radiated disapproval. 'She will see you.'

'What did you mean, Grace?' I asked. 'You said stripped.'

'And you another of them!' She tucked in her loose lips and nodded. Her hair was iron-grey and thin. 'Don't tell me you haven't come to pick up a choice bit you'd like.'

'I've brought something. I'm not intending to take.'

'Well, that's a turn-up for the book, I must say. The relatives have been coming here in droves. Vultures over a carcass, but she keeps on living. I hope you realize she's ninety-five now. Don't expect too much of her. But at her age, everybody's expecting her to go at any time. So it's a good idea to get in while you can. "Dear Angelina, I've always fancied that little table in the parlour."' She mimicked the avaricious hypocrisy perfectly, and Angelina's weak and inoffensive response. '"Then do take it, Flora—or Mary or Rose or whatever. It's no use to me now." No good to Angelina, no. But what about me?'

With no one she could tell it to, she had bottled up this grievance for too long. It erupted like the bursting forth of a too-long kept champagne, the pressure of fermentation having built up as the wine grew more bitter and sour. Perhaps Grandmother's will left everything to Grace. All of which I die possessed. Very soon she would die possessed of nothing.

My smile was mechanical. 'I told you, Grace, I've *brought* something.' I produced the canvas, now without its frame, from under my arm. She hadn't noticed it. I'd expected relief, but instead of relaxing she stiffened. Wrinkles smoothed along her jaw at the tension. ,

'It's one of those,' she grumbled.

'Yes.'

'You mustn't . . . no, not show her that . . . please.'

I was completely confused. Why should I not show it to Angelina? 'She'll be pleased to see it again, Grace. Come on now.'

'You'll remind her.'

I glanced at Margaret for assistance. She was as tense as Grace, but it was an anticipatory tension, her eyes bright and high patches of colour on her cheeks.

'Remind her of what?' Margaret asked, her voice empty, strained dry.

But Grace had recovered. 'It's up the stairs and to the right. The room at the end. She likes a bright room.' She nodded a distant disapproval. Brightness was too revealing.

She watched us out of the room with suspicion. I followed Margaret up the stairs. Ahead there was a short corridor, lit only by a small window at the far end. Before we reached it there was a cross-corridor, where we turned right. I tapped on the door at the end, eased it open because my grandmother was expecting us, and we went in.

It was a corner room, adapted over the years as a bed-sitter. Angelina was in a wheelchair, which for some reason shocked me. But what had I expected? She'd not moved from her chair the last time I'd visited, when she'd been a mere seventy-five. She was sitting half-turned away, watching something through the window, and without the aid of spectacles. The chair appeared too big for her; she was bolstered with cushions on both sides and in the small of her back. Perhaps it was this that made her seem so small. She had shrunk into her clothes. Her hands, gnarled and claw-like, were resting on the arms of the chair. Her face, in profile, seemed barely to have changed. A thousand wrinkles had taken up the sag, so that it was easy to see she must have been very beautiful when young. A soft-focus lens, and I could have made her that again. She had the long, straight nose I'd inherited, the small chin, the long neck.

She had seemed not to be aware of us. 'There's that magpie again,' she said, her head nodding, nodding, as though on a spring. 'Why is there only one, I wonder. Perhaps the poor thing's lost its mate.'

I spoke quietly. 'It's me, Gran. Tony.'

There was nothing wrong with her hearing. Her head snapped round. The chair swung to face us at a touch of her left hand. Her eyes were deeply set now, the blurred grey of age, but she saw me clearly, I could tell—the way they swept me from head to toe, the way she switched her attention to Margaret, critically, hungrily. She saw so few strangers.

'Charlie's boy? Then it's about time. That's not your wife. Why haven't you been to see me? Come closer, where I can see you. My eyes aren't what they were.'

But she'd been able to see the magpie in the garden—what had been the orchard, I realized from a quick glance, but which was now a jungle. Her faculties seemed to be in order, though she had the trick of the very old of jolting from one thought to the other abruptly. They have to express their thoughts as they present themselves, in case they become forgotten and lost.

I moved forward into a position where she could consider me in detail, nodding and humming to herself.

'Yes, you're Tony. Not changed a bit. You nearly left it too late, my lad.' She gave a little splutter of laughter, and dabbed her lips with a lace handkerchief that could well have been as old as herself.

'I could hardly come before, Gran,' I said gently. 'Not without a certain amount of disloyalty. Do you remember what you said about my wife?'

Her eyes danced, her lips quivered. 'I remember very well. And I'll bet I hit the mark. Oh yes. Another woman knows. But I see you've found a better one. Come along, dear, don't stand over there. What's your name? Speak up. Don't be shy.'

'Margaret. Margaret Dennis.'

'Not married then?' She meant to me.

'It's Ms.'

'Now don't you use that modern slang to me, my girl. If you're his mistress, stand up and say it. Pride. You girls, these days! No pride. I shouted it out with pride, let me tell you. And why not?'

'She's not my mistress, Gran. She's a business associate, an expert on paintings.'

Gran was enjoying herself, though. There was no stopping her. 'So now we have experts. In my day we were artists or non-artists. We didn't speak to non-artists. Are you a non-artist, young lady?'

When I glanced at her, I was surprised to see that Margaret was smiling. 'You could put it like that. I study other people's paintings. We can't all reach the heights, you know.'

That seemed to satisfy Angelina, who nodded, and looked down at her lap for a moment. Then she raised her eyes again. 'Well, sit down, why don't you. Old people don't care to look up. Of course, I was always small. You could say I've always looked up to

46

my men. Freddie was tall, like you, Tony. Oh, so like you! And Arthur was huge. But I looked up to Freddie in a different way. I suppose you know he was a genius. Oh yes. Now, get a chair for the lady, Tony. Where've your manners gone? You never used to let me stand without rushing for a seat. Don't you remember, that fight in the café . . . the café . . .' She faltered to a halt. For one moment she had confused me with Freddie.

I went to find a chair. They were all rush-seated and uncomfortable. I heard Margaret say behind me: 'Freddie?' She said it very casually, as though not to disturb an already insecure intellect. 'You can't mean . . . Frederick Ashe!'

Grandmother's voice was suddenly alive with delight. 'You know him? You've met him?' She stopped so suddenly that in the silence the scrape of the chair was harsh. 'But he's dead, of course. So long . . . you weren't even born.'

'I wasn't born,' said Margaret softly, on an indrawn breath.

I had placed the painting on the surface of a chest of drawers, which was above the level of Grannie's eyes. She hadn't noticed it. Now, before I could reach her to intervene, Margaret snatched it up and offered it to Angelina.

'This is his,' Margaret stated with

47

confidence.

I put the chair behind her knees and slowly edged it forward. She sat, without a glance at me. I stood at her shoulder. Angelina had not reached up to take the painting, but allowed it to rest on her knees, her hands still gripping the arms of her chair. Her head was bent. There was silence for so long I thought she might have nodded off. At her age, that was possible. Nodding, she was, but it was not from sleep. Nodding, nodding, with tiny whimpers, and I watched the fingers of her left hand tighten on the chair arm until the blood flowed from them.

There was a gentle rustling sound, and I realized she was whispering to herself.

'The cottage. Oh, it's the cottage. That first day . . . You were sitting there. Under that window. Painting. Of course, painting. When were you not, Freddie? I was wearing my blue gown. Do you remember that? It caught on the briars. There they are, on the right. Oh Freddie, Freddie . . . so long ago . . .' She raised her head and looked at me. No—her face turned to me. She didn't see me, could not, with those swimming eyes. 'So long since I saw this. Where did you find it? I gave it to Charlie.'

'My father—' I began, but Margaret was briskly practical.

'Is it his? You're talking about Frederick Ashe, aren't you. Is it his, Angelina?'

48

The eyes focused. She dabbed at the corners.

'Of course. Stupid girl. You ought to know that.'

I reached past and lifted the painting from Angelina's lap, and caught a glimpse of Margaret's profile. It was stiff with concentration, her lips pale. I heard her sigh.

'You knew him, did you, Gran?' I asked in a chatty voice. 'He gave you this painting, I suppose, and you gave it to my father . . .'

'Now, now!' She was skittish, lively. 'You know very well how it was. Everybody knew, but they didn't say anything. Not to my face. Oh, this takes me back. Yesterday . . . it could be yesterday.'

She smiled into the distance. Yesterday was any day in the past, but the painting had been cleaned, and was as fresh as when it had been painted. Yesterday was the day it had been painted, or the day before that.

'Tell us,' said Margaret in a small voice. But I touched her shoulder. Angelina needed no prompting. The memories—so crystal clear from so far in the past—came pouring out. Her voice had more life, was younger. Her head came up with something like pride, perhaps a personal pride in her youth and beauty.

'Father had a large estate. I was seventeen. Yes, all of seventeen. On holiday from Saint . . . oh, something. Learning to be a young

49

lady. I walked the estate, and it was so boring. You cannot believe how boring. Daddy had told me a young painter had rented the cottage in the lower meadow, so I went to look, for something to do. And there he was, painting. He was very ugly. The beauty was inside. That little turned-up nose! The big ears! Of course, I was taught to paint at school, but young ladies had to use watercolours—so much more genteel. This painter was working in oils. He wasn't very tidy, and I felt I had to be the lady of the manor, so I told him it wasn't too bad, but he must try harder. That was what they said to me at school. "Angelina, you must try harder." Miss Trench. You know Miss Trench, of course. No? Perhaps she's retired. I never liked Miss Trench—she never laughed. I didn't see Miss Trench again. Well, fancy that, I'd never realized. But she would not have approved. Oil painting was not for the young ladies of Saint Edith's. There, you see, I've remembered.'

Her lips quivered in a smile at the memory of her school. Her eyes closed. Surely she couldn't nod off to sleep now! But her head lifted, and she went on.

'Frederick said he'd bet I couldn't do any better, and young ladies at private schools didn't learn anything useful. He was Frederick then. I called him Freddie in Paris, though. And I said I could if I tried, and he

50

bet me I couldn't. So I said how much, a shilling? But he didn't have a shilling, and he said a kiss, so I knew I was going to be kissed anyway, win or lose!' The voice changed to a crisp reprimand. 'And don't smile at that, young lady. It was very daring, and he *did* let me try, sitting down and doing a tiny corner of his painting for him, and he said it was very good and gave me my kiss, and said if I came the next day he'd lend me an easel and brushes and a canvas, and I could paint my own picture. So I did—and we did, all through that wonderful summer. We painted together.'

She looked round vaguely for the painting, and seemed confused that it was no longer on her lap.

'That was one of them,' she said, moving her left hand vaguely.

'You painted it together?' asked Margaret disbelievingly.

'No, no. Silly child. Didn't I say! We sat side by side, two canvases, his palette on a table between us, and shared his colours. What he did, I did. I copied his brush strokes as well as I could. Or he copied mine. Later, it didn't seem to matter which. We found we went together. Naturally. It was destiny, and there were pointers. And that's how it was, until the end.'

She put a hand over her face and bent her head. Margaret seemed about to say

51

something, but I squeezed her shoulder, and we waited. At last Angelina went on: 'He insisted. It wasn't his war, I told him. Wars don't belong to artists. But he joined the French army and I never . . . never saw him again.'

'But—' began Margaret.

I cut in quickly. 'You must have loved him very much, Gran.'

'Like a child, like a woman. You couldn't possibly understand. He was my life. I never painted again.'

'So there were two sets . . .'

She didn't answer directly. 'Mamma disapproved. Consorting with a vagabond, she called it. My father understood, I think. Yes, Father was a wonderful man. We painted all that summer. Eight paintings.'

'Eight pairs?' I asked.

'Yes. Of course. I've said that. But Mamma had her way in the end. She made my father give Frederick notice to quit. And he'd got nowhere else he could go, and hardly any money. To me, it was the end of the world. Where would he go? I asked him. He said Paris. He said he had painter friends in Paris—if he could only get there. Claude Monet and Maurice Bellarmé. So I went to see my father and told him, and he gave me money for Frederick to get to Paris, much more than was needed, because he understood what I was thinking, you see; I could tell that in his sad eyes. But he wanted only my happiness. Two days later I took my wicker-work basket of clothes to the cottage, and we went to Paris.'

We went to Paris. Such simple words, but in 1910 it would have been an act of great courage to a young woman brought up as Gran had been. She had had to be with her man. It was as simple as that, and Gran expressed it simply.

'We nearly starved,' she went on, 'but Freddie got work at a bistro, and I tried to sell the paintings. I sold six. Six out of all that work! For about ten francs each. But Father sent me money from time to time. Mamma never wrote. She didn't even come to my wedding, and never spoke to me again. And the war came . . .' She drew breath sharply, her lips quivering. She was silent. Her time sequence had become confused.

'The initials,' I prompted after a moment. 'The signatures on the canvases.'

She flashed me an abrupt smile, direct from her beloved Paris. 'But that was our thing, you see. Tony, you should know all this. Our initials were the same, only backwards, which Freddie said was destiny. So we each signed our canvases the same, an A and an F on top of each other. We always worked side by side. He said I inspired him. He said he couldn't do it alone. Dear man. But really we did them together. His brush strokes were mine, and mine his. Sometimes, for a laugh, we would try switching them over, halfway through. But that didn't seem to work. Isn't that strange? I've never understood that.'

'You painted a great number?' I asked gently, feeling Margaret straining to get in with her questions.

'Oh yes. About eighty finished pairs. More. I destroyed the sketches before I came home.'

Margaret moaned softly.

'That was in 1917?' I asked.

'Well yes. Freddie died. I told you that. I had to come home. A single young lady in Paris couldn't have a child, could she?'

'Of course she couldn't,' I agreed calmly, although my heart was pounding.

'So I wrote to Father, and he sent me the money to come home, and said he would find me a husband, who I knew would have to be absolutely dreadful, to take on a young woman carrying someone else's child. And that would be for money and status, but I didn't care about anything any more, and Father arranged everything. He was in the importing and exporting business, and he sent some of his men to pack the canvases, which was about all I had left, and I came home, to this house, and became Mrs Angelina Hine—Mrs *Arthur* Hine. Fortunately, he didn't live long, though long enough to father one son on me—that would be your uncle Henry, Tony. Yes. Henry.' She sniffed, and shook her head.

The shaking gradually subsided and her head fell forward. Her breathing changed. She was asleep.

'For heaven's sake, Tony!' said Margaret. 'The paintings! We can't leave, not knowing.'

Grandmother Angelina murmured something. I said: 'What was that, Gran?'

'We had a bonfire,' she told me distinctly, lifting her head.

'The paintings?' asked Margaret in a weak voice.

'They were in tea chests. Eight tea chests. Father imported tea. His men came and packed them for me. I marked one set of four as Freddie's, with a cross, so that I would know. But my husband hated Freddie. As he would, I suppose. As he hated Freddie's son, when he arrived. Your father, Tony. It was like acid to him, knowing the paintings were up there in the loft. All that I had left of Freddie, except the child. But he couldn't destroy the child. It had to be Freddie's paintings. In the end he was near insane about it, and said I'd got to burn them. Myself. With my own two hands. That was because he'd been unable to give me a child himself. He said I must be doing something to stop it. Ridiculous. But do you know . . . that very night . . . I'm sure it was that night, he was so fierce and triumphant with me . . . that was when I got pregnant again, the night

55

I burned the paintings.'

She puckered her lips, pondering fate.

'The canvases!' Margaret whispered.

'He asked me—demanded—what crates Freddie's were in. I'd marked four of them. A cross. Did I tell you that? But I couldn't bear the thought of destroying Freddie's work. So I told a lie. I said *mine* were in the tea chests with a cross. I could bear to lose mine. I remember that night. It was dark in the garden. Down there, in the orchard, that was where we did it. He was up in the loft. I stood on the landing and wept. I heard the chests being smashed open. He was roaring something, fury I suppose. He threw the paintings down at my feet. Grace and I took them down to the orchard. We made a pile. Eighty canvases make a big pile. He came and poured paraffin on it, but he wouldn't strike the match himself. He said I had to. He watched from up here. This very window. I lit them . . .'

Her eyes were sightless. She stared into the past, her jaw set, the wrinkles in her skin now more deeply etched. Her left hand gestured towards the painting I'd brought.

'That was the one I saved. I kicked it behind a tree, and in the morning, when he'd gone to one of his shops, I went out and wrapped it in newspaper and hid it in the garden shed. I was weeping so much I couldn't see what I was doing. Then, years

56

later, when your father was sixteen and decided to leave home, I told him to take it with him.' She sighed, breathed deeply for a moment, then was asleep again.

Margaret hissed: 'For God's sake, she can't go to sleep now!'

Angelina murmured and raised her head. 'And then I had nothing left of Freddie, with Charlie gone. He'd destroyed everything.'

This didn't seem to make sense, because she had just told us how she had managed to save Freddie's paintings. She would have had those. But I didn't have time to question this.

Angelina put her head back and rested it against her small pillow, and stared sightlessly at the wall, until I realized she was sleeping with her eyes open. Slowly, as I watched, the lids descended.

We stood and watched her. I said: 'We've tired her out.'

'She can't leave it there. Wake her up, why don't you!'

'Let her sleep.'

'You fool,' she said, whispering intensely. 'Can't you understand? He was no idiot, her husband. He probably double-guessed her, knowing she'd tell a lie about which paintings were in which chests.'

'Does it matter?'

She flung her hands towards the ceiling. 'They're probably still in the loft—the other set. We've got to know the truth, which they

57

are. I'm going to wake her.'

I grabbed her arm. 'It doesn't matter,' I snapped, 'who painted what! You're obsessed.'

She allowed me to draw her towards the door, but she was furious. From behind us there was a bubbling sound from Grannie. We turned. Her eyes were open, and she was smiling.

'Such a clever girl,' she murmured. 'That's exactly what he did.'

CHAPTER FOUR

Now we were drawn back by Angelina's alertness. So far as she was concerned there had been no gap in the conversation. She even raised her arm in a gesture of companionship. We were her friends.

'Did you know this, Gran? On that night, when you burned the paintings, did you know you'd destroyed Freddie's?'

She shook her head. 'Not then. Not until years later.'

'You didn't go into the loft to check?'

'At that time, it was a comfort I didn't wish to disturb. And I was afraid. Of him.'

'Then when did you get to know?'

'Later. Much later. After Charlie left home, after Mr Hine died.' He had become

Mr Hine, I noted. 'I went up then. Tried to, but I fell. It's very steep. That's why I'm in this chair.'

Then how had she found out? But before I could ask, I realized that Grace must have gone up for her. 'Was it Grace?'

'Yes. She told me the marked crates had been broken open. So he'd won after all.'

Margaret moaned feebly. But Grace might have made an error. 'The others are still there?' Margaret asked quickly, desperately clinging to any remote possibility.

Smiling now, sleep far away, Angelina nodded. 'Which is why I'm so glad Tony has come. I told myself, if Tony comes he shall have the paintings. Who else should they belong to but the grandson of the person who painted them?'

'I can't let you—' I began, but Margaret was still in there fighting.

'You're giving them to Tony, Mrs Hine?'

'That was what I said.'

Margaret turned away, and I heard her rustling in her shoulder bag. I said: 'It's very good of you, Gran, and if it's in your will . . .'

'I'm not going to trouble changing it now. Don't be a silly boy. Take them with you.'

'I . . . can't!' Not past Grace, not after what she'd said about vultures.

Margaret tugged at my shoulder and thrust something into my hand. It was a sheet torn from a notepad.

'What's this?'

'It's a formal deed of gift. I've scribbled it out, and it might not be legal wording—'

'To hell with your formalities.'

'It's a matter of provenance, proof of ownership.'

'You heard what she said. They're not works by Frederick Ashe. Not from his magic brush. So you don't have to worry.'

She was agitated, her eyes wild. 'I don't know. I need time. Get her to sign it, Tony, damn you.'

'What is it?' demanded Gran. 'Let me see. Get me my glasses, they're over there somewhere . . .' Her fingers reached for the paper.

Before she could take it I crumpled it and thrust it in my pocket. The idea of getting my grandmother to formalize a gift was repulsive. I was family, her own grandson. I took her reaching hand in mine.

'Thank you,' I said. 'Thank you, Gran. I'll treasure your paintings.'

She smiled, and her hand fell limply from mine. She had smiled herself to sleep.

. 'Let's go,' I said.

'You must be insane!'

'There's no money in it, no glory in the find. They're only paintings by Angelina Foote.' I picked my own from the top of the chest of drawers. 'So you were right about this being a Frederick Ashe. Too bad, as it turns out.'

Talking steadily, I got her out of the room, and closed the door quietly.

'You'll regret this.'

'What I regret is that I ever went to that Antiques Road Show in the first place.' I shuffled her down the stairs.

'Your paintings . . .' she tried.

'When she dies, I'll collect them. Nobody will want them, not eighty Angelina Footes. Ah, Grace, we're off now. She's sleeping. We can see ourselves out.'

Grace watched us out of the door. In spite of what I'd said, she refused to deny herself the pleasure of closing it with firm finality.

Margaret stalked to the car, lips tight, small patches of white at their corners. She slammed the door furiously.

As I slid in beside her, she rounded on me fiercely. 'You damned fool, Tony. You complete and utter idiot. You should have got her to sign it.'

'She gave me the paintings. Isn't that enough?'

'It is not! That Grace, she'll probably get the lot in her will. Everything that's left in the house, and those are, that's for sure.'

'She'll hardly want a load of old paintings. And Gran gave them to me.'

'You can't prove that in a court of law. And how d'you know Grace wouldn't want them?

You know nothing. It's all contradictory. Can't you see . . . we've proved nothing. Oh, to hell with it. Let's go and get something to eat.'

Being Margaret, she naturally headed for the most expensive restaurant in town, which stretched my pocket somewhat as of course I had to pay my share. But we got a corner table, and being expensive they were also discreet. We were allowed to eat without undue interruption.

'We know nothing,' she said again. 'Your grandmother's memory could have been faulty, and I think she was confused, anyway.'

'She sounded lucid enought to me. For her age.' The soup was cold. Margaret said it was supposed to be.

'For her age,' she agreed. 'But as soon as she saw the painting she said: "It's his."'

'So? Apparently it is. Frederick Ashe's.'

'She later said she needed her glasses to read the bit of paper you so cleverly stopped her from signing. So she may not have seen the painting clearly. She saw the magpie, so she's probably long-sighted.'

I wasn't sure I liked the soup, and left half of it. 'She also later said she was convinced she'd burned Frederick Ashe's paintings, but mine was the one she saved from the fire. So she would know it's one of his without seeing it very clearly.'

'She saw it was the cottage. No question of that. She mentioned the briars. When she said it's his, she could have meant the cottage and not the painting. As it was. He was renting it.'

We sat back and waited for the roast lamb. I said: 'Now you're trying to persuade me that my painting isn't a Frederick Ashe, and that she burned her own stuff after all. You're contradicting yourself. Surely an expert such as you can't be mistaken!'

'Oh, you can laugh. But you heard what she said. She copied every brush stroke. She used the same paints. We don't know how much alike the two sets of paintings are.'

'But *she'd* be able to tell, surely.'

'Of course she would,' she agreed, tossing an absent smile at the waitress bringing our lamb.

'Well then,' I said, after she'd left. 'My Gran said she wrapped up my painting the morning after the bonfire, and hid it in the shed. At that time she believed she'd destroyed her own. If in fact she had destroyed Frederick Ashe's, she'd have realized when she was wrapping it. Her sight was probably good at that time.'

She smiled as she chewed, waited until she had swallowed, then pointed her knife at me. 'Yes, but she told us she was in tears. So she might not have been able to see.'

'Why was she in tears?'

'What?'

'If she thought, at that time, she'd fooled her husband, why the tears?'

'You're very unimaginative, Tony. She had been degraded. She'd been forced into destroying something precious to her, whether it was a set of her own paintings or a set of Ashe's. And don't forget, she did say he'd treated her violently the previous night. Really, Tony!'

She was, at least, in a less abrasive mood now. I allowed myself a smile very close to a grin. 'You're trying desperately to convince yourself you've not made a mistake, and yet you're now saying my painting might not be a Frederick Ashe.'

'I have not made a mistake. I have personally studied the four available genuine Ashes, in the art galleries. However well she copied his brush strokes, they could not be so exactly alike in style. There are dozens of considerations, confidence in line, the strength of the approach, the impasto . . . I could *not* be mistaken. Yours is by the same hand as those other four.'

I thought about that, and decided I didn't want a pudding but was dying for a smoke. I couldn't see what she was getting at. She couldn't have it both ways.

'Haven't you missed one very important point?' I asked.

'I don't think so.'

'It's this. Gran said she never managed to get up into the loft, to confirm for herself which were destroyed. So what we're discussing depends entirely on Grace. She might have made a mistake about the tea chests. She might even have lied to Gran, though heaven knows why. But there's only her word, from a quick look in the loft, which is probably very dark anyway, to say that it was the Frederick Ashe paintings that were burned. Suppose she was wrong. Then Gran *did* destroy her own, and mine—having been saved from the fire—is therefore one of hers.'

'I've told you. I'm certain yours is a Frederick Ashe.'

'But only because you're comparing it with known Frederick Ashe paintings in the galleries.'

'Only?' Her eyes were very big. Her voice held a hint of danger. 'And what d'you mean by that?'

I admit I hadn't much faith in what I was about to say, but I couldn't resist the impulse to take a dig at her precious art expert establishment. I kept the smile out of my voice.

'What if the art gallery paintings are Gran's, and not Ashe's? Then where would you be? After all, Gran said *she* sold six. Isn't it likely she would sell six of her own, if her Freddie's were so precious to her?'

'Not unlikely at all,' she agreed

65

complacently, surprising me.

'I'll have to stop calling him Ashe. He was my grandfather.'

'That much seems true.'

'So where's my artistic heritage now—both grandparents artists!'

'Good for you.'

'No need to sulk.'

'I was pleased for you. For both of us. Pleased that you've at last come round to the point I wanted to make.'

I eyed her with suspicion. 'What point?'

'That it's absolutely imperative for us to get a good look at what's in that loft.'

'Oh now . . . hold on.'

'She gave them to you. They're yours.'

'All the same . . .'

'We don't know how close your grandmother's work was to Frederick Ashe's. Hers could be terrible imitations. One look, and I'd know. But they're yours, in any event, so we ought to go and collect them.'

I took a deep breath. 'If you think I'm going to stand in front of Grace and say I've come to empty the loft . . .'

'I wasn't suggesting that.'

'Then what?'

'She has to leave the house some time.'

'Good Lord!'

'I'll tell you this, Tony. I feel I'm on the verge of a great art discovery. One way or the other. If necessary I'll break in at midnight and sneak up there on my own, but for you to do it you could at least claim you were collecting your own property.'

'At midnight?'

'It need not be so late.'

'Why can't we just go and see Grace and say we simply want to do no more than look in the loft? Not take anything away. You did say—you'd only need one look.'

'I was talking figuratively.'

'Figuratively in what way?'

'I'd want to get them back to my place, clean them up, examine them in detail. Check them against yours.'

'You're hopeless.'

'With you or without you, I'll get into that loft.'

'Without me, you could only look, and leave them there,' I pointed out.

'There you are then.'

There I was. Stuck. I have to admit that I too wanted to be certain. I owned a loftful of canvases which could be wildly valuable, or worthless apart from their sentimental value. Whatever happened, I was the grandchild of a famous painter, but it would be less unsettling to know which grandparent had become famous. Only the fear of Grace prevented me from marching up to the house and demanding my rights, and the fear of the law. How could I prove Gran had given them to me?

'So how do we do it?' I asked, when we were sitting in the car.

'We watch the house, and wait till Grace goes out.'

'It could take days.'

It occurred to me that if I'd been Grace I would have listened at that bedroom door, suspicious that Angelina might be giving away more of the precious inheritance. It also occurred to me that Grace might be well aware that she had a loftful of Frederick Ashe paintings, that she was equally aware of their value, and that eighty times twenty thousand could cushion her declining years, and that she could well spend all of them cruising the world on it. First class.

But I didn't say anything on this aspect of it, only decided, as we had planned, that indeed our actions had to be kept secret from Grace.

It was only because of this that I spent the afternoon and most of the evening skulking in the shrubbery just inside the drive of Mandalay. Margaret was parked, bored to the eyebrows I hoped, in the drive of an empty house just down Forster Grove. My thoughts reflected my condition: damp, cold, and depressed. I was considering that if I'd been Arthur Hine, intent on banishing all evidence of Frederick Ashe from my house, I would have burned the lot—both sets. It was unlikely that my Gran, distressed at the time, would have counted them, especially as she was being helped by Grace. A pile of a hundred and sixty might well look like what one would expect of a pile of eighty.

Strangely, as I examined this idea more deeply, I found it a little comforting. If this were to prove correct, all decisions would be lifted from me, and I'd be back with my single canvas. Frankly, I didn't care who'd painted it.

The front door opened. The time was something after nine, and it was now dark. Heavy clouds had been massing, intensifying the gloom, but before she turned off the hall light I saw that Grace was dressed for outdoors, in a bonnet and a long, ancient topcoat. She slammed the door, and her shadow moved towards the dilapidated garage at one side of the house.

I edged my way back towards the entrance, then turned and ran.

'She's going out,' I panted, yanking open the car door.

'Don't panic.' She was smoking a cigarette, the first time I'd seen her doing that. 'Come in and sit down, and don't slam the door too hard. She'll probably be driving past here, it's a dead end farther up.'

We sat with the engine purring softly. Grace drove past in a very old Morris Minor, the model with the split windscreen. Margaret pulled out into the road, and we followed. It wasn't difficult. Grace's maximum speed was 25 mph.

We were reaching the outskirts of the town, with a few shops making their appearance when Grace swung right and parked in the space beside The Dun Cow.

'Right,' said Margaret, looking for somewhere to back and turn. 'That's Grace out of the way for a while. I bet she does this every evening, after she's tucked Angelina into bed. Down here for her two halves of Guinness and a natter.'

And who could blame her?

To my surprise, Margaret drove into the drive at Mandalay. If Grace returned early, we would be trapped. But clearly, Margaret anticipated that we should load the Volvo directly from the front door. She also anticipated finding an open window round the back, which she did, almost as though she was an expert at this kind of thing. Doctor of Crookery.

'You climb in, and come through to open the front door for me,' she instructed.

I nodded. As of now, she was in charge. My nerve was failing; I'd have made a rotten burglar. In practice, it was easier than I'd anticipated. Some latent memory guided me though the hall. The front door had a cylinder lock, so we would be able to close it behind us with no sign that we'd ever been there.

At the head of the stairs there was a small light left on. It guided us up the creaking treads, and along the short, facing passage. The cross-corridor was dark. I groped for a light switch, and suddenly Margaret snapped on a torch she'd brought from the car, searching out switches.

'I'll go and look in on Gran,' I said softly.

'Why on earth . . . ?'

Because, if she was awake, I wanted to say something like: I've come for the paintings, Gran, so if you hear any noises . . . So as not to frighten her. 'You look for the loft,' I said, not prepared to argue about it.

She made a clicking sound with her tongue, and went in the other direction. I opened Gran's door very quietly. The room was not completely dark, as there was a light on the small table beside her bed. She lay on her back, only her face showing. I went forward, making no sound, and stood over her.

The bedclothes were neatly tucked in, and she made hardly any disturbance in their smooth symmetry. Her tiny head seemed buried in the soft pillow. I bent down and carefully lifted away a lock of thin hair that had fallen over her eyes.

There was hardly any indication that she was breathing. Abruptly concerned, I bent my ear close to her lips, and was just able to detect a shallow inhale and exhale. Very old people barely disturb their environment with

71

their presence.

I turned away and left the room. The door-latch made a faint click.

Margaret was waiting for me, impatient and now nervous.

'It's at the end of the corridor,' she said. 'She's asleep.'

'There's a ladder.'

It was not so much a ladder as open stairs, as there were treads instead of rungs. The climb was almost vertical, and once again it was my turn to lead.

'Hurry,' she said.

'I'll need the torch.'

There was no handrail to grip, just open steps. With one hand reaching upwards and forwards, I mounted to a trapdoor. It opened easily. I had to be careful to lower it gently as I hoisted it beyond the vertical. A waft of stale dust enveloped me.

My first stab with the torch discovered a light switch on one of the upright rafter supports. The wiring was naked. I touched the switch, rather surprised when two bare bulbs went on. It was a poor light for such a large area, but it was more useful than the torch. The complete floor area was boarded, so that we were able to move around without difficulty.

I had expected to find four tea chests standing proud in a vast emptiness. But a hundred years of family discards were scattered around, and we had to search. They were together. Four tea chests. Sealed. There were no crosses on them that I could detect.

Quite close, lying where they'd been thrown, I found the shattered and discarded remnants of what could have been four other tea chests. The metal corner bracings identified them. On these remains I could see no crosses, either.

But Gran hadn't said what she'd used to mark the crosses. If it had been chalk, the dust and decay of seventy years could have eliminated all traces.

'We forgot to bring something to open them with,' said Margaret, her breathing heavy and fast.

'There must be something we can use.'

There was. It might have been the same crowbar Arthur Hine had used to break open the other chests.

The tops came off with creaks and groans and bangs. All four were filled with canvases. Margaret's hand was shaking when she reached inside and drew one free.

It had dust on it, and there seemed to be some darkening of age. Or it could have been the poor lighting. I clicked on the torch and held it close to the canvas. She swept her palm over it. The signature was the same overlapped A and F as on mine, the date three years later.

'Well?' I asked.

She didn't reply at once. Perhaps I was expecting too much of her. At last: 'I don't know!' she said, pain in her voice.

I left her to it, and got the tops off the other three. They weren't packed tight, and old dresses that had been Gran's had been used to restrict movement. One of them was blue. I drew out another canvas at random.

'Try this one.'

She shook her head, and merely glanced at it. 'It can't be!' she said in despair, staring at the one in her hands. 'It's the same. The same style as yours. And yet it can't *be*. Yours was rescued from the fire. This is the other lot. Tony, it's impossible.'

'We'll have to unpack 'em, and take them down in bundles.'

'Do it how you damn well please,' she said in sudden anger. But the anger was at herself and her inability to make a decision. 'Sorry. But, Tony, can you get them down yourself?'

'I'll need help. A full chest is too heavy. Why can't you lend a hand?'

But I knew why. When her head turned so that she could glance at me—and away—the torch caught her eyes. It was all in there, her growing panic and despair. With all her years of study behind her, the precious expertise she'd nursed was letting her down. She could not make a firm and confident decision. 'You can't do that,' I said quietly, guessing her intention.

'There's only one person who really knows.'

'Even she—'

'She would know. At a glance.' She shook my arm. 'A minute. Is that too much to ask! Old people sleep and wake and sleep again. I'll be gentle.'

I turned away. 'We're wasting time.'

She took it as agreement and, taking the canvas with her, dangling from her fingers, she backed away down the steps.

I did what I could, piling them in heaps of ten beside the opening, backing down, reaching them through, and doing it with no hands for support. There were fifty standing beside the steps when she returned.

'Well?' I said, my back to her. She didn't answer. I turned.

Even in the poor light I could detect that she was pale. Her eyes seemed sightless, her mind not with me.

'You woke her?' I prompted.

'Yes. Oh yes. They wake easily, old people.'

'And what did she say?'

'I don't know. I don't *understand*.'

'Relax, Margaret. Did she get a good look

75

at the painting?'

'She seemed to.'

'And?'

She shook her head, her lips puckering.

'With her glasses on?' I prompted.

'They were on the side. Yes, I gave them to her. She took one good look at it and started shouting out . . .'

'Perhaps she took a good look at you, too, and couldn't remember who you are. I should've gone with you.'

'Shouting for Grace.'

'Just that?'

She nodded, her lower lip betweeth her teeth.

'Perhaps you frightened her. Did she use your name?'

She shook her head. 'Only Grace's. Shouting.'

'For help, I suppose.'

'She was angry.'

I grinned at her, trying to shake her from the mood. 'All right, so you didn't get anywhere . . . so what! I hope you didn't leave her upset.'

'I soothed her.'

'Right. Then we'll have to rely on you. Now why don't you take some of these down to the car. I'm getting the hang of it now.'

She spoke not one word during the rest of the transfer. There were eighty-one. I counted them as we loaded the Volvo, then went back to the landing to check that there was no visible evidence that we'd been there, put my head inside the door of Gran's room—she was again peaceful and quiet—then put out the lights we'd used, closed the front door behind me, and joined Margaret in the car.

She was smoking again. I said: 'No doubt your scientific methods will reveal the truth.'

I meant it as encouragement; she took it as sarcasm. She gave a small, bitter bark of angry laughter, and backed the car out of the drive.

The Morris Minor was just taking the bend farther along the Grove. It was a matter of seconds. From later events, it became obvious that Grace had spotted the Volvo's headlights swinging out of the drive, but at the time she did nothing to obstruct us. We drove past each other as though neither car existed.

It was nearly midnight when we drove up to Margaret's cottage. We hadn't said much during the journey. I was busy fighting my conscience. My moral performance so far had not been commendable. I helped her into the workroom with the complete set, plus my original canvas, and we placed them in piles on her benches.

'Phew!' she said. 'Some job here. I'll be at it all night.'

'I take it I can't be much help?' I said it hopefully, the hope being that she would say no.

'You can make coffee, hold things, encourage.'

I flung the lock of hair out of my eyes with one hand. 'I'd rather hoped to get some sleep.'

'Sleep!' She stared at me with wonder. 'Don't you care?'

'In any event, I'm the grandson of two marvellous painters.'

'And that's all? Oh, Tony, how can you be so unfeeling! It matters. They're all yours. Either you've got one Frederick Ashe and eighty-one Angelina Footes, or the other way round. And it's Frederick Ashe who's become famous. Don't you understand? Some of the great artists had pupils, who naturally learned to paint like their master. Sometimes they're almost indistinguishable. But the pupils are all called "the school of so-and-so". So your grandmother is going to be "school of Frederick Ashe". However good she was.'

'She was, wasn't she? Good, I mean. In any event.'

She made an impatient gesture. 'Oh, you're hopeless. Put it like this. That one painting of yours, if it's a Frederick Ashe, would be a find. I bet you'd get fifty thousand pounds for it in auction. In that case, the whole eighty-one Angelina Footes wouldn't be worth more. But if the eighty-one are Ashes, then what sort of a find would that be? It'd rock the art world. You'd be—what?—worth a million and a half. Maybe more. And you say it wouldn't matter!'

'Of course it'd matter,' I said gently. 'I assure you I'm all agog. Couldn't be gogger. But I'm still a professional photographer, with a contract to fulfil. I thought I would hire a car—'

'You can't just turn your back on all this.'

'I shall return.' Why had I become caught in this facetious mood? Because I couldn't take her seriously? That was it, surely.

'You don't need to hire a car. I'll drive you where you want to go.'

But I needed my independence. I wanted to be free of her forceful influence. Above all, I had to get away on my own, and consider from the outside a world for which I felt no sympathy or understanding. The pragmatism was stifling me. I'd always believed the art world to be bound by love of beauty and perfection but apparently, like everything else, it was wrapped around with money.

'You'll be busy. I'll need at least a full day at my photo lab, and you'll need a night . . . and a day?'

Then she stood back and looked at me fondly, shaking her head.

'Oh, Tony, Tony, you're quite incredible. Go away and play with your photographs. But come back with expectations. Because, whatever happens, it's more important than

79

your crabby little photographic business.'

With these parting words ringing in my head, I went to my room.

CHAPTER FIVE

In fact, I did hire a car, thus straining the muscle of my credit card. There was no question of Margaret driving me. By the morning she was grey with exhaustion, having cleaned most of the paintings, and I nearly had to carry her to bed. All I got out of her was the fact that she still had no proof, either way, as to the identity of the artist who'd painted the eighty-one.

I walked into town, no more than a mile, hired a red Ford Fiesta, and headed for my own territory.

My place had a small window on two sides of the corner where Beech Street meets Albert's Fold. There's a door beside it opening into a reception area with a narrow counter dividing it in half. On the counter is a notice. 'If red light shows, please press button and wait.' The red light is above the door the other side of the counter, and indicates that I'm working beyond it. In no event must light be allowed to enter at the wrong time. There was, that day, plenty of time during which the red light was glowing, because I had six spools of film to develop and around two hundred colour prints, six by four, to produce. The buzzer was silent until late in the afternoon.

I was well into the swing of it, having stopped only for a sandwich and coffee at a place just down Albert's Fold, when the buzzer went. I shouted: 'A minute.' Then, with the print out of the fixer and into the wash, I could open the door.

He was in his thirties, I'd guess, a large and solid man with too much colour in his face and flashing a pessimistic smile that came out all twisted. He was wearing a dirty anorak and a tweed hat.

'Mr Hine?' he asked. 'Anthony Hine?'

I nodded. Customers did not usually need to confirm my Christian name.

He flashed a leather-bound plastic card out of his inside pocket, and said: 'Detective Sergeant Dolan.' And flashed it back before I could get a good look at it.

'Excuse me.' I reached out and waited. He grinned, and produced it again. I checked the photograph. It could well have been him. 'Thank you,' I said. 'I hired the car, you know, not pinched it.'

'I'm sure you did. Are you the grandson of Mrs Angelina Hine?'

Tingles ran down my spine. My palms rested on the twelve inches of counter between us, but I couldn't prevent my fingers from curling.

'Yes,' I said stiffly.

'Then I'm sorry to have to tell you that your grandmother died last night.'

His eyes didn't leave mine, and he probably noticed they'd gone out of focus. I was thinking that Gran had possibly been dying when I bent over her, dying when Margaret allowed her to return to her last sleep. And we'd not known. Could we have done anything . . . ?

'Sir?'

I cleared my throat. 'I'm sorry. I saw her only yesterday.'

'So I understand.'

'You've come from there?' My eyes focused. His head was tilted, the hat slid sideways, he poked it back. 'It's quite a distance—how did you trace me?'

'An address book. And this place is in the Yellow Pages . . . you weren't at home, you see.'

'No.'

'Your wife said you'd left her. In fact, walked out.'

'That's correct.' Had she said I'd gone off with another woman?

'You left with a painting, I understand.'

So . . . not with a woman, with a painting. 'It's mine. My father handed it on.' He smiled encouragingly, so I continued—couldn't stop myself. 'Which was why I went

82

to see my grandmother.'

'The painting?'

'To check who'd painted it.'

'That . . . and the others?' he prompted.

My reception area is so small that there's no room for chairs, just the twelve inches of counter and its button. I was backed up against my darkroom door, but our faces were still only a yard apart. There was no retreat. He smiled. It seemed to peel the skin from my bones. I couldn't say: what others? He clearly knew.

'We discussed the ones in the loft,' I admitted. Admitted? It felt like an admission.

'In what way?' He waited, but it was all too complex for me to go into. 'To what end?' he suggested helpfully.

'She said I could have them. A gift.'

His eyes at last slid aside. Some of my best work graces the walls, twenty by sixteens. He eyed them with approval. 'But a photographer,' he said, 'especially an expert, wouldn't give wall space to a bunch of mouldy old paintings.'

'This one would.'

'But you didn't take them with you when you left.'

'It would've seemed too . . . well, eager.'

'They're not there now. In the loft. I looked.'

'You were told to look?' I guessed.

'Certainly. By the companion. Grace

83

Fielding. She saw you leaving, the second time. Late. After ten. Did you realize she saw you leaving?'

I shrugged. 'I thought so at the time. Does it matter? I mean, they were mine. I went back and collected them. I didn't fracture any laws.

'Breaking and entering. Burglary.'

'I didn't break anything, and surely I could enter my own grandmother's house.'

He pursed his lips. 'Try theft,' he suggested.

'But they're mine.'

He lifted both palms, smiled, and said: 'And there we have it. Are they yours? That is exactly the point.'

It had been hot in the darkroom, but was cool out there, and I was down to my shirtsleeves. Nevertheless, the shirt was sticking to my back, and he was watching with interest the drop of sweat trickling down my nose. I'd been trying to keep Margaret out of it, but now I needed her, and had to mention her.

'They are mine. She said she wanted me to have them. I've got a witness.'

It seemed not to impress him. 'Miss Fielding told me you went there with a woman. I don't think there can be any dispute that your grandmother wanted you to have them. But she's dead. The legal processes take over. There's a will. Grace

84

Fielding tells me that she gets all of which your grandmother died possessed. That's the phrase. In this case, she died possessed of the house, and everything in it at the *time* of her death. In the house, Mr Hine. Do you see what I'm getting at? If she died before you took those paintings out of the front door, then what you were doing was theft. You were stealing from Grace Fielding.'

I was taking slow, deep breaths. For him, the speech had been long, and I'd had a chance to recover my wits.

'She was alive when we left.'

'You're certain of that?'

'We looked in on her twice—three times, but I didn't go near the bed the last time. She was breathing very shallowly, but she was alive.'

'Hmm!' he said. 'Yet Miss Fielding arrived just after you'd left, that second time, went straight up to Mrs Hine, and found she was dead. Now don't say she couldn't tell. She's experienced. She can take a pulse. Your grandmother was dead.'

'I see.'

I saw very clearly. There had been only minutes in it. Grace could make a legal fight of it. She surely would, if she believed the loft paintings were by Frederick Ashe, who was becoming collectable. Grace, in fact, might well have spent some time, that afternoon, persuading Angelina to retract the gift. She

85

would certainly have been furious when she spotted the Volvo leaving, and then discovered, as she must have done, that the loft had been emptied of paintings.

'I see,' I repeated. 'So you've come here to charge me with theft?'

'Oh no. No, no,' he said emphatically. 'It's not as simple as that. I've spent a long while with Miss Fielding. She told me that after you left, the first time, she guessed what you'd come for, so she spoke to your grandmother about it. In the end, your grandmother agreed to write to you, and tell you she'd changed her mind about giving you the paintings. Miss Fielding was upset about the number of valuable items that'd been given away already. Are you following this, Mr Hine?'

So Grace had listened at the door. 'Closely,' I assured him.

'The old lady, you see, might well have been breathing shallowly, as you said. It wouldn't have taken any great effort to prevent her from breathing at all. A hand over her mouth and nose, that's all it'd take. There would probably be no struggle. What I'm trying to say to you is that the ME has said there're signs that she was suffocated. The post-mortem will clarify it. We thought you ought to know. For now, we're treating it as a murder enquiry.'

He was saying this in the same unemotional

86

and casual way he'd been using before. Perhaps, to him, the death of a woman of ninety-five was a very minor occurrence; she'd been so close to it. But to me it was the opposite. She had had so little left. Every passing day made the trespassing minutes more precious. And she'd been robbed of the diminishing time left to her.

'Mr Hine?'

I shook my head, clearing my eyes. 'I'm listening.'

'You can see the point, I'm sure. The possibility is that you went there, the second time, and she woke, and told you what she intended to do. Which was to cancel her gift. But you wanted those paintings. How did you put it? You would give wall space to them. You *wanted* them. So you would not want her to retract her gift in writing.' He cocked his head, and waited. It was quite clear what he meant.

'Are you making a charge?' I managed to say.

It was then that the basic unreality of the scene swept over me. I was standing aside, mouthing words that had been scripted for me, and I could discover no emotional background to lend them force. For the past forty-eight hours I had been moving in an insecure world, prompted by impulses and reactions rather than reason. I'd been carried along by it, finally retreating into my

87

darkroom to be embraced by my firm and structured life. But I'd opened the door on to the world again. My routine life should have been there, too, to be lived or confronted or opposed. But real. Now there was no home and no family, only a fantasy involving paintings and a throw-back to my ancestry. And I was now being virtually accused of murder. Did I laugh in this man's face, did I demolish his reasoning with well-structured but dignified rhetoric? No. I merely said in an empty voice: 'Are you making a charge?'

The way he shook his head was not denial, it was disbelief. He'd seen everything, but I was a new discovery.

'You'll naturally be shocked, Mr Hine. You'll need time to think. All I'm asking is that you keep yourself in touch. I may need to find you again.'

At last I laughed, but it was the natural humour of a man who can find amusement in his own dilemma. I *was* amused. 'I've only got one place where I can lay my head, and I can't give you the address. I've been driven there, and I've walked away from it. I can find it again. It's near Kidderminster, I know that much. And there's here. Follow me home . . .' I stopped, and gestured helplessly. 'Follow me to Dr Dennis's place and that'll be it. For now.'

'This Dr Dennis?' he asked. 'This is the witness you spoke about, at your grandmother's?'

I nodded. We were now talking naturally, me trying to be helpful, as would a normal law-abiding citizen, he probing gently without pushing it.

'It's Dr Margaret Dennis. She's an art expert.'

'Well-known?'

'Internationally,' I said, with reflected pride.

'Then we'll be able to trace her. And trace you. This association with her—can I ask?—is recent?'

'Very. Her interest is professional.'

'Your private life—'

'Is none of your business. I merely mentioned it in case my wife—'

'She told me there was a woman.'

'The same.'

We stared at each other. I could read his thoughts. I smiled, allowing them to mature. He pushed his hat on more firmly.

'If you get any more news,' I said. 'You know—the post-mortem, I'd like to know.'

'I'll see you're kept fully informed, Mr Hine. Closely.' He nodded, opened the outer door, and left.

I returned to my darkroom, where I had a high stool in front of my bench. My legs felt weak. I wanted a smoke, and filled my pipe. It's rarely that I smoke in there, because of the poor ventilation. This time I did, unable to get back to my work, and attempting to clear the situation in my head. I was trying not to think about Grannie Angelina's death.

I had declared that I was not really concerned about the provenance of the eighty-one canvases. In either event, they had been painted by one of my grandparents. But this didn't mean that I wasn't concerned about owning them. In fact, there was a deep and hard core of possessiveness growing inside me. They were mine. Gran had wanted me to have them. Yet now there was a hint of dispute over their ownership. Grace could well put up a legal battle about them, monetary value or not. They'd been the last straw of a series of gifts extorted from Gran, trading on her generosity. There was going to be trouble from Grace, and hell, I'd got all the distracting trouble I could handle.

Determined to be professional, and refusing to brood uselessly, I forced myself to return to the prints, and, as always, became completely absorbed within a couple of minutes.

*   *   *

The cottage—I had to continue to think of it as that—was dark when I arrived there, but Margaret came at a touch of the bell-push in the porch. I heard her rapid footsteps up the staircase. She opened the door, snapping on the light at the same time.

'Where have you been? For God's sake . . . Tony, I needed you.'

She might well have been my wife. I smiled, smoothing the mood. 'It's a big job. Ten hours solid. I'm whacked.'

She was jumpy, her eyes jerking around, her hands moving in small gestures. Her make-up was minimal, her hair mussed, her clothes stained. One hand held a cigarette between two fingers. Her lips plunged for it, and she drew smoke in greedily. She turned away. It was almost a command to follow. We nearly trotted through the kitchen, and I had only a moment to notice the scattering of quick snacks and empty cups, and the saucers lined with cigarette stubs.

Inside her workroom there was a flat glare of white, pitiless light. She closed the door, the gesture being allied with the closing of my darkroom door. Inside here was her life, but whereas, for me, there had been another life, for her this had long been the nucleus of her basic existence.

She had completed the cleaning, the whole eighty-one, and had them ranked all round the walls, perched on her benches. They glowed, they danced. Sunlight shone from them, mocking her artificial tubes. Here was Paris in the spring and summer, and on into six or seven autumns, but it was a Paris where the sun always shone. Frederick Ashe—or

Angelina Foote—had loved sunlight, had tried to recreate it, and had succeeded. I stood, caught in awe.

'You've had a busy day,' I said at last.

'I have.' Her voice was harsh. 'I've had five under the spectroscope, I've analysed the pigments . . .'

'But we know they shared the same palette.'

She moved a hand in quick rejection. 'There was a chance, damn it.'

'But . . . nothing?'

'Not one clue. Hers or his! I've agonized over brush strokes and techniques, the force of the impasto, the . . . the vision. They could be his. His, Tony!' Her voice was unsteady. She had worked too hard and too long. 'But look round them. Go on. Take your time. Tell me what you see.'

I glanced at her. There was a bitter harshness to her voice that I didn't like. Then I walked round slowly. These were mine. All this beauty really belonged to me. Did I say they mirrored Paris? Well yes, but there were a few that held a tang of England. There was one that held more than a tang. I turned with it in my hand.

'You put my original one amongst them,' I accused her.

She flicked me an empty smile, bent, and picked up a canvas from behind a chair. 'No. This is your original one.'

One in each hand, I turned them over. She was correct. The one she'd just handed me was mine. I knew that because there was a small scorch mark on one of the wooden stretchers, which I'd never been able to understand, but now did.

'Look at them,' she said fiercely. 'Go on. Tell me if you can see a difference between the two.'

Of course there were differences. No two brush strokes can be identical, no loading of the brush, even from the same palette, equally full. Nevertheless, they could well have been painted by the same person. Yet there was one difference, one that was immediately apparent to a photographer. Perspective.

'They were painted from slightly different viewpoints,' I said, not because that proved anything, just as something to reassure her. Certainly, from the wildness in her eyes, she needed reassurance.

'I saw that. D'you think I'm a complete fool!' Her voice was too loud. She modified it. 'There's more of the side of the cottage in the one than the other. One tree is farther over to the left than in the other. It fits, Tony, for heaven's sake. They sat side by side—say three feet apart—so of course they would see the view from slightly different angles.'

She had reasoned this out. At the end, she was managing to speak reasonably. Then she

93

spoilt it by waving wildly round the room and crying out: 'But I ought to know which is which! It's driving me mad. I'm an expert. People pay me to fly round the world. I say yes, this is genuine, that is a fake, and they take my word. I ought to know, blast it, and I don't.' Then I saw that it was fear in her eyes. 'I ought to know, Tony,' she said with a catch in her voice. 'I *have* to know.'

'Perhaps one of them was left-handed,' I suggested, introducing a light touch.

'What?'

'Sitting side by side, using the same palette, one of them would have to lean over awkwardly to reach it. But if one was left-handed, it'd solve it for them. Perhaps that was why they always shared a palette, placed between them.'

'Don't be a fool, Tony. Please.'

'Just an idea.'

'You don't realize what we've got here, do you! It's a great art find, the find of the century. We can't keep it a secret and hide them all away. Some time I've got to produce them and say: yes, that's Frederick Ashe, and that one's Angelina Foote. Me. The expert. And I'll need to point out why I say that, and be confident. Confident! And I'm lost. I can't get hold of anything positive I can latch on to. Don't you see, Tony? I don't know which of those two in your hand is Ashe's. And I should be able to!' she wailed, whipping her

94

hands up and sending her hair flying.

'If one of them was left-handed . . .'

'Oh for God's sake.'

'. . . and we know which . . .'

'Will you please—'

'. . . we'd at least know—or be fairly certain—which of these two was done by who.'

She paced a while. My suggestion seemed to have sailed right past her. She stopped, pointing a finger at me. Maybe it was the light that made her seem so pale, but after all she was conceding a defeat.

'There's only one thing for it. We'll have to go back to your grandmother and ask her—show her both—and ask her which is which.'

She was asking me to do this, and her reluctance was in no way linked with her belief that I might be hesitant to comply. She was hating herself for admitting the necessity.

'I'm afraid we can't do that,' I said gently. 'She died last night.'

She sucked in her breath so sharply that it fluttered her lower lip. 'Then she was . . . dying, when we saw her?'

I wasn't going to go into the ramifications. 'I don't think we could have helped her.'

'Oh hell! The poor old thing. I upset her. You don't think that could . . . oh no. No! I don't know . . . I can't see . . . there's nothing I can think of. Oh . . . Tony!'

She stood before me, arms now limp at her sides. Her eyes were brimming with tears, though whether at my grandmother's death or at her feeling of helpless defeat I couldn't tell.

'You'll think of something.'

'I've thought and thought.' Her hands came up in small fists in front of her. 'I've racked my brains, nearly driven myself mad . . .' Then she moved to stand facing me, raised her fists, and thumped my chest. I allowed the two canvases to slip from my fingers, slide down my legs, and flop gently to the floor. I took her elbows, then slid my hands up to her shoulders.

'It's going to be all right, Margaret.'

She searched my face for confidence she could cling to. 'But it's not! she moaned. 'Everything's . . .' Her voice sank to a whisper. 'Everything's going to nothing.'

Tears welled on to her cheeks. This was the young Margaret, home from art school as a failure. I was her father. She needed comfort and understanding. And who better than me to understand, who'd made my photography a retreat from unpromising reality? But her case was worse than mine. Hers was not simply her obsession, it was her life and her only reality. She had worked for it, fought for it, hacked herself a notch in the hierarchy of art knowledge, and always she had to be aware that the higher she climbed, the farther her fall if she made one incorrect identification. She was exposed and vulnerable, and however successfully she had trained herself into a practicality and severity fitting her status, beneath it there was a woman refusing to admit her basic frustration.

So I kissed her on the forehead as a comforting father, kissed her on the eyelids with gentle understanding, and on her lips as no father would kiss her. There were aeons of desperate longing in her lips, and her hands tightened around my neck in a frantic desire for security and self-confidence.

I lifted my face from hers. Her eyes were huge.

'In the morning,' I pronounced, as one who knows, 'it will seem different. You'll see.' My voice betrayed none of my own lack of self-confidence.

She didn't answer. She clung to me again, and the morning was a long way away.

CHAPTER SIX

We stared at each other across the breakfast table. She was relaxed, her face naked of make-up, her hair in a tangle that I found delightful.

'You said it would look different,' she said.

'And it doesn't.' But it was delivered with a smile.

Whatever I'd said to her in the night, I had not mentioned the possibility that Gran's death might not have been natural.

'I've been thinking about it.'

'Oh? When?'

I grinned at her. 'Between times.'

'I'm not sure that's a compliment.'

'But I was thinking for you.'

'Hmm!' She nodded, sipped coffee. 'Such as?'

'Two things. This left-handed business . . . no, don't laugh. It's valid. Listen. If both were right-handed—or both left-handed, of course—they could well have switched positions from time to time, to share the strain of reaching over. If so, we're in trouble. But if one of them *was* left-handed, and the other not, the odds are that they always painted together in the same positional relationship. You're with me?'

'Oh certainly. With you, but not convinced.'

'Then consider this. We don't know whether my original one is Ashe's or Grannie's. But if we did, you'd have a clue. Am I right there?'

'If we knew that, you idiot, we'd have the truth here and now.'

'But there are six others around. Presumably those have all been assessed by other experts, your peers, whose judgement you'd respect. Yes?'

A spark of interest had entered her eyes. It died when she realized it would mean deferring to other opinions. 'I see what you mean. But how does it help?'

I had to work it out as I spoke, clarifying the situation in my own mind.

'Let's look at what we've got. Things we know. We know two sets were painted, and from what you say they're almost indistinguishable from each other.'

She nodded glumly. 'You're right there.'

'We also know that my original canvas is not from the same set as the eighty-one. We know this, because it's matched with one from the loft set, apart from the fact that it was painted from a slightly different viewpoint.'

'I can't argue with that.'

'But what we don't know is whether the other, already-known, Ashes are part of the loft set, which would make the original complete set eighty-seven—'

'Angelina said more than eighty.' She nodded her permission for me to continue.

'Or from the other set, the same set as mine, and not destroyed because they were sold in Paris, long before the bonfire.'

'If we knew, what would it prove?'

'Accepting . . . accept it for the moment . . . that the other six can be attributed to Frederick Ashe, then we'd know whether to attribute the whole loft set to him, or only my original one.'

'How would we know?'

'By whether the six match with six in the loft set, and by the question of the viewpoint of the painter.'

To my surprise and disappointment she looked down miserably at her cup, and moved it around with one finger at the handle. She looked up.

'I'm afraid I've already thought of that. Something like it, though not the left-handed business. I was frantic for ideas. Do you know what it's like . . . no, of course not. I thought I was going insane. So I phoned all four of the art galleries. And there's a snag.'

'You'd have to go there?'

'Not that. They haven't got the paintings now.'

'Sold? They'll know who—'

'Not sold. Stolen. In the past two years. All four. Clever, slick and efficient robberies, aiming for those specific canvases. The Frederick Ashes.'

I thought about that. It took only a second. 'A collector. Somebody interested in Frederick Ashe.'

'Naturally.'

'But there's still the other two. In a private collection, you said.'

She made a dismissive sound, pursing her lips. 'There's a man. He's known in the

100

trade. He sends a representative to bid for him when there's something he wants, with simple instructions—no limit. He can afford to. His wealth is legendary, but where he got it from is doubtful. There've been rumours, ranging from drug-smuggling to stock exchange irregularities. Rumours only. But he has a house, almost a fortress, and rumour, again, has it that he owns a huge collection of paintings. The snag is, nobody's ever been allowed to see them. But of course, whatever his wealth, he can buy only what's offered for sale. It's he who owns the two other Frederick Ashes, and legitimately. The odds are that he's got the whole six, now. So what can we do there? I ask you.'

I looked at her across the table. Elbows on the surface, her hands cradling a coffee mug, she was staring wide-eyed at me, and making a tiny moue of embarrassed surrender. And that was exactly what she was doing; she was *asking* me. Some time in the night she had come to terms with herself. She could not wholly admit that she was beaten, not to the extent of calling in fellow experts. They might shame her by displaying greater knowledge and a more firmly established scholarship. But she could dare to display her weaknesses to a friend—an intimate friend—who wouldn't be ashamed to use unartistic methods of proof. So she was asking me, but meekly, in a way suggesting surrender to a stronger character than herself—a man. It was this part of it that was false, but I didn't let her see I realized it. In practice, I was becoming personally involved with the puzzle, and didn't mind playing the game, if that was what she wanted.

'I don't fancy tangling with a man like that,' I said, 'but we don't have to discard it out of hand. Call it number three option.'

'Number three?'

'I can see two other ways of going at it. One of them is the left-handedness. It might be possible to show that one of them *was* left-handed. If so, we apply it to the pair of near duplicates we've got, and it'd tell us who painted which.'

'Small chance there.' She nodded. 'What else?'

'My gran said Grace had told her it'd been the Ashe painting that went in the fire. It was from that set that mine was rescued. Right? We thought Grace could have made a mistake, or even have been lying. So she's obviously the first one to tackle. Ask her, and see what comes from it.'

Interest sparked in her eyes. She thrust back her chair. 'I'll take a shower. We'll use my car.'

'No. I intended to do it alone.' I smiled at her, taking the edge off it. But all the same it was a challenge. Was she going to take charge again, now that I'd made my suggestions? Or try to.

'I'd like to hear what she says.' Then she made a gesture of dismissal. 'All right. If that's how you want it.'

'I've got an excuse—a reason. It will be natural to call and offer my condolences. They were together for more than sixty years.'

'Of course. I'm being thoughtless. You must go alone. But it'll be awkward for you.'

'Perhaps.' '

More than awkward, embarrassing. She had fed the police with information that had virtually led to a murder charge against me. She was certainly going to make trouble over the paintings. No, awkward was a pallid word for it.

When I was ready to leave I put my head inside Margaret's laboratory, where she'd once more plunged into her work. I'd suggested that things would look better in the morning, but this was artificial daylight, and everything looked the same. Had I realized it, the solution was already there for the taking, but at that time we hadn't run out of options, and neither of us looked closely enough.

I drove away to see Grace.

The day was sunny, and I'd hoped it would make the place look less devastatingly gloomy. But it did not. The trees had grown wildly with their freedom, and no sun penetrated. Pessimistic, then, as to my welcome, I was not surprised when Grace tried to slam the door in my face.

I put my foot inside, and used my shoulder as a buffer. 'We've got to talk, Grace.'

'Thief!' she shouted.

'We ought to discuss the paintings.'

'There's nothing to talk about. You stole them. Go away.'

'We *are* talking about them. Now wouldn't it be more sensible to do it sitting down? Like civilized human beings.'

She would not like it to be suggested that she was uncivilized. She had been the companion to a lady. Didn't that make her a lady, too? The pressure eased at my shoulder, an eye appeared at the gap.

'You're a thieving swine,' she said temperately, 'but I suppose you'd better come in. Never let it be said I wasn't polite.'

I entered. The emptiness of the house was overpowering, with an atmosphere of aching loneliness that was Grace's own. Could she bear to live with it here alone? Would she wish to? The house would certainly be hers. She could sell it. She would not be derelict. Or so I told myself.

She led me into the drawing-room where we had first waited. It was full of whispering stillness and of chill rejection. Grace seemed unaware of any inhibition. She took one of the four remaining Regency dining chairs and sat primly on it, leaving me to do the same, or to stand. I chose to stand, to give myself room to move around. At least I could disturb the air, my clothes making rustling sounds to which the room listened hungrily. Grace waited. She'd made her opinion known. She sat still. There was no indication of mourning. The curtains were as wide as they'd been before. The room itself mourned, though it hadn't seen Angelina for . . . how many years?

I went straight to the attack, though gently. She was not a fragile woman, as my grandmother had been, but she was not young.

'I've been told,' I said, 'that you're making a claim to the paintings.'

'They're mine. Everything that was in this house when she died. Mine. You can't get round that.'

'Then surely it all rests on exactly when she did die,' I suggested.

Her head snapped up and her eyes gleamed. 'I saw you leaving. The car pulled out of the drive. I recognized it. I drove up to the front door. A minute, perhaps. I went straight up to her. Ran. I didn't trust you. Another minute. And she was dead then. She died before you got them out of the house. So there.'

She was in no way senile. She knew how things stood. I smiled at her. 'It's almost as though you're saying I killed her, Grace.'

105

'I wouldn't put it past you.'

'Come now. That's a serious accusation. Why should I? What would I gain?'

'The paintings from the loft, that's obvious. They're mine. You bring them back here, or I'll have the law on you.'

'But she said she wanted me to have—'

'Said,' she jerked out, her face quivering with the triumph. 'Only said. She'd said to me she'd take it all back. In writing.'

'I see.' The pen being mightier than the word. 'But how could I have known she'd promised you that, Grace? If I didn't know, I'd have no reason. Surely you can see that.'

'You woke her up. Got it out of her.'

I paced a little, trying to make my feet disturb the silence beyond our voices, but the carpet was heavy.

'You've worked all this out,' I conceded.

She nodded, jowls quivering. 'You're not getting one over on me.'

'I'm not trying to.'

'It sounds like you are to me. But you can be sure of one thing—I'm having them back. Or I'll want to know the reason why.'

'The reason why,' I said, though the remark had been rhetorical, 'is that I'm satisfied I've got a legal and moral right to them.'

Her feet stamped so hard on the carpet that she nearly shot herself out of the chair. 'We'll see about that. Just you wait.'

106

'What can they mean to you, Grace? A bunch of old paintings, that's all they are. It's not as though they're valuable.'

She leaned back, crossing her arms as though she'd said the lot. 'It's the principle of the thing.'

'Unless you believe they *are* valuable, Grace.' She glanced away. 'Is that it?'

She sniffed, and her lips sucked in, then prodded out again.

'Do you believe they could be valuable?' I persisted.

'How would I know?'

'Well now. That's the point. There was a bonfire. Do you remember the bonfire, Grace? But of course you do. Mr Hine threw a batch of paintings down from the loft, and they were burned. He thought he was throwing down the set painted by Frederick Ashe. You know who he was, I suppose?'

I waited. Her eyes were fixed on a patch of mould in the far corner of the room. They flickered back to me, and away again. 'Her lover.' It was delivered with contempt.

'But Angelina thought she'd fooled him—fooled her husband—and believed she'd burned her own paintings. Though perhaps he was too smart for her, and threw down the canvases painted by Grannie's lover.'

'He wasn't stupid, Arthur wasn't. She called him a shopkeeper. To her, that was an insult. But he was a clever man. Owned six shops. A clever man.'

'I'm sure he was.'

'And don't tell me he married her for money,' she said violently, once more facing me fully, her hands free and gesturing. 'He never made any scret of it. I heard him tell her that. Arthur always called a spade a spade. He said she was like spoiled goods, that they had to pay him to take her off their hands.' She smirked. She'd memorized the exact phrase.

'So,' I said, after a small interval during which this endearment was allowed to settle, 'so, he was possibly clever enough to double-guess her, and he threw down the Frederick Ashe paintings he knew she treasured.'

'Yes,' she said, pride in the inclination of her head.

'Do you *know* he did that?'

'Not know.' She was cautious. 'Not really know.'

'And yet—and my grandmother told me this, Grace—and yet she said that you went up into the loft for her, because she couldn't manage it herself, and you came down and said the Frederick Ashe ones had gone.'

'How would I know that?'

'Because she'd told you that his had a cross on the tea chests.'

She pouted sullenly. 'As like as not.'

'Did you tell her those were the ones that'd gone?'

'I seem to remember I did.'

'Come now, Grace. It's something you wouldn't forget. Did you go into the loft and check if the chests still there had a cross on them? Or not?'

'I went into the loft, yes.'

'And did they—at that time—have a cross on them?' It was now becoming difficult to moderate my voice.

She lifted her chin. The wattles fell back. 'I didn't trouble to look.'

I took that in, letting my mind juggle with it a little, but it came out again unblemished.

'And yet you told Angelina that it was the batch of Frederick Ashe paintings that she'd burned.' I made that a statement.

She answered with impatient definition. 'Yes.'

'But you didn't *know* that?'

'No.'

'Then why did she say it?'

I had the feeling that it was not I who'd led her gently to that point, but she who had teased me along to the question. She smiled. I'd got to it at last. But there was such secret malice in the smile that I nearly recoiled.

'Because I knew it would hurt her,' she replied, nodding in emphasis. 'And I knew she'd never be able to get up there and check for herself.'

'But why in heaven's name should you want to hurt her?'

'Because I loved Arthur, and he loved me, and Angelina killed him.'

'Figuratively speaking, of . . .' I stopped and stared at her. The hard buttons of her eyes challenged me. 'You did say killed?'

'If pushing him down a staircase is killing, that's what she did. I saw her do it. She killed him.'

I had to turn away. She had led me into a uncharted realm of conjecture, and I was afraid to go ahead. It was something I didn't want to know.

'You don't want to believe it, do you?' she jeered at my back. 'Your precious grannie, the angel. Just because of her name. Angelina!' she cried in disgust. 'She was no angel, I'll have you know.'

I turned back to her. Her name was Grace, but there was no grace here. She leaned forward, tightly embracing the venom. Spittle decorated the corners of her lips.

'Tell me,' I said quietly, facing it full on.

'Why d'you think there's no carpet on the stairs?'

'What?'

'His blood. It wouldn't wash out. She had it taken away.'

'His blood.'

'He was carrying a drinks tray—glasses, bottles, everything. She was just behind him at the top of the stairs, at his shoulder. He'd never let her walk in front of him. A lady always goes first, he used to say. You follow, my angel. He called her his angel. That was a laugh, but Arthur always had a sense of humour, you can say that for him. There've been times—'

'Grace!' I cut in, and for the first time I was unable to control my voice. 'For God's sake keep to the point.'

'There's no need for blasphemy.' Then she gave a bitter laugh. 'I want you to understand.'

'Oh, I do.' Arthur had hated his angel all their married life. Or loved her, in spite of himself. If he'd not, why the corroding jealousy for a man long dead? I decided not to probe that matter with Grace. 'The stairs,' I said more quietly. 'Arthur and his tray.'

She nodded, her lower lip loose. 'He'd got no spare hand for the banister. He was a big man, heavy. I was behind, along the corridor. I saw her take his elbow. He glanced round. She twisted him, and put all her weight into his back, and he was gone. She shouted at him all the way down.' She stopped abruptly, then whispered: 'Shouted *at* him. Hatred. Yes.'

'He broke his neck?'

'What?' She tore herself from the memory. 'No. It was the glass. The jugular. You know the jugular?'

111

'Not exactly, Grace, but I'm sure you do.'

'I might have saved him,' she said in a dead voice, 'but Angelina was having hysterics and grabbed hold of me, and wouldn't let me go. Hysterics! Not her! It was on purpose. Hard as nails, she was. I couldn't get to him, she hung on so, and his life ran away down the carpet.'

'You mentioned the carpet,' I put in quickly. 'When was this, Grace? Roughly.'

'On the sixth of May, 1934.'

'Your memory is very clear, I must say.'

'It was the day after your father's sixteenth birthday. The day after he went away.'

'I see.' I caught at the tide of it, hoping to get as much as possible before the ebb of tears. 'So the batch of paintings, the ones remaining after the bonfire, had been in the loft for how many years . . . fifteen? Sixteen?'

'All of that.'

'The bonfire was soon after my father's birth, I understand.'

Again I had the impression she was encouraging me, leading me on. She was leaning forward like a crumpled gnome, her face bright with intentness.

'That would be the time,' she agreed.

'And in all those years my grandmother, who must have been uncertain which paintings she'd destroyed, didn't go up and check?'

'How could she?' She raised both palms

112

and slapped her cheeks in an ecstasy of revelation. 'Arthur had a padlock put on the trapdoor—right after the fire, that was.'

'Yes. He would. That sounds like his line of thinking. So that, after his death, when Grandmother had the key . . . that was when she tried to get up there?'

'So stupid. She couldn't wait.'

'And she fell?'

'Yes. She fell. It seemed like a judgement on her.'

'Very true. You saw that one, too?'

'I was right behind her.'

'Right behind? On the steps, d'you mean? And she didn't take you down with her?'

Her face was so solemn it must have hurt. 'She was reaching up with both hands to the padlock. I could see—her feet were six inches from my nose, so don't say I couldn't see—her left foot was slipping off the tread. I shouted, but I was too late, and she went. I sort of, you know, flattened myself against the steps and hung on. She went right over me.' She waited, challenging me to criticize her own role in this, to mention how close her own hands must have been to my grand-mother's ankles. I said nothing. She sighed. 'It was her spine. She was paralysed all down one side.'

Thus making her completely dependent on Grace. Why had she not dismissed her, and taken on a more amenable and amicable

113

companion? Fear? Fear of what Grace had seen when her husband died? And Grace—she had stayed because of the power she could wield, the taunts, subtle and outspoken, she could throw around, the misery she could inflict by telling my grandmother that she had, with her own hand, destroyed her lover's life-work in a bonfire. And Grace had not even bothered to check the truth of this!

No wonder the house held an atmosphere of doom. The two women had lived with this between them, holding them in its grip for over fifty years. Hatred is a stronger emotion than love. Hatred feeds on itself; love needs replenishing.

And yet . . .

'You told me you loved him,' I said, trying to discover something in this house that hadn't gone sour. 'And he you. Were you lovers?'

'Sometimes he visited her. They slept in separate rooms.'

'And when he was not with her . . .'

'He was with me.'

'A passionate man—'

'Don't throw your fancy words at me, young man,' she cut in fiercely. 'We were young, and we were in love. Sex, that's what all you young people look for and think about. We could not have gone on, in this house together, if we'd not had each other.

Oh I know, you got your dear Angelina's story, her grand passion, like a story book. And *that* you approve. Don't deny it. I can see it in your face. Why should it have been any different for us? We loved each other. I think . . . if it hadn't been for me . . . he'd have gone insane in this house. We laughed and we cried together, and we whispered our secrets to each other. And I watched him die on that staircase.'

For the first time there was life in her face. Suddenly I could see that she would have been pretty, with that mobile, chunky face, pretty in a joyful, outgoing way, generous in her giving and in her enjoyment of life. It was a fleeting glimpse, the most painful moment of my visit. Then it was gone. I took out my pipe and stared at it, not daring even to consider lighting it.

'And when you were whispering together, Grace, laughing together, didn't he tell you how he'd tricked Angelina, and thrown down from the loft the ones she *didn't* want to burn?'

Her mouth fell open and she gobbled, positively gobbled in an attempt to control her tongue. 'No!' she managed to get out at last. 'That's not true.'

'But that's the sort of thing he would talk to you about, Grace. It's the exact type of intimate joke you'd exchange.'

Then she was on her feet, both arms raised,

her scarred and arthritic hands clenched, and she flew at me. Not in the way Margaret had flown at me. This was furious outrage. She had trusted me with her intimate thoughts, and I'd seized on them and used them against her. But I had to know. The damned thing was becoming an obsession. I wanted to help Margaret. Yes. But there was something more important than that now. The paintings, in one way or another, had been the cause of one death and a crippling accident—even a second possible murder. All these thoughts flitted through my head in the couple of seconds it took me to capture her flying wrists, to find myself inches from her distorted face, feeling the spittle from her fury spattering me, and then to try to shout her down.

'Be quiet, Grace! You'll do yourself an injury. Take it easy, for God's sake!'

Then her face, made for it, crumpled into tears, and I almost had to catch her as I helped her back to her chair. She found a handkerchief from inside her garments and pressed it to her face, sobbing and sobbing to a point where I realised it had become false. She didn't want to look up at me.

'But it's true,' I said softly. 'You've got to admit it, Grace. He would have told you.'

I waited, and eventually she shuddered and raised her face, dabbing at it futilely. 'He never did.'

'I can't believe that.'

116

'You can just please your damned self,' she said distinctly, separating each word with emphasis. 'Now will you please go.'

I did so, after a last, doubtful glance at her, but I waited in the hall knowing she would have to watch me out of the door. She came after me, briskly now, her head up again.

'Oh . . . one thing, Grace,' I said.

'What now?'

'She was paralysed down her right side. I noticed that. So at the end she'd learned to use her left hand. What was she before her fall, right—or left-handed?'

'What're you up to?'

'I just wondered.'

'She was right-handed, if that does you any good.'

I smiled at her. I didn't expect to see her again, unless she took me to court over the ownership of the paintings.

When I turned from her, a large, dark car was parking behind mine in the drive. The first person out of the rear door was Detective Sergeant Dolan.

CHAPTER SEVEN

For a moment I was uncertain what to do. Did I nod, walk over to my car, and drive away? But that would signify an abandonment of Grace. I advanced on to the drive, and waited.

A tall, thin and sour man got out of the other side of the car. He stared at me across the roof, said something quietly to Dolan, and on his reply gave instructions. Then he and the driver, who was a woman in a plain costume, not a uniform, advanced on Grace. I heard the thin man ask whether she was Grace Fielding. At her murmured response, they disappeared into the house.

'So here you are,' said Dolan, as though they'd been scouring the countryside for me.

'As it happens, yes.'

'Just off?'

'That was my intention.'

'Spare a minute? Come and sit in the car.'

We sat side by side in the back of the police Granada. He was treating me as an old and valued friend.

'A social visit, was it?'

He was offering me an escape route. 'Not really.' I tried to get my pipe going, my system shouting out for nicotine. 'I came to discuss the paintings.'

He gave a soft chuckle. We weren't staring at each other, so a smile would have gone to waste. 'Not a friendly discussion, I'd guess. The Super's going to be mad, you smoking in his car.'

'Let him. I don't mind getting out and driving away.'

118

He touched my elbow. 'He'd like to hear that I'm keeping you fully in touch.'

'There're developments, then?' I wound down the window and blew smoke at the open air.

'The post-mortem report's in. A verbal one, anyway.'

I glanced at him. 'And?'

'She was suffocated. A hand over her mouth and nose. There was no struggle.'

'I don't suppose there would be,' I said, feeling sick at his casual tone.

He seemed to be marshalling his thoughts, as there was a pause. Then he slapped my knee. 'Have you tried the beer in The Dun Cow?'

'No,' I said cautiously. 'Haven't had the time.'

'The draught bitter's good, and they've got a pin-ball machine.'

'Exciting. That'd tax your mind.'

'She goes there every night. Two halves, and she plays the machine. Thumps the side, as they do. It's supposed to achieve something.'

'Yes. This is Grace Fielding you're talking about?' Watching his nod, I struggled for a mental picture of her, half a pint in one hand, and thumping the other palm against the machine. 'Are you telling me something?'

'The machine's painted brown. The paint's flaking. All that thumping, I suppose. And it's not often dusted.' He cleared his throat. 'There were traces of dust and tiny flecks of brown paint in your grandmother's lungs. We've taken samples from the machine for checking.'

He must have been a wow in court, with his precise and exact explanations. There was only one question I needed to ask.

'You're taking her in?'

He shook his head. I'd turned to face him. He said: 'I shouldn't think so. If that'd been the intention, the Super would've sent me. No—he's playing it softly. He's a sneaky devil. If he gets a straight admission, that would change things. But I doubt he will. She struck me as a hard woman.'

'She doesn't admit much. But she was upset—'

'You upset her?'

'Not purposely. One thing led to the other. I doubt she can stand much more, but I don't think you'll get an admission.'

'So he'll go gently. Just questions. He knows we've got no case, as it stands. Nothing the court wouldn't throw out. At this stage, anyway.'

'Why're you telling me this?'

'You're an interested party.'

'Don't kid me, Sergeant. The police don't show their hands unless they want something. What d'you want from me?'

He grinned, and to his credit came out with

120

it. 'The paintings. Information on them. Why is she making such an issue about them?'

So we were back to the paintings. There was no getting away from the subject. 'My grandmother had been giving away bits of furniture and ornaments and things, all of which cut down Grace's possible inheritance. The paintings—me taking them away—was perhaps a camel's back situation. She spotted us driving away. She couldn't stand the thought. The way Grace put it, it was the principle of the thing.'

'Hmm!' he said. I hadn't supplied him with the fact that these gifts had been Angelina's only way to hit back at Grace's malice. But perhaps he guessed. 'Are they valuable?' he asked.

'I don't know. Perhaps. It's a question of who painted them.'

'Perhaps she knows they're valuable. Grace Fielding, I mean.'

'That's what upset her, me trying to find out. But she wouldn't admit to knowing a thing about them.'

'We might be able to persuade her.'

'Beat it out of her?'

He raised his eyebrows. 'If necessary,' he said solemnly. 'You on her side or something?'

I laughed. 'You're tricky, Sergeant. I said it as a joke.'

'I'll try it in the canteen, and let you know

how many laughs I get.'

I sighed. 'She'd looked after Angelina for most of her natural life. She'd hardly kill her now . . .'

'Unless she knows they're valuable. From fury. A last straw, as you said.'

I was silent. I could hardly tell him that Grace wouldn't destroy the person on whom she could vent her hatred. He would think I was mad. At last I ventured: 'I don't think she knows what they are, valuable or not.'

'You *are* on her side.' He spoke accusingly, wonderingly.

The house had witnessed too much distress already. I shook my head.

'She was your grandmother, for Pete's sake!'

'I'm aware of that.'

'You're a bit slow on the uptake, that's your trouble. Haven't you realized . . . if we take her in, charge her, and get an admission that she killed Mrs Hine—or if we eventually get a conviction—then it'll show that your grandmother died after you'd left the house, and then there'd be no denying your legal right to the paintings.'

'I hadn't thought of it like that.'

'Then think about it.'

I stared at him, not sure any more that he was the friendly and understanding man I'd thought him. Understanding, yes, but in a sly, furtive way. He was trying to use my emotional responses to force me into revealing every fact that Grace had told me. One of them might clinch the case. I had no reason to feel any sympathy for Grace, but I couldn't find it in me to hate her.

'All right. I'll think about it,' I promised, and opened the car door. From outside, I leaned into the open window. 'And if they turn out to be valuable, I'll let you know.'

I left him a waft of smoke, walked to the Fiesta and got inside, and only then realized that I was blocked in by the Granada. So I had to sit and wait, with nothing to do but think.

I realized, thus thinking, that the provenance of the paintings had now become imperative. It was no longer a question of value, nor a matter of assisting Margaret in her ego problems, but a matter of laying a ghost. Those canvases had sparked too much tragedy. I had to know to what extent it was justified.

At last the superintendent and his driver emerged. They did not have Grace with them, but she stood there at the door, still open six inches, and peered out at them. When the Granada backed out, she shut the door firmly. It indicated that she considered me a very minor menace, in comparison.

I reversed out, and set off back to Margaret's place, stopping only to post off the proofs for the factory at Maidstone.

It occurred to me that opening the front door was the first time that day she'd taken a breath of fresh air. Her stance was dejected and weary, her face blotched, her make-up nil, her eyes red with strain.

'You're late,' she said. 'I've got something cooking. I only hope it isn't spoilt.'

'It can't be that bad, I'm starving.'

She stood back from me. I could tell she was poised to demand how it had gone, but she restrained her impatience until we were halfway through the meal. At last: 'Well? Did you discover anything useful?'

'By useful, would you consider an accusation by Grace that my grandmother killed her husband?'

Her fork was poised, waved, then she said: 'Is the old fool completely insane?'

'I think not. There was a hint, too, that it was Grace who caused Angelina's accident.'

'A hint?'

'She almost boasted about it.'

'Dear Lord, what a house!'

'I don't think I want to see it again, ever.'

I then went on to tell her what had happened during my visit there, to the best of my recollection. Her dinner grew cold on her plate. Not mine; I ate between bursts of speech.

'And did she know what crates Arthur Hine took the paintings from?' she demanded, before I could get into that bit.

I considered how to put it. 'She said she didn't . . .'

'Of course she knew!' Margaret burst out.

I looked down at my plate. 'She wouldn't need to know. Her purpose was to *say* to Angelina that the Frederick Ashe paintings had been destroyed. She wouldn't need to know the truth.'

'Then why is she so possessive about them?' she demanded. 'She must know they're valuable, that's all I can say.'

'How could she, Margaret? You people, living in your tight little art world, you seem to believe the great British public can't wait for the latest news about art. It's not so. The odds are that Grace doesn't know how well-known Frederick Ashe has become.'

'Oh, you're a fool! Don't you want to know the truth?'

'Very much so.' What I didn't want to do was watch her face, so I went to get the coffee. 'But not by conjecture. Proof positive.'

'Which we're never going to get. That woman knows the truth, and you let her get away with evasions.'

'She told me one thing,' I claimed equably, putting a mug under her nose. 'Angelina was right-handed.' She looked down. 'It's not much, but it's something. Unless she was lying, of course.'

I sat down opposite to her again, uneasy at

125

her hair-trigger temper. When she still hadn't spoken after two minutes, I asked: 'And your day—how did it go?'

She looked up smiling, but with an obvious effort. 'Something, possibly, achieved. Very little, but I got something. I drove up to London. There were catalogues to be consulted, and the records of art gallery collections. I wanted to find reproductions of the four Ashe paintings that were stolen.'

'And you did?'

She pouted. 'Black and white in three cases, and only a description in the fourth. But it did seem, working from memory of course, that they could have near duplicates in the loft set.' At my eagerness, she shook her head. 'It means nothing. Most artists paint more than one canvas of their favourite scenes. It doesn't have to mean . . .' She stared past me, her eyes vacant, and licked her spoon absently. 'It occurred to me to search for biographies. They're sometimes very useful. The authors use reproductions of little-known works, because the pictures are important to the reading matter, not because they're fine works.' It was clearly a practice of which she didn't approve.

'I can see you found something. Let's have it. Whose biography was it?'

She smiled like a temptress, her eyes narrow, her tongue flicking her lips. 'Maurice Bellarmé. Your grandmother mentioned him.

He was apparently a close friend. There was a reproduction of one of Bellarmé's paintings that he simply called *Angel, 1914*. She was very beautiful, Tony. And there was another. *Frederick Ashe, 1914*. It was this one that caught my attention. It was a picture of Ashe working on a canvas. They often did this, the artists in those days, using each other as models. And Tony, Ashe was painting left-handed.'

She produced this nugget of interest as though it didn't glitter with the perfection of a pure and definite clue. I opened my mouth, and she put a finger to my lips.

'I don't want to make too much of this, Tony. After all, if they'd both been right-handed, he'd probably have sat to her right when they painted together. Then he would be the one to reach across for the palette, out of politeness.'

'Politeness to their womenfolk wasn't rejected in those days.'

She didn't rise to it. 'But with him being left-handed, it's almost certain he would sit to her right. Almost.'

'If he sat to her left, they'd both have had to reach across,' I agreed.

'Exactly. So we could surely take it as proof.'

'Almost certainly.'

She raised her eyebrows. We were both being very cautious, because we were aware that we were taking Grace's word for it that Angelina had been right-handed.

But I had a ghost to lay. Ghosts demand truth, because they can see through deceptions and evasions, see through each other.

'Let's take a look at the matched pair we've got,' I suggested, and she was up off her chair so fast it nearly went flying.

It was me she'd wanted to persuade. Or rather, she had wanted me to persuade myself. Already she had made her decision, but her attitude had changed since we'd first met. Then it had been a matter of plain and uncontestable statement: this is, and this is not. Her confidence had carried her foward, and she would not have expected to be forced into persuading. Now she was confident, but it was qualified. I was the one who now had to be persuaded. It was, perhaps, flattering. But it was out of character.

We put the two paintings of Frederick Ashe's cottage side by side, in the way they had been painted, which was apparent from the slightly different points of view. We separated them by a distance of three feet from each other, the approximate amount apart they would have been on their easels when they were painted. In these positions, the difference in perspective gave them a fresh reality.

My own canvas—I checked the scorch

mark on the back—was the one on the right.

Margaret sighed, and seemed to sag. Frederick Ashe, left-handed, and sitting to the right of Angelina, must have been the one to paint my canvas.

'So that's it,' she said. 'That's the answer. Ashe painted yours, and it was rescued from the fire. So the rest of his, apart from the six we know about, were destroyed. You've got eight—one Angelina Footes.'

'Haven't I!' I said with pride.

'Don't you care, damn it?' she shouted.

'Not much.'

'The whole damned batch wouldn't fetch as much as your one Frederick Ashe.'

'Probably not. School of Frederick Ashe. You said that.'

'Oh . . . you're impossible.'

'What d'you expect me to say?'

'At least . . . at least show some sort of disappointment. What's the matter with you? You nearly had a fortune in your hands, and now you've got . . . what?' She made a wide, sweeping gesture, almost swinging herself off her feet. 'A load of tat, not worth getting rid of.'

'I didn't intend to. However it turns out, I have a houseful of paintings by both my grandparents.' But no house to display them in, I recalled. Fleetingly, I wondered what Evelyn would say if I took home eighty-two paintings. How many canvases per wall would that be, counting the bathroom? I must have smiled.

'And it's nothing to smirk about,' she snapped.

'You're taking it too seriously.'

'Of *course* it's serious.'

'Ah! Perhaps you're thinking of the time you've wasted. Time lost and no fee. Tell you what, take any half dozen. Go on—'

She slapped my face.

Startled, I could do no more than stand there rubbing my cheek. She had her lower lip in her teeth.

'Sorry,' I said. 'But you're so . . . so intense. I was trying to lighten . . .'

'It matters,' she whispered, half turning away.

She had poised herself on the springboard of her career. One leap into the heights of a major art discovery, and she need never descend again. She'd been in orbit. But the springboard had collapsed, and her enthusiasm was drowned. To me, too, it mattered, I recalled. My ghosts demanded their absolute proof.

I said gently: 'This doesn't have to be positive. Let's look at it logically.'

'You and your damned logic.' But now she was more calm, even with a hopeful undertone in her voice.

'Grace could have been lying. We know she lied to Angelina, one way or the other. It's in

130

her blood—lying. If she knew Angelina was left-handed, it would be almost instinct for her to say she was right-handed.'

'Weak,' she decided emphatically.

'All right. Weak. Try this, then. That reproduction you found in the biography of Maurice Bellarmé—it was of Frederick Ashe. But that could've been printed backwards. It happens, you know. I had it happen with one of my pictures in a photo magazine.'

She pouted. 'That's unlikely. You're trying to encourage me, aren't you, Tony! Oh, I know you. Getting to, anyway. You don't like to hurt people. You're too soft. And I know you're as disappointed as I am. But you pretend. You *are* disappointed, and if you interrupt I'll kill you, Tony. You're not as disappointed in me as I am. This is my job, and I'm supposed to be an expert. Expert! I've failed. All right, it's taken me a day or two, but now I can face it. I'm finished, and that's it. There's nothing else I can do with these paintings of yours, or decide to do. So . . . as far as I'm concerned, that's the end of it. We assume the loft batch is Angelina's and . . . I don't know . . . I'll sell them for you, if you like. I don't know!'

The thought crossed my mind that if she was so certain she had 'failed', how could she be equally certain that the loft batch was Angelina's? But I didn't say so. Her brilliant mind was coldly analytical, and there wasn't

131

much room for warm logic. What I did say was: 'It's not the end, you know. There's still that man you mentioned, who has those two—and perhaps all six—of the accredited Frederick Ashes. We go to him—'

'You must be mad.'

'I don't see why we shouldn't.'

'You don't go to a man like that and expect to be welcomed and shown round his collection. The Queen couldn't get in there without the SAS behind her.'

After contemplating this image for a moment, I said: 'I'd thought of something more subtle. All we want to know is whether his two (or his six) have got near duplicates in the loft set. As my original one has. If so, then it indicates that the loft set must be Grannie's, because we have to accept the six are Frederick Ashes.'

'Indicates! Indicates!' she said impatiently. 'And how could you tell, just by looking at them, that they've got near duplicates?'

'We ask him.'

'We take all that batch of canvases to him . . .' She stopped, realizing that this was not what I'd implied.

'No. I'm a photographer. Remember? I'll take shots of all eighty-one, full frame, and do prints. They'll be good, I can promise you that. And we take him the prints. We say nothing. We let him do the talking.'

'I don't like it . . .'

'What harm could there be in trying?'

'I'd just as soon abandon the whole thing.'

I grinned at her. 'Rightee-oh. So we load 'em all in my car, and I'll do it round at my lab. It'll be inconvenient, but I'll manage somehow. Then I'll go and see him myself.'

'No,' she said.

'No?'

'I'll . . . I'll come with you. I'll have to. What if he lets us see the canvases! You wouldn't know what to look for.'

'Of course. I'd forgotten that. But I'm such an ignorant pig . . .'

She thumped my arm. 'Where's your camera, you big fool?'

One thing about her, the volatility of her temperament maintained the interest. Nursing my arm, I went to fetch my Pentax. I was still having to carry all my possessions around with me in the car.

CHAPTER EIGHT

She expected me simply to walk round her workroom, shooting away and capturing perfection. It's not like that. Strictly speaking, it should have been done with the camera mounted on my enlarger stand, each canvas face up on the base, and with a spotlight each side. But I was equipped with

133

no such niceties. I used a 50mm lens on the Pentax, and loaded in a slow film for finest grain and maximum definition. This meant that I would have to handle fairly slow exposures, as the diaphragm had to be stopped down for a decent depth of field, to allow for any lack of squareness to the subject. I couldn't use a flash on the hot-shoe, because it would throw back reflection, and I didn't want to use an extension flash because of the fall-off of light intensity across the canvases.

Margaret couldn't understand my laboured precision, so I explained. She still didn't understand. I did one at a time, perching them on a chair, leaning them against the back, and relying on her flat and white artificial light. It worked out at one-tenth of a second of f11, which was too slow for hand-held shots, so I used the tripod.

Eighty-one frames. It seemed to take an eternity. Three spools.

'I'll get straight on to this in the morning,' I told her. 'Another all-day stint.'

'Right. You do that. I'll try to find out who owns those two Maurice Bellarmé canvases.'

'Why trouble?'

'You said . . . the picture of Frederick Ashe in the biography could've been printed backwards.'

I grinned at her. She wasn't missing a trick.

We went to bed. Together. It seemed natural and inevitable. Mostly, we slept. Our second night together, and we were both so exhausted that we slept! Yet, come to think of it, we had become so attuned to each other's moods and characters that there was a hint of strain between us that inhibited relaxation. At least, so I felt. For once, I did not feel she had been completely honest with me, and it was in attempting to decide in what way that I fell asleep.

My automatic alarm woke me early. I was a self-employed man, used to fixed hours as a regular routine, and I had work awaiting me in my darkroom. I took a shower, got a quick breakfast inside me, and took her up a cup of tea at eight. She groaned and rolled over when I kissed the back of her neck. Her eyes were smeared, her cheeks puffy. The jet-black hair, I noticed, showed lighter traces at the roots.

'What time . . .' Her eyes cleared. 'You're dressed!'

'Early birds. It's eight o'clock.'

'Can't you ever rest?'

'No.' This was true. How could I rest when I was competing with Evelyn in the rivalry for income? The fact that I was no longer doing so hadn't yet seeped into my system. I still could not relax. Damn Evelyn. 'I'll be off,' I said. 'It's another big day in the dark.'

'No wonder you're so pale. Hurry back.'

'You know I will.'

I kissed her on her naked lips, savouring the perfume of her, and turned away quickly. Why ruin my applaudable efforts for an early start?

It was a fifty minute drive. When I pushed open my photo-lab door, there was a bulky brown envelope dragging against the floor. Not delivered through the post. No name on it.

On my narrow counter I slit it open. There was a note with the contents, from Evelyn.

Tony,
For God's sake make arrangements for your post. If you want a complete break, then do it. From next Monday I shall return all your mail as gone away. Which you have. I want to organize my life on that assumption.

Evelyn.

It had been a mistake even to have started using my home address for business purposes, simply because Evelyn maintained an office there. Now I would have to arrange with the Post Office for my stuff to be forwarded to my tight little workplace. One good intake of mail, and I wouldn't be able to get the door open.

There were two new commissions, one of them a lucrative and technically difficult assignment for a glossy magazine, to cover a pop group's tour. Just try working in that psychedelic lighting! Forcing myself not to think of this, nor of Evelyn, I got down to work in the dark room.

They were good, better than I'd expected. I did a complete set at six by four and glossed them, put them in an envelope, and left. It had taken me nine hours. I was drained, and pains kept running up my back and across my shoulders. I went in for a coffee before tackling the run back to Margaret's. These long stints in the dark room did terrible things to my eyes.

'Get a dark room assistant,' Evelyn had said. 'You're the photographer, not the stinks-room mechanic.'

But part of the job was the quality of prints. It was something of which I was proud.

'Good?' Margaret asked as she let me in. 'Are they good?'

I simply handed her the envelope, and followed her down the stairs. She poured us drinks, and while I sat quietly and tried to make myself unwind, she went through them. She looked up with a smile.

'I didn't expect this. The colour's marvellous.'

I shrugged. 'It's done with chemically-linked dyes. They can't be perfect, but you have to try to get the best there is from the

137

materials.'

'I could put a lot of work in your way—'

'Not that sort of thing, thanks. It's mechanical. I like variety. It keeps the interest going.'

'But these—'

'I could bang those up to twenty by sixteen, and print on specially grained paper, and most people would just as soon have them as the original painting. But I suppose that offends your sensibilities?'

'Somewhat. But if it gave pleasure—'

'Condescending, that's what you are. The poor, non-aesthetic horde, who don't appreciate your art!'

She flushed. 'What's got into you, Tony? You'll hardly let me finish a sentence, and when I praise you—and genuinely, I assure you—you throw criticisms at me.' The patches of colour were high, and her eyes seemed out of focus.

I looked at her above my glass. If I hadn't known better, I'd have said she was on drugs. It was some sort of emotional high that possessed her. Had there been a breakthrough in her endeavours?

'Sorry,' I said. 'It's been a heavy day.' A bad one. I couldn't get Evelyn's message out of my mind, and I hadn't found time to get to the Post Office. But most of all, with my brain tired, I was unable to find sympathy for Margaret's art-establishment oriented ideas. I was clinging desperately to my ghosts. The blooms of high colour on her cheeks were still there. 'I see *you've* had a good day,' I added as a palliative.

She looked away. 'If it's any satisfaction, I haven't. I've been tracking around, trying to locate the whereabouts of those two Bellarmé portraits. All I can come up with is that they're in a private collection. Somewhere. So there's no joy there.' She grimaced at me. 'You're hungry?'

'Yes. Very.'

'It's all ready. You see, I'm still considering your welfare.'

We ate in silence, which gave me time to realize how expertly I was able to ruin relationships with my moods. The trouble was, I could put forward no good explanation for them. I could well have kept my mouth shut. But no. Perhaps I'd been too pleased to see Margaret again, and had relaxed, allowing built-up tension to take control. I'd known for some time that I'd been trying to do too much on my own, the photography, the processing, the paperwork and accounts. But I'd been reluctant to seek assistance. I treasured the complete pattern of expertise. Proud, that was it. Big-headed, even. It doesn't do to face yourself over an Irish stew.

I gave myself excuses. My whole life was being set aside to cater for this provenance business. Did I resent this? No, to hell with that. The paintings were mine. I had to know the truth.

After a lemon meringue pie—she was quite a cook; it was perfect—I tried a suggestion.

'I suppose it's too much to ask you to call in another expert? A second opinion.'

Her eyes were dark under her eyebrows when she glanced up. 'Yes, too much. You shouldn't need to ask that, Tony.'

Over the coffee she told me what she knew of the big man we would now have to approach. His name was Renfrew Coombes. He lived in a large house on the edge of Exmoor in Somerset, and so far as Margaret knew the police had no active interest in him at that time. Several art historians had attempted to gain access to his gallery, but had been shown the inside of the door, even if they'd got beyond the outside. He was no longer an active villain, but it was said that his old team—as it was politely called—was still with him. He was protected, though there was no longer any suggestion of violence. He never answered his own phone. His secretary was illiterate, inasmuch as no replies were ever received, not if they concerned the collection.

'Then we go and knock on his door,' I suggested, 'and we see what happens.'

'Tomorrow?'

'Only because it's too late tonight. I've got a business to maintain.'

She said idly: 'And if the eighty-one turn out to be true Frederick Ashes, would it tempt you to retire?'

I grinned at her. 'I'd turn amateur, but I'd still be a photographer.'

'And I,' she said, 'would still be a consultant on art.'

'Even more so.'

'Yes.'

We parted on the landing. There were no words said on this arrangement, it just happened.

'An early start?' I asked.

She nodded. 'We've got to find the damned place.'

We used her Volvo, because Margaret thought we needed to make an impression. On such a man as Renfrew Coombes, nothing less than a gold-plated Rolls would have made an impression but, really, she wanted to do the driving.

It wasn't as difficult to find as I'd expected. We stopped in town so that I could fix the forwarding address business with the Post Office, and I popped into a stationer's to get an Ordnance Survey map covering Exmoor. One inch to the mile. It covered every tiny hamlet, and I noticed that a number of them had Coombe in their title. I studied it as Margaret drove, and discovered something about the sort of man we were going to visit. He had decided to retire from crookery. It befitted his self-esteem to retire to somewhere bearing his own name. This he had managed to bring about.

It is a simple thing to change the name of a country. They do it every month in Africa. It is also possible to change the name of a county, if a boundary adjustment also adjusts the political balance. It even happens that towns change, by being squeezed out—Wellington in Shropshire is now no more than an appendage to Telford. But just try changing the name of a village. Then you have the villagers to deal with, and they won't even let you change the name of their local pub.

So Renfrew Coombes had searched around, and discovered that there was a village called Renfrew Coombe. It was simple to drop his final *s* by deed poll. I learned, later, that he'd bought the freehold of the whole village, just so that his address would be Renfrew Coombe, Somerset, England.

It was such a man whom we hoped to impress and persuade.

We discovered the village as we popped over a stone-built hump-backed bridge. A wriggle in the road, and there it was, a row of cottages, one public house, and a tiny village store. We slowed, wondering whether to ask directions to the big house, but I sensed the atmosphere and whispered for her to drive on.

142

A fair number of the original residents were still hanging on. You could tell which they were, those people on the street who looked like furtive extras in a film set, equally nervous in spite of the lack of cameras, but uneasy with their new neighbours. Coombe had managed to empty a few of the cottages, and fill them with his own men. These, too, were obvious. They were the ones with newly colour-washed walls, the brightly painted front doors, and the professionally landscaped diminutive gardens with roses sweeping up the walls. The occupants of these cottages lounged in doorways, from time to time flicking cigarette ends at their fuschias, then disappearing inside to their phones to report a sight of a stranger. Strangers were suspect. The publican, too, lounged in his doorway. The pub was now part of the film set, might even have been no more than a false front. Beer might still have been obtainable inside, if the regular citizens weren't too dispirited to find out. Or maybe the cellar contained an armoury.

Shaking myself from these fanciful thoughts, I looked ahead. 'There,' I said. 'Just beyond that rise.'

What I'd seen might have been the ruins of a castle, but it was the only sizeable building in that hilly, tangled landscape. It was possibly half a mile away. The road became increasingly unappealing, perhaps as a discouragement. The map showed it to continue onwards, but the surveyors had allocated it no more than a dotted line.

One or two buildings speckled the rises each side, and could have been farmhouses, though their bright and recent paintwork made them suspect. I was aware of being observed with suspicion.

It had once been a castle, guarding a ford and offering a grim front to the north. It had been built on from time to time, with scant attention to previous styles, and perhaps had more recently been improved by an intake from Renfrew Coombe's millions. It was depressing and unwelcoming. A mist would have improved the prospect.

We drove through an opening in the surrounding high wall, directly into a large courtyard. I would have expected a gate across that opening, with a guard. But against what would Coombe need to protect himself? Certainly not burglars; they would appreciate the risk. The law? There was nothing specific to level against him. Ordinary visitors such as ourselves? There was a very large, solid and iron-studded door to serve that purpose. It could be closed firmly on an unwelcome face.

Which was what happened.

Margaret had performed a wide, smooth swing round the courtyard, which was entirely stone-flagged and liberally mossed, but which once must have rung to the hooves of armoured cavalry. We stopped opposite the door and got out. Nothing moved. I could hear no bird-song, no bleating of sheep or barking of dogs. The door towered above us under an inadequate porch. There was no bell-pull or button, only a large knocker in the form of a lion's head. I lifted it, and banged firmly. Twice. The echoes sang away inside the house.

After a minute or two we heard the approaching clack of steel-tipped heels. The door opened without a creak. The man staring at us was tall, thin, in his fifties, bald, and wearing a black butler's jacket with too much spare material around the chest. He said nothing. We failed to impress.

'We would like to see Mr Coombe,' I told him.

'He doesn't see visitors.'

'There's something I'd like to show him.'

Bushy eyebrows were raised. He watched my hand reaching towards the bulky shape in the side pocket of my anorak, and his eyes changed. The door slammed shut. We heard his heels retreating, steadily, unhurriedly.

I banged again. The heels retreated. Once more. Still the heels. Again. The heels stopped. Finally, I gave it a regular tattoo. The heels began to approach.

By this time I'd decided what had worried him. Renfrew Coombe had enemies, undoubtedly. The package in my pocket was

145

suspect. This time I was prepared, and had one of my six-by-fours ready in my hand. The door opened. His right hand was behind it. I held up the print.

'Show him this and he'll see us.'

'Bugger off.'

'If you don't, I'll send it by post, and he'll be looking for another flunkey.'

He eyed me with venom, then, as it seemed innocuous, he reached out a tentative hand. I released the print. The door closed. The heels retreated.

We walked round the courtyard, stretching our legs after the long journey. The moss was slimy and the flags uneven.

'You think he'll see us?' she asked.

'Daren't refuse.' But I wasn't as confident as I sounded.

'But will he let us leave again?'

'We've got the paintings.'

She wrapped her arms round herself and shuddered. 'I can't see we'll gain anything.'

'Maybe not. It's worth a try, though.'

We were over by the courtyard entrance when the door opened again. He stood there and crooked a finger. I put a hand to Margaret's arm. Walk slowly, make him wait, show confidence.

The inside was a surprise. I hadn't expected the grand hall still to be rush-strewn, and perhaps the suits of armour would have been retired. But the full transformation was staggering. Only the walls and the windows were the originals. The echoing heels had been slamming hard on to black and white checkered marble. The walls had been treated to a pine coating, and the wide, black oak staircase, as it must have been at one time, was now decorated with chromium supports to a black leather-faced pair of hand rails. The full-width stair carpet was purple nylon. The scattered furniture was chrome and plastic. I wouldn't have been surprised if each leaded diamond pane hadn't been double-glazed. Large, white-painted radiators stood where the armour had mounted guard.

It seemed inconceivable that a man with such anarchic taste could own a unique collection of art treasures that he coveted. But of course, he didn't covet them. They were not there to be looked at and admired, they were there because other people would have liked to have them, and Coombe had them. That was their purpose.

The steel heels led us past the staircase and through a door at the side. He waited until we were inside, received a signal from his boss, then the door closed behind him.

This was Coombe's personal office. It had received professional attention from a colour-blind interior decorator. Rugs too precious to be walked on hung against the naked stone of the walls, the spaces between

147

them occupied by tall white columns, each bearing a goldfish bowl with a single exotic fish in it. The splendid proportions of the large and tall windows were ruined by low valances and net curtains dyed red. There were a lot of windows; it was a long, high-ceilinged room. At one end was a round fountain, into which the little boy tinkled endlessly away. He'd been lacquered pink. The wall-to-wall carpeting was one huge flow of white, like a snowfall. The desk too was white, though it had started its life in the study of one of the Louis. Chairs, cane and rush, stood around in negligent disorder. Only two chairs were comfortable, these being deep leather easy chairs with studded backs. In one sat a young, pale man with polished hair and a bored expression. In the other, not behind the desk, sat the man who must be Renfrew Coombe.

By this time I had become resigned to failure. A man who could live in these surroundings could not be expected to have any appreciation of art or understanding of it. He wouldn't know a Toulouse-Lautrec from an Aubrey Beardsley. It was on his personal knowledge that I was relying. My confidence sagged. He seemed to confirm my assessment by holding up the print and saying: 'What's this?'

I walked forward. I was no longer aware of Margaret's presence; perhaps she was stunned by the room. Standing in front of him, I answered: 'It's a print, a photograph of a painting I own.'

It was then that I became aware that his was an orthopaedic chair. His feet rested on its extension, his back was moulded to its adjustable contours, as far as such a back could be manipulated. He was a gross man, whose fat had absorbed his outline to the point of inhibiting his movements. The hand holding the print almost engulfed it, the thumb obscuring most of the surface. His face was a pear, with the jowls resting on his shoulders. Whatever neck there had been was absorbed. No shirtmaker could have produced a collar that wouldn't be ridiculous. He was wearing a white, polo-necked jumper.

Angrily, he stared past the thumb at what was revealed. 'So what?' he barked, his voice deep and throaty.

'It's a Frederick Ashe. As the owner of the only ones in a private collection, you might be interested . . . I thought.'

'Tcha!' he said in contempt, then he tore it across, across again, and tossed the pieces over his shoulder.

The youngish man—I now realized he could have been forty—moved uneasily, then subsided again. In the corner of my eye I saw Margaret studying the manikin. She was keeping her options open.

149

'Feel free,' I said. 'I have the negative as well as the canvas.'

'When I buy, it's at auction. Now get out of here.'

Reaching over the chair arm, the young man had rescued the portions of my print. He hooked a low table towards him and jigsawed the pieces together, then he glanced up at me. His eyes, ice-blue, contained interest, and I knew that all was not lost.

'There's another eighty of them,' I said, keeping my voice casual. 'Eighty-one canvases in all. I've got photos of all of them. Want to see?'

I drew out my packet slowly, so as not to trigger any violent reaction. I held it up. Coombe stared at me, then waved his hand. 'Paul.'

His assistant reached towards me, forcing me to go to him. Smiling, I slipped the set out of its envelope and handed them over.

With the expertise of a card-sharp, he put them down on the table and fanned them out. Then, delicately with spatulate fingers, he edged each one sideways so that he had a full view, and moved along. Six of them he slid fractionally downwards. I barely noticed the action. Then he swept them together again, rose to his feet with athletic grace, and went over to his employer.

There was whispering, and grunts in response, then Coombe said something and

150

Paul walked with silent stealth from the room.

We waited.

Coombe was not an entertaining host. He interlocked his hands and placed them on his stomach, where they rested like a coil of hosepipe, and closed his eyes. I moved over to Margaret's side. She glanced at me. Her eyes were dark, her cheeks pale.

'A waste of time,' she whispered.

'I think not. He hires the brains, and Paul's his curator.'

She looked away, shuddered when her eyes fell on the fountain, and murmured: 'I'll scream if I don't get out of here soon.'

But it was a long wait, and she didn't scream. Paul at last returned. He held the batch of prints in one neat block, and went directly to his employer. There was more whispering. I edged closer.

At last Coombe raised his eyes. They were flat and empty. Paul, with a smirk, handed me the pack of prints. I slid them into my pocket.

'Right,' said Coombe, rumbling aggressively. 'So you've got eighty-one forgeries. Why should I be interested?'

'They're not forgeries.'

He went on as though I hadn't spoken. 'I'll take them off your hands. Eight thousand the lot. Take it or leave it.'

'Why should you want them, if you think they're forgeries?'

151

That was a mistake. The hands uncurled and the fingers flexed, like dying snakes. His face was suffused with blood. Paul took my arm quickly.

'Out!' he said.

We left. Margaret led the way. Paul stood in the hall and watched us on our trip to the door. A roar of fury sounded behind him, and he retreated, the door closing quietly.

Steel-tips was waiting to see us out. He bowed mockingly. We left. I knew why Coombe wanted to relieve us of the canvases, forgeries or not. He could not risk them coming on the open market, and thus throwing doubt on the authenticity of his own. Even, perhaps, of demands coming from high places that his own should be inspected.

I said: 'Drive away slowly and keep going. Stop when we get the other side of the village.'

This she did. By that time I'd confirmed what I suspected.

I had, as was my normal practice, banged on the back of each print my rubber stamp, which includes all the details required to trace a negative in future. Such as the number in the batch. In this instance, I'd done a print from each negative, so that the prints were numbered simply 1 to 81. I now possessed 2 to 81, number one being in four pieces on the formica top of that low table.

But they were no longer in exact order. Paul had paid special attention to the six he'd noticed. These six were now together at the bottom of the pile.

'Got him!' I said in triumph. 'We now know he's got all six of the Frederick Ashes. And we know which ones from the loft set are paired with his.'

Margaret didn't seem as pleased as I'd expected. 'But we don't know whether his are painted from right or left biased viewpoints of your six.'

'But surely they must be the same as my original canvas, a right-hand viewpoint.'

'Hmm!' she said doubtfully. 'But sometimes artists do more than one painting of something they like. Those six could've been picked out by that evil-looking young man just because they're similar to the six Coombe has.'

'You do take some convincing.'

'And you, Tony? Are you convinced? Don't forget, you're as good as agreeing with me that the loft set are all Angelina Footes. I hadn't noticed you agreeing with me lately.'

I grimaced at her, changed it to a grin. 'So we need to have another go at it. Is that what you're saying?'

'Another go at Coombe? Heaven forbid!'

'But don't you see, we've now got something on him. We know he's got those four stolen paintings.'

'So?' she asked, with no warmth.

'We phone him. We put it to him that on this evidence the police could apply for a search warrant. In exchange for our silence, we demand that he should let us . . . or me, if you like, and I'll take photos . . . let me, then, have access to his collection, and—'

She jerked the car into violent movement. I shouted: 'What the hell!' But she was glancing at the rearview mirror.

'There's a car just come over the bridge,' she said. 'I'll have to lose him.'

'You're crazy.'

'Don't you realize what you've stirred up! And you talk about threatening such a man! He wants those canvases.'

'Over my dead—'

'If necessary,' she said. 'If necessary.'

She set out to lose the other car. It was faster than the Volvo, and more powerful. But they didn't stand a chance. Thugs have a fine regard for their own lives, but Margaret had none for ours.

CHAPTER NINE

In order to reach the village of Renfrew Coombe we had had to take the Porlock to Lynton coast road, and strike off south into Exmoor. After that, there had been only one route. This road, out on the moors, is about twelve feet wide, and you either follow it or bump along through the scrub. Closer to the coast the road is no wider, and tall hedgerows encroach very intimately. So when I say that Margaret set out to lose the car on our return journey, she could not do so until we were nearing Porlock, because they could afford to hang back, knowing she had no alternatives.

But Porlock is approached by way of Porlock Hill, from this direction being downwards. The hill is steep, and it winds. Cyclists are advised to get off and walk, and the few escape roads—steep ramps of sand to slow you down—are signposted. They occur where the fall becomes 1 in 4, and always on a corner so tight that you can catch a glimpse of your own rear wheels as you take them. Most people tackle the whole thing at around 20, up or down. But Margaret had no patience for this sort of thing.

She took it in second gear with the revs flying high, driving on brakes and throttle so that the whole three quarters of a mile was done in one screaming, wriggling dance round the bends. I didn't think a Volvo Estate would do this sort of thing, but it did. Approaching the top of the hill, the car behind had closed up. Where he thought we might disappear to, except through Porlock and on to the Minehead road, I couldn't imagine. He made the mistake of trying to match the Volvo, and we lost him at one of the escape roads, which he took, or nearly. It made an expensive noise behind us as we slowed through the village of Porlock.

'Was that really necessary?' I asked.

'We daren't let Coombe know where the paintings are.'

'Oh!' I said in dismay. She had prodded free a thought.

She slowed even more, glancing sideways. 'Oh what?'

'My rubber stamp, the one I bang on the back of my proofs—it's got my home address on it, and both my phone numbers.'

She nodded. It was just what she might have expected. 'Then you'll have to keep away from your home.'

'Didn't intend going there.'

'Perhaps not. But every time you come to my place you'll have to make sure you're not followed.'

Life was becoming increasingly complicated. 'Every time I come?' I asked. 'I thought you'd pretty well drained every drop of knowledge from the canvases.'

She drove a mile before she replied. 'We'll see. We've got to discuss this.'

Which we did, when we reached her place. Now that we knew which photos had attracted Paul's attention, she could concentrate on those. She had never seen the two Ashes he owned legitimately, and the catalogues contained no more than a description. But she had certainly seen the other four, in the galleries from which they'd been stolen. As far as she could tell from memory, those four were now in the hands of Renfrew Coombe. If they were not, why had Paul shown such interest in pictures of canvases almost matching them?

We had got back in time for a quick lunch, and were now sitting out in the sun on Margaret's patio, which overhung the valley. I was feeling lazy, which made me uneasy. Lounging around in the middle of a working day felt strange. My disorientation increased. I could see this business hanging around for ever.

'There's only one thing for it,' I said at last. 'We'll go to see him again . . .'

'We will not.'

'. . . or I'll go to see him again, and say we—or I—believe that his Frederick Ashe paintings might not be genuine. The odd lie never does much harm. I'll tell him that if I can see them, there's a method of making sure. I wouldn't tell him anything about the left and right viewpoint theory, but with a bit of luck he'll be worried enough to let me take a peep—'

'I forbid it.'

'Forbid?'

'It's too dangerous for you.'

I noticed that she'd now excluded herself.

'I don't see that.'

'He wouldn't dare to let you see inside his gallery.'

'Paul could bring them out. Just his two legitimate ones would be enough for what I want. I'd simply compare them with the photos, and confirm that they're right viewpoint versions of the ones in the loft set. That'd make 'em the same as my original one.'

Her lower lip tucked between her teeth, she turned and stared at me. 'Promise me you wouldn't go inside the gallery.' Her eyes were very dark.

'If you wish. I don't see that it matters.'

'Oh, you are slow! What does he know about you? You could be an undercover man from the Arts Section of Scotland Yard. You might see something that'd make you a dangerous liability.'

'If he thought I was a policeman, he wouldn't dare to touch me.'

'All the same . . .'

She was flushed, her eyes moist and bright. I couldn't understand her attitude. Was it concern for me? To be sure, we had a natural empathy for each other; we could bear to be in each other's company without strain. Looking back, I realized that this was partly what had stood between Evelyn and myself. We had both had to work hard for a continuing domestic peace. Not so with

158

Margaret. Our intimacy had grown rapidly, but I didn't think it had developed to a position where she could be concerned deeply for my safety.

At last she said simply: 'I don't want you to go.'

'Because you now know enough about the paintings to stake your reputation that the eighty-one from the loft are not Frederick Ashes?'

She looked away from me over her valley, then reached sideways to her cigarettes on the metal table between us. She spoke with her eyes still averted, so softly that at first I wasn't sure I'd heard her correctly.

'I know enough about that loft set to be certain of one thing. Nobody would ever dare to say they're *not* by Frederick Ashe.'

'Pardon . . .'

'Don't be a fool, Tony,' she said sharply, snapping her head round, dragging the cigarette, still unlit, from her lips. 'You know what I mean.'

I stared at her dumbly.

'You do!' she cried. 'We could put them on the market as Frederick Ashe canvases, and not one art expert anywhere would dare to dispute it.'

Then she spent quite a while getting the cigarette going, giving me time to absorb this new concept.

Where, now, was all her high-flown

professional morality? At no time had there been any reason to question it, and in fact her probity had ruled every action she had taken. Now, all of this was to be jettisoned, was it? And why? In order to make a quick fortune for me and a fair commission for her, but mostly to secure her treasured acclaim for this remarkable artistic find! How could that be? I just couldn't imagine her smiling at a gathering of her enthusiastic peers, when inside she would be squirming. Oh, the bitterness of the thought that she was betraying her trust as an international expert, she whose word was pristine truth!

'Less,' I said, 'The six that're duplicated in Coombe's collection, and my single one.'

'What?'

'To prevent any backlash from Coombe, any protests, any awkward questions . . . to play safe, there would have to be no duplicates.'

I'd confused her. 'Yes . . . of course,' she said.

I shrugged. 'Suits me, then. It'd save all the trouble of seeing him again.'

'There's that, too.' She smiled. Though she tried to conceal the fact, there was relief in it. But there was not enough behind her eyes, no affection, no hint of passion, to make me accept that her relief was for me.

'I really must catch up on my work, anyway,' I went on casually. 'I'll spend another day at my photo-lab.' I laughed. 'Oh, don't worry, I'll make sure I'm not followed. You can work out how you're going to unload seventy-four of the canvases on to an innocent world.'

She grimaced. In spite of what she'd said, it was not a task she would enjoy. But during the rest of the day, she did much to reinforce the impression that her concern was for me personally. She became more affectionate and attentive. She probed me about the details of my profession, and seemed fascinated. From her bedroom door she looked at me in a way not usually lavished on me, and throughout the night she protected me with her strong arms. I had no fears. It was no longer necessary to have future contact with Renfrew Coombe, and I was going to become a millionaire. Wasn't I?

I regretted only that my recent incursions into the art world were turning me into a cynical bastard.

In the morning I covered what I was beginning to feel was my regular commuting run, and as usually happens when you're overwhelmed by work, more commissions had arrived in the post. One of them was a lu-lu, the pictures for a brochure covering holidays in Norway, all expenses paid, plus a generous fee. The satisfaction this produced was slightly dimmed by the recollection that I was shortly to become a millionaire. I would be able to buy the travel firm! It was also undermined by the fact that it arrived by way of Evelyn, who had included another charming note.

Tony,
I need a settled address to which I can direct the serving of divorce proceedings. Of course, to claim desertion would be futile, after so short a time, so I have had a man follow you, and evidence of adultery is available. Please let me know whether service of the writ may be made at your business address, or at the home of Dr Margaret Dennis.
Your immediate reply will be appreciated.
P.S. Please do not claim that my address is still yours, as I have had the locks changed.
P.P.S. Aleric sends his regards.

E.

I threw it to the floor and stamped on it. The disaster it spelled out was not my divorce, but the fact that Margaret's address was now known to a third party. It was dangerous. I went quickly into the darkroom, where I had my phone on the end of the bench, intending to call Margaret to warn her. It rang beneath my fingers and I snatched it up. If it was Evelyn . . .
'Mr Hine?' A man's voice, like dark brown

velvet. Another commission? I unearthed my best voice.

'Tony Hine speaking.'

'Ah! Fine! This is Paul Mace. You'll remember me, perhaps. At Renfrew Coombe.'

'I remember you.' I was cautious, no longer being particularly interested in what Coombe might have to offer.

'Mr Coombe has been thinking about your proposition.',

'I don't remember making a proposition, I simply told him what I have.'

'And which he would like to acquire.'

I took a deep breath. 'Mr Mace, I own eighty-one Frederick Ashe canvases. These I intend to offer at auction, and your employer will no doubt put in a bid—'

'You don't understand.'

'It's you who doesn't. Tell him I don't intend to include the duplicates of the Ashes he now has—or believes he has. I don't want to embarrass so important—'

'Will you listen!'

I stopped. It had been difficult to maintain the formal style, anyway. Then I said: 'I'm listening, but any offer under—'

'He's making no offer.'

'No?'

'I've been told to instruct you to bring all your canvases here and leave them for our examination, and possible destruction.'

163

'Instruct me! Now listen here, you slimy little—'

'We have your wife.'

'Just listen . . . you what?'

'We are holding your wife here as a . . . how shall I put it . . . ? as guarantee of your sensible behaviour.'

I laughed. His timing had been perfect. I laughed, and he made clicking noises of disapproval with his tongue.

'We shall hold her until—' he began.

'You can hold her for ever, as far as I'm concerned. Hasn't she told you . . . obviously not. I've left her. She's suing me for divorce. I don't *want* her back, you loon.'

'Come now, Mr Hine.'

'Then go and damn well ask her.'

'We have your son, too.'

'And you can keep him as well.' This I said with equal force, but I was recalling that Aleric had Frederick Ashe's nose and his ears, so it did seem that he was my son, after all. But he had a different view of life from my grandfather's, I told myself. 'He'll love it there,' I said. 'You'll be able to train him as one of your heavies, or hit-men, or whatever.'

'Really, this is absurd,' he bleated, no longer brown velvet, but brushed nylon.

'Isn't it!' I agreed.

'You'd better speak to her.'

'Who? Evelyn? No thanks.'

'Here she is now.'

And there she was. Evelyn had always been addicted to smooth, legal invective, each word cutting quietly to the bone. All this polish had disappeared. She was a very angry woman.

'Tony, I'm going to kill you for this!' she shouted. 'You and your blasted paintings. Give the man what he wants, and let me go home. You hear me?'

'I hear you, Evelyn. Tell me what happened.' '

'Be damned to what happened. Just do as I say.'

'Tell me what happened.'

'How can I talk—'

'What happened, for heaven's sake?'

She turned her face from the phone, but didn't cover it. I heard her shout: 'Get out of this room, you nasty little creep. Out!' A pause. I heard the distant slam of a door, so unlike Paul. Then she was back to me.

'I'll tell you what happened, if it amuses you. Two men came to the door. They told me to put my coat on. *Told* me! I protested. They used force. Force on me, Tony. I shall never forgive you. They entered my house against my will. Aleric was there. They used physical violence on him, then they took us out to the car.'

'He's hurt? Aleric—is he hurt?'

She snorted. 'Nothing hurts him. He was unconscious when they took us out, but he'd

broken some fingers. Not his own. Do no
interrupt, Tony. Let me say it. They brough
us here, wherever here is, and they tell m
we'll be driven home when you surrende
some paintings you seem to have. Painting:
Plural. I don't know what it means or wha
it's about. You've only got one damne
painting, which I'm glad to see the bac
of . . .'

'Evelyn!'

'So just you do what he wants, or by Go
I'll sue you for damages due to negligence—

'Evelyn!' I shouted. She was silent.
waited, and could hear her breathing.

At last: 'Well? Make it good, Tony.'

'It *is* good. What if I tell you I now ow
eighty-one paintings, all valuable? Possibl
total value around a million and a half. That
pounds sterling, not lira or pesetas. Pound:
Do you seriously imagine I'm about to gi
them away?'

In saying this, I was assuming that Pat
Mace would be listening on an extension lin
It did no harm to set him worrying. All th
same, it was a mistake. Evelyn hissed gentl
between her teeth.

'Are you telling me the truth?'

'Though I haven't been able to prov
they're valuable,' I added quickly.

But the damage was done. 'No wonder h
wants them.' I could almost hear her min
ticking over.

166

'It's not quite like that.'

'So what can we do?' she asked, my ally now in our combined distress.

'I take it you've already told him the legal aspects of what he's done, and explained how you'll have the police on him when you get out of there?'

'What are you talking about? It's what *you're* going to do that matters. What *are* you going to do?'

She was thinking in terms of ransom, how many paintings was she worth, and how many would we have left, and what sum of money would they get us? Her mind was already running in terms of a resumption of cohabitation.

'I don't intend to do anything about it. I've explained that to your friend Mace.'

'You're not . . . you'd leave me . . . well, let me tell you . . .'

'It's quite simple,' I explained patiently. 'When he realizes he can't use you to force my hand, he'll let you go. Simple.'

I felt her shudder, felt it right through the phone system. She did that when she was forcibly taking control of herself. Then she spoke quietly, in her most biting tone.

'No! No, Tony. I see through you now. You're intending to share it all with your marvellous Dr Dennis. Doctor of what, may I ask? You'll have to tell me, some time. But not now. Now, you're going to listen. Do

167

what I say, or you'll have nothing, you and your fancy woman. You're forgetting something, Tony. I know her address. If you do not bring the canvases, or whatever they are, and bring them now . . . *now*, Tony . . . I'll tell him. And his men will fetch them. I'm quite certain that's where they'll be. Do I make myself clear?'

The situation was very clear to me, but not exactly as Evelyn assumed. I had wanted a good excuse for going there again, and now, with a bit of luck, I had been able to implant in Mace's mind my confidence that I held eighty-one Frederick Ashe canvases. My bargaining power with these was stronger than Coombe's with Evelyn. This, too, I had firmly implanted.

'I will come, Evelyn,' I said.

'With those—'

'As quickly as possible. That'll be at least four hours from here.'

'Four hours!'

'You don't know where you are, but I do. Four hours, at the very least.'

Then I hung up before she could extend the delay, and immediately dialled Margaret's number. Quickly and succinctly I explained what had happened. I told her to make arrangements to take the canvases somewhere else. Somewhere safe.

'I know just the place.' She sounded a little breathless.

'Oh? Where?'

'Sotheby's.'

'But you can't . . .'

'They know me. They'll take 'em in.'

But that hadn't been the reason for my protest. Such a distinguished firm of auctioneers, with more than adequate security, could quite well protect the canvases. The trouble was, she was rushing me. I still wanted my proof, even if she didn't, and I wasn't keen on the way she was confining the options. Before I knew it, they'd be putting them under the hammer. She seemed to sense my reason for hesitation, and laughed.

'Oh, don't worry. They won't even look at them. It'll just be a batch of canvases, miscellaneous.'

'If you say so. But if I've got to go there and see this Coombe character again, I might be able to get some more information.'

'I don't like you going at all.'

'But you'll agree I've got no option.'

I could almost hear her grimace. 'I suppose not, though what you hope to achieve I can't imagine.'

To tell you the truth, I wasn't sure, myself. But somewhere in the back of my mind was a feeling of outrage that he should have abducted my wife and used her to apply pressure on me. To be sure, my opinion of her was not at its highest, but she was still my

169

wife. And Aleric? I wasn't sure about him, my long-implanted opinion of him controlling my thinking even now. But the outrage still applied. Certainly, I couldn't turn up with the canvases, as demanded; I'd now virtually put them out of reach. All I could hope was that I could talk my way through and out of it. One thing was certain, though—I had to go.

'I'll play it by ear,' I said, adopting a false confidence.

On this inconclusive note, we hung up. I spent a little time printing another copy of the photo that'd been torn up, and left. I managed to close and lock the front door before Detective Sergeant Dolan tapped me on the shoulder.

'Lucky I caught you,' he said amiably.

I couldn't agree to that, so I grunted. 'I'm in a hurry.'

'I'll walk you to your car.'

But what he had to say took longer than that, and we finished it sitting inside my hired red Fiesta.

'There's news?' I asked.

'You're not going to like it.'

'Say it, damn you.'

'Touchy, aren't we! All right. Grace Fielding has committed suicide. She left no note, so we don't know why. But we can guess.'

'It all got on top of her,' I decided emptily.

I knew why, didn't even have to think about it. My taking of the paintings had indeed been a last straw. All those years of wasted life, and the reward for them had been pared away, culminating in my grand effort in clearing the loft. Perhaps she had realized they were of value, and I had them, and it was all going to be too much strain to wrest them from me. Despair had overcome her, and she'd taken her own life.

'How?' I demanded.

We had reached the car, and I had to lean on the roof.

'Apparently she'd climbed into the loft for something or other . . .'

Looking for crosses on the crates perhaps, I thought, but I said nothing.

'. . . and she seems to have found a length of rope up there, and tied it to one of the beams—damn it, Hine, d'you want me to describe it? She jumped through the trapdoor hole. Her feet were tapping against the loft ladder.'

I got into the car, hoping I wouldn't be sick inside it. I'd badgered her to that end. Don't tell me otherwise.

'What took you to the house?'

'The forensic evidence. The dust and the specks of brown paint.'

'You mentioned them.'

He slid on to the seat beside me, having been talking through the open door. 'Funny

171

thing, the paint didn't match up, the stuff from the pin-ball machine against the flecks in your grandmother's . . .'

'I know what you mean.' I was fumbling with my pipe, but the tobacco wouldn't find the bowl.

'And what she expected to find in the loft I can't imagine. Certainly not canvases.'

He had his chatty mood going again, smooth and gentle, but with the persistence of a road drill.

'I couldn't say,' I mumbled.

'A pity she didn't wait for my news,' he observed.

'For God's sake!' The pipe wouldn't draw. I stared at it in disgust and groped for my brain. 'What did you mean by "apparently"? Apparently she climbed into the loft, you said. Seems to have found some rope. You sounded doubtful.'

I felt him shrug. 'Just that it's strange. At her age, it'd be an effort even getting up there. And she had sleeping tablets available.'

'She normally took them?'

'Your grandmother did.'

'Simpler,' I agreed. 'It would've been.'

'More pleasant, perhaps,' he decided. 'Less unpleasant, say.' He touched my arm. 'You get my point?'

'I get it.'

Nevertheless he insisted on enlarging on it. 'I can see you're blaming yourself. Oh yes you are. You got those paintings out of the house pretty smartly, because you knew she would object. You knew it would upset her. You knew there was going to be a protest, probably legal, as to the ownership . . . and, incidentally, where are they? And what're you doing with them? I hope it's nothing to do with disposing of them, because that'd make it look as though you knew she was going to commit suicide. Which would be ridiculous, of course. The sad thing about it—and I'm sure you'll appreciate this—is that she was in a fairly strong position regarding the ownership. It was beginning to look as though your grandmother was dead before Grace Fielding arrived back home, so that the paintings would be considered as part of the inheritance. I wonder whether she'd have taken her own life if she'd realized that. And she would have realized it, if I'd got there in time with the forensic evidence.'

He said all that in a steady, ruminative voice, as though he was merely musing to himself out loud. I might not have been there. But he knew very well that every carefully considered word was like a hammer blow at my conscience. There was nothing I could say.

He slid out of the car, swung the door, but caught it before the latch got it, drawing it open again.

'For your information, she seems to have

died intestate, so I doubt there'll be any dispute about your ownership of the canvases. Unless further evidence comes to light.' He nodded. 'Of course.'

'I . . .' But he'd slammed the door.

Cocking his hat on the side of his head, he strolled away, rolling slightly. I sat there. It was a long while before I found I could start the car and drive away with any confidence.

Heading towards the M5 and Somerset, I had to try to convince myself I had an adequate reason for going there.

CHAPTER TEN

It was nearly three in the afternoon when I came within hitting distance of my objective. For several miles I'd been fighting those tight curves and the steep rises and falls, and it was quite abruptly that I came out on to the moors above Renfrew Coombe, with the turn-off to the village a mile ahead.

The hedges had disappeared as though trimmed by giant shears. Each side, now, was a low bank of gorse, and there was no difficulty in turning off on to the green-brown carpet and stopping to consult my map. I wanted to be absolutely certain of my location, and my possible escape roads. There was a likelihood that I'd need them, as I hadn't Margaret's driving ability to rely on if I found myself in trouble. I got out of the car to pin-point the village.

It was somewhere below me in a cleft between the round-topped hills, which marched away in all directions. This high above sea level, they were all capped brown with gorse, not yet green, and since it was early June they were possibly not going to be able to achieve it. In the valleys, as though they'd tumbled from the peaks, were folds of green trees, too far below for me to identify them, but a solid, bright green, so probably deciduous. They fell down the lower slopes like a tossed green duvet in a ditch, and it seemed that no habitation could exist beneath their tight mass. Yet my map confirmed it. Renfrew Coombe was below me, or rather, below a point half a mile farther on.

I drove that half-mile, and there found a bare, red-earth, pull-in space, into which I nosed the car, gently, because the fall in front of me was steep. I got out and had another look. The brown slope fell below me at an angle of thirty degrees, directly into the cleft of the valley. Now I could see slate roofs and sun-caught thatches beyond the belt of trees. The map indicated a distance of less than a mile. As the crow flies, the saying goes, but from there he'd be falling.

I backed out and drove on, downhill now, steep and winding, and again abruptly between high hedges, and then between trees, massed each side and meeting above me, the sun pattern on the tarmac dazzling. Then there was the bridge and the village. I hadn't before noticed how constricted the cottages were, with the hill slopes so tight behind them and the rock-strewn brook facing them across their meagre street.

My approach was noted and relayed. When I rounded the final bend and turned into Renfrew Coombe's courtyard, the front door was already open, and the goon stood waiting.

'Mr Mace is expecting you,' he said, almost bowing. It was an honour, he implied, for me to be invited beyond the door.

Paul Mace was standing at the rear of the echoing hall, but this time the other side of the stairway. There was no friendliness in his eyes as he gestured towards me in a peremptory manner. Then he reached back to open the door.

It was a sun room, in that the roof above it had been removed, and glass substituted. Everywhere was glass, and the room looked even larger than it was because some of the glass was mirrored. Green tangles of growth had been encouraged to climb the walls and to hang from the glass ceiling. Potted exotic plants crowded from all sides. The humidity was high, and the temperature controlled at about 100°F. From the branches of a tree that might eventually bear bananas, two marmoset

176

monkeys gibbered at me, peering suspiciously at a stranger.

'They're outside,' said Mace, his voice tense with distaste. 'Outside' was a place of which he did not approve.

There was a tall door consisting of a single sheet of plate glass, and beyond it a wide spread of terrace. It was slabbed with imported granite, was wide, and sported a balustrade and half a dozen Greek statues, which could well have been stolen there and shipped clandestinely. Beyond it, down a wide sweep of ten shallow steps, was a lawn.

To achieve a flat, smooth lawn it must have been necessary to chop into the hillside. On this lawn they were playing croquet, my wife and Renfrew Coombe.

Surely I hadn't been mistaken when I'd thought his chair to be orthopaedic. Certainly, from his bulk, I'd assumed he was incapable of standing on his own two feet. Yet here he was, massive even against a backfall of huge oaks, planting those great feet firmly and smacking a ball vigorously, though inaccurately. Evelyn was laughing. She must have been winning, because losing was never, for her, a source of joy. But Coombe was enjoying it. He could, after all, afford to lose a game here and there, when nothing rested on victory. My impression was that he was being gallant, and deferring to her lack of experience. Evelyn was as close to

177

simpering at his jovial attentiveness as I've ever seen her.

He need not have deferred. Evelyn could take on anything and succeed. All she would need was a sight of the rules, and as long as there was a sufficient number of 'provided thats' and 'notwithstandings' she'd have them tamed at once. Her cold and analytical mind would then compute the angles and impacts required, and before you'd know it she'd have you retrieving your ball from the shrubbery.

In this instance there was no shrubbery, just a steep drop into a million or so trees, so that when Coombe watched his ball disappearing over the edge he raised his meaty shoulders, jutted his flabby lower lip, and growled heartily: 'You win. You're too good for me.'

'Who could be good enough for you, Renfrew?' she asked, taking his arm, hanging on it like a poor, weak feminine person, and allowing him to pilot her up the steps.

Ye gods! I thought. They fancy each other! I'm on a winner, here. Though of course, she was probably only undermining him with her charm. But why didn't I ever encounter that charm? She was flushed with it, short of breath from it. It was years since she'd been short of breath with me.

'Mr Hine is here, sir,' said Mace, his voice cold.

'D'you think I hadn't noticed! Clear off,

Paul, there's talking to be done.'

'I think I should be here to advise—'

Talking down to his employer from the terrace was one thing, but now Coombe had reached the top step. He loomed over his slim and effete curator. 'You'll do as I say,' Coombe told him, and after one glare at me Mace turned and walked away round the corner of the house.

As my eyes followed him, I noticed that one of the statues was attended by my son, Aleric, leaning against it. This all seemed strange to me, that he and his mother should, supposedly, be under restraint, when Aleric could simply have disappeared into the trees. Though perhaps there were invisible guards, or Aleric had been told there were and didn't care to risk it. He flipped a hand in my direction.

'Hi, Pa! How's it going?'

'Fair, son, fair.'

'We will sit,' Coombe announced, 'and talk in a civilized manner.' He led the way to one of the round, white-painted metal tables and drew back a chair for Evelyn. She smiled up at him as he slid it behind her. Then he sat himself, and the chair sighed. I sat opposite to them. It was a triangle of three people, yet my impression was that I was opposite them. Strange.

Coombe pressed a bell-push. 'We'll have tea. I import my own Darjeeling. You'll

179

like it.'

Evelyn smiled. She liked it all, it seemed. 'My short stay is coming to an end.' There was sadness in her voice.

Aleric realized that he was not invited to join us, but he strolled across and found a closer statue to embrace.

Coombe said: 'You'll stay to tea, then your husband can drive you home, with a standing invitation—'

'I've got a feeling she won't be going home,' I cut in.

'What!' Evelyn slapped her palm on the table surface.

'Though it seems to me you won't be displeased,' I assured her.

'What the hell d'you mean?'

I looked away from her furious eyes. 'I haven't brought the canvases.'

I expected Coombe to be choleric in his anger, but all he did was rumble a little in his chest, then smile in a most unpleasant manner.

'That was very stupid of you,' he said gravely.

'They're no longer available.'

'You're lying, of course.'

I shrugged. Something that Detective Sergeant Dolan had said came to my assistance. 'They're kind of involved in a bequest. The Chancery Court, or something like that, is holding them until there's an

180

inquest—'

'For God's sake, Tony!' Evelyn cried. 'Don't talk legal gibberish to me. You're just trying to be clever. I can't *afford* to get stuck here . . .'

'Now, now, Evelyn,' said Coombe heavily. 'Afford is an irrelevant word. You stay as my guest. Until I say otherwise,' he added smoothly to me. But his eyes were twin buttons of black ice.

'I can't stay here!' Aleric suddenly put in agitatedly. 'My bike! What about my bike?'

We ignored him.

'There's something you ought to understand,' I said quietly.

'Understand!' Evelyn reached across and snapped her fingers beneath my nose. I'd never seen that done before. 'All I understand is that you're being deliberately awkward.'

'I was talking to Mr Coombe. He's the one who needs to understand.'

'Let him speak, my dear.' Coombe clasped her other hand in his, where it disappeared. 'But first, here's something for *you* to understand, Mr Tony Hine. Your wife has told me she's shortly to be free of you, and will have more spare time. I'm in need of legal advice, and she's agreed to represent me in all legal matters. Various departments and institutions are trying to tie me down with their complications, and she will help me. So when you speak to me, you're also speaking to her. Have I put that correctly, Evelyn?'

This was a different man from the one I'd met before, who'd seemed to rely on Paul Mace too readily, and whose only weapon had been a hectoring voice. He was smooth and he was patient. He was deadly. I couldn't decide who was fooling whom, as clearly a man such as Coombe would already be surrounded by a barrier of legal finagling, and a woman as astute as Evelyn must have realized that.

'The point is, Tony,' she said, 'that when I divorce you, I shall claim the paintings as part of my settlement. I've explained this to Renfrew, and you . . . from the way you're speaking . . . must realize your legal hold on them isn't very strong.'

Did I tell you how clever she is? This wasn't a warning to me, it was a stall she was presenting to Coombe. He had only to be patient, and all would fall into his ample lap. Heavens, I thought, she had realized I was in danger from him, and she'd thought this up as a protection . . . for me! I looked down at the table, not wishing her to read the expression in my eyes.

'The snag is,' I explained, looking up, 'that the paintings I've got *could* be worthless, in which case we're sitting here arguing about nothing.'

At this point a manservant appeared along the terrace with a large tray, which he placed in front of Coombe, who glanced at him.

'You took your time,' he snapped.

'I'm sorry, sir. The cream had gone off.'

'Well, watch it, sport.' He turned, smiling at Evelyn. 'Will you be mother?'

It was revolting.

'Could well be worthless,' I persisted. 'There were two sets painted at the same time, by two different people, one of them Frederick Ashe. It's almost impossible to tell one from the other. All I've had to go on is the one painting I've always owned, which is duplicated in the new set of eighty-one. Is anybody listening to me?'

Evelyn was concentrating on the teapot, Coombe on the strawberries and cream and on her.

'Listening,' Coombe growled.

'It's impossible to say,' I went on, raising my voice a little, 'at this stage, with any certainty, if my own painting is a Frederick Ashe, and its mate in the other batch what you might call a copy. And this'd apply to the rest of the eighty-one, of course. The odds are that this new lot are copies, and worthless.'

Coombe flicked his eyes at me from beneath the thick bushes of hair that he called his eyebrows. 'You would naturally say that. I'd prefer my own opinion.'

'Which is just why I came. To help you form it.'

'But you haven't brought the paintings, so

183

how would you do that? Milk second for me, my dear.'

I took out my envelope of prints and slapped it down on the table. 'With those. There's one photo of each of the eighty-one, as you know. One of them is duplicated by my own, and I've got reason to believe your six are, too.'

'My *what*?'

At last I had his attention, full frontal, all that unlovely face in one concentrated scowl. It had not been intentional. I knew I'd made a mistake, before the words were out, and possibly a fatal one.

'What did you say?' he asked heavily.

'He said: your six,' Evelyn offered, smiling at me sweetly.

He glanced at her warningly, then said to me: 'Why do you say that?'

Honesty, I decided, would deflect his fury from me. 'On my previous visit here, when I got this batch of prints back, six of them were out of order, all together at the bottom.'

His face was now red. He mouthed something, and jabbed at his button. 'Paul!' he snarled.

'And as,' I went on, trying to keep the momentum going, 'the only four you hadn't got have been stolen from their rightful owners, and as you're the sort of man who can arrange such things, I naturally assumed you were simply putting together a full set of

184

Frederick Ashe.'

Paul appeared in the doorway of the sun room.

'Though of course,' I qualified, 'it now seems they might not be Frederick Ashe paintings at all. If,' I explained placidly, 'the new set of eighty-one are.'

Coombe crooked a finger, then pointed it at the terrace surface in front of himself. Paul advanced and stood there. His face was pale and pinched, so he must have sensed the atmosphere.

'You,' said Coombe, 'are a bloody fool.'

'Sir?'

'You gave him back his photographs with six of them—yes, I said six—in one set at the bottom.'

'Oh.' Paul stared into the distant trees, where a corpse might lie hidden for years.

'So now,' growled Coombe, 'while you're still around, you'd better arrange for another room for another guest, because we daren't let him go. And get a team out to collect those canvases.'

'No point,' I said quickly.

'What?' His head swivelled at me with the ponderous weight of a swing bridge.

'They're no longer at that address. Gone to Christie's, I think. Or was it Sotheby's?'

Coombe bounced to his feet, the metal chair clattering away, and vented his fury on Paul. 'By god, I'll break you for this! Every

185

soddin' bone. They'll put 'em up for auction, and I'll have to bid for every bleeding one, you ape, you stupid, worthless moron.'

Paul's immaculate suit seemed to become a size too big for him. Perspiration dripped down his nose. 'I'll . . . I'll . . .'

'You'll what? Raid Sotheby's?'

'Or Christie's,' I suggested helpfully. 'Or both.'

Paul made a whimpering sound.

'There's an easy solution to it,' I offered. The head again swung towards me, shoulders following. 'You pay me their estimated value, a million and a half, and I give you a deed of assignment. Evelyn can draft it—'

'Damn you, I'll see you dead first.'

Evelyn put in: 'Aren't we becoming too agitated over this? Simply because Tony *believes* you have all six of the Frederick Ashe paintings, it isn't necessarily a danger to you.'

Coombe stared at her blankly. 'He can go to the police. D'you think I can risk them coming here—with a search warrant! Talk sense, Evelyn, or keep your mouth shut.'

She flushed. I could've told him he'd made a mistake. But she persisted. 'What can he take to the police? A story of photos in a certain order? A theory he's worked out from that? They'd laugh him right out into the street.'

Slowly, as though hypnotized by her calmly confident court voice, Coombe relaxed.

186

Recognizing this, Paul Mace scuttled for the fallen chair and brought it back for his boss's superior backside, and after a moment Coombe sat. But his face was still dark with anger.

'After all,' she added, patting his hand, 'he hasn't actually seen them.'

Once again, I realized, she had come to my assistance. All sorts of unpleasantness had been lining up for me, and one thing I could not afford at that time was to be restrained forcibly. But in assisting me, she had, though she couldn't have understood the importance to me, successfully put a stopper on my plans to get a sight of the actual paintings in Coombe's gallery.

In fact, this was really why I'd gone there. It would have been possible to make my position clear on the phone, but I'd had the hope that I'd be able to con my way into his gallery and check his paintings against my prints, in this way confirming—or otherwise—that his were painted from the same relative viewpoint as my own original one. This, Evelyn had effectively blocked. All the same, there's no harm in trying.

'I don't know what all the fuss is about,' I complained. 'What if I did see your Frederick Ashe collection? There'd be nothing to gain, me dashing off to tell the police. All I'm interested in is finding out whether my eighty-one are Frederick Ashes or not.'

All that did for me was to provoke one of Coombe's better glares. 'You must be soft in your head. How'd you come to marry such a gormless idiot, Evelyn?'

'I can't remember. Certainly I can't imagine, now, any good reason.'

'Well . . .' I said. 'I'll be off then, seeing that nobody loves me around here. All I'll say is that I'm not parting with any of my canvases until I know the truth about them.'

If Coombe was a gambler, that might get him, I thought. The risk of allowing me to see his six, against the possibility of making a profitable deal. It didn't work. He backed only certs.

'You'll stay where you are, until I've decided what to do with you.'

He snapped his fingers, having seen Evelyn use it so effectively, and he and Paul Mace moved to one side. I stared at Evelyn, and she at me.

'It's all gone to your head, hasn't it!' she said sadly. 'A week ago, and you were the same old plodding Tony I've always known, now you've got this obsession—'

'The truth, that's all I want.'

'The truth is that you've got me in this mess, and you don't seem to care if I stay in it.'

I tried to work out how much I cared. 'Mess? You seem to be enjoying yourself.'

She smiled thinly. 'I might get some

well-paid work out of it.'

'Don't be a fool!' I rapped back sharply, annoyed that she, so perceptive normally, could be so easily taken in.

'Don't you call me—'

'He's leading you on. The easiest way to hold you here, that's what it is.'

She was shaking her head. 'Oh no, Tony. If you think we're not watched every minute, you're mistaken. And overheard. What we're saying now, somebody, somewhere, is listening to.'

It was a warning. I shrugged and got to my feet, ostensibly with impatience but in reality to check her statement. Nobody was in earshot, nobody was watching us. I thought she was mistaken, but Aleric caught my eye and inclined his head fractionally.

I had been paying too little attention to our son, taking him for granted. But he'd heard what we'd been discussing, and knew what was going on. He heaved his weight from the statue and strolled over to me.

'You sure are in trouble,' he said, making it sound admirable.

'So it seems.'

'Then give him the paintings. It's no skin—'

'You heard. They could be very valuable.'

'Oh . . . sure . . .' He shrugged lazily, and looked sly.

'And incidentally, I now know that both
189

your great grandparents were artists.'

'You don't say! What do I do, roll about in ecstasy?'

I should have become used to his casual dismissal of everything not in his restricted sphere of experience, such as discos and fringe drugs and motorbikes.

I grimaced at him. 'Please yourself. I thought you might be encouraged to think you could one day amount to something.'

'A painter? Garn!'

'Have you seen my grandfather's paintings in the gallery here? Or possibly my grandmother's, of course.'

'Haven't troubled.'

'They wouldn't let you near them, anyway.'

He winked. Nodded. What he said contradicted the visual evidence. 'Never get in there.'

I began to wonder whether he had something to say, to tell me, and had been laying a smokescreen. I spoke resignedly. 'I suppose you're right.'

'When y' get outa here, Pa, can you go and see about the bike?' he asked.

'Bike? Yours?' It seemed totally irrelevant in its context.

'I left it in the drive. It'll get nicked.'

'Yes. Well certainly, I'll do that. But will they let me go?'

'Sure to. With you here, they're gettin'

nowhere. Put it in the garage for me, Pop, will ya?'

'It'll be locked. Your mother always locks it.'

'The key's on the hook in the kitchen.'

'But she's changed the house locks. How do I get in?'

His gaze slid sideways, as though he was considering this obstacle. 'You know the big glass door that faces the trees. At the back.'

That was what his eyes had rested on, the plate glass door. We had no such door at home, and no trees at the back. 'I know what you mean.' I knew, now, why he'd introduced his motorbike into the conversation.

'It'll be open,' he said with confidence. 'You'll see. Just try it.'

I thought about that. What was he suggesting? I tested him out. 'The neighbours'll think I'm a burglar.'

'Not if you come through the trees.'

'After dark? I'd get lost.'

'You gotta torch, ain't ya?'

'It'd be seen.'

'Odd flashes. You could do it. Three flashes—who'd see them?'

'If somebody did . . .'

'Not in the trees. Nobody'd be there, would they?'

'And all this for a blasted motorbike!'

'It's important, ain't it?'

'Depends on the point of view,' I told him. He grinned. This was the first time he'd treated me to a genuine grin of pleasure instead of a leer. 'Yeah, an' I reckon it's time you thought of mine, if I can think of yours.'

He'd certainly given some thought to mine. I gave him a considering look. For too long he'd been an unpleasant object in the background of my existence, best ignored. I hadn't tried to probe his depths, because his creed demanded a shallow outlook on life. It appeared I might have been negligent. He had known exactly what was going on, had weighed up the pros and cons, and had made a decision. He was on my side, even though there were facets of my character he could not know about. He hadn't wasted his time here. He had learned the details of the set-up and worked out how the security might be probed. Not bad for a nineteen-year-old layabout.

'You'll be getting bored here,' I suggested.

'Yeah. You got to do somethin' though, ain't ya!'

I agreed, and would have pursued our growing intimacy if Coombe's voice hadn't summoned me. 'Hey you!'

I turned. A decision had been reached. I went over to him. 'You called?' Evelyn turned, frowning, on her chair.

'We're going to let you go,' Coombe said, 'because there's only you can get those paintings back from Christie's or wherever. Which you will do. Understand me? You will bring them here and let Paul have a look. He says he can tell if they're Frederick Ashe paintings or not.'

'He's seen the photographs. They ought to tell him.'

Paul Mace stood, his lips thin, his eyes brooding. 'Not good enough. I need to touch the paint. Feel the texture. It's an instinct. Not many of us have got it.'

But the strain showed around his jaw and in the tic at the corner of one eye. He was laying everything—possibly even his life—on his ability to make a decision. Or perhaps he was counting on the fact that there was nobody around there who could dispute it.

I tossed in a challenge. 'And what if I don't come back?' What could Coombe threaten now? Evelyn's life? Aleric's? I wondered whether he was sufficiently certain of my reactions if he did.

Coombe didn't fall into the trap. 'Then we come after you. You can't hide away for ever. I might be able to save Evelyn the trouble of divorcing you, and she'd get them as an inheritance.'

Nicely put, I thought admiringly. Nothing messy, such as breaking a few limbs. I would simply die. I turned to Evelyn. 'I'd like my painting to go to Aleric, Evelyn, please.'

She stared at me, her lips moving but no

sound emerging. I was aware that my remark had been based on something close to hysteria, and Aleric understood.

'Say, Pop, that's great!' he burst out.

Then, to my surprise, Evelyn picked it up. She had never before ventured into light farce. 'I always told you that you ought to make a will,' she said.

'Oh, get him out of here!' Coombe growled angrily, and this Paul Mace did with obvious relief.

The goon stood at the open front door, watching me drive away. Aleric stood behind him, his thumb up.

CHAPTER ELEVEN

I drove to Lynmouth to get something to eat and to buy a torch. It was early in the holiday season, and not crowded. Time needed wasting, so I spent it watching the river flowing out of the gorge, and strolling round the harbour. But when the sun was low on the horizon my nerves pressed me into action. There was no point in trying to reach Coombe's residence until late, when all but a minority of the guards would be asleep, but I had no idea how long it would take me to navigate that valley from the road above. I was relying on one basic fact; all I had to do

194

was keep heading downhill, until I reached the trees that Aleric had mentioned.

I realize now that I must have been in a state of euphoria, brought about by the sheer magnitude of Coombe's villainy. To a person like me, he was so far from anyone I had ever before met I was quite unable to contemplate him as a serious obstacle. I was nervous, but strangely confident. I was over-simplifying.

It was dark in the Coombe valley, with only a glow on the horizon beyond the hills facing me, when I edged the nose of the Fiesta into the parking place I'd used before. This in itself was tricky, as I dared not use lights, and yet it had to be far enough in from the roadway as not to attract attention from any night travellers. I did it by moving a few inches, getting out to check, moving another foot, until I had the front wheels right against the fall-off. I checked that I had with me all I needed.

The bulk of my photographic equipment I'd left locked away at my photo-lab, and I'd brought along only my little Ricoh. A photographer would feel naked without at least one camera. This Ricoh is useful in that it slips away into my anorak pocket with scarcely a bulge, is light, and yet is a true 35 mm job with a good lens, though with rather a wide angle. I'd also pocketed my smallest flashgun, with an extension lead. As I've explained, for what I had in mind—and

I'd had it in mind all the while—a flashgun used on the hot-shoe of the camera is unsuitable. I was fully equipped, my torch in my other pocket.

All I needed was the resolution to start. Standing there, watching the valley becoming more and more black, I suddenly doubted my ability to carry it through. I was wearing jeans and my cleated walking shoes, so was well equipped in that way, but I was not a hill climber, and it was damned frighteningly dark. There was only one thing to do, which was to get going. So I did.

What became evident at once was that the gorse—I assumed it to be gorse—which formed a solid carpet six inches thick, not only dragged at my feet, but was slippy. I found, also, that it was difficult not to break into a run, the slope being so steep. The fact that I could no longer see the ground meant that each foot went down blind, and they never seemed to reach a firm surface when I expected them to. The jarring began to shake my spine. It was more effort to steady my progress than if I'd been climbing.

I was only a hundred yards down from the road when a new difficulty arose. During daylight I had looked down, and the impression had been of a smooth surface all the way to the trees. I discovered that this was not so when my right foot, descending in its turn, met nothing. I pitched face forward, and it was only reflex action that enabled me to twist and land on my left shoulder. The drop had been only a foot, but the shock was great. I tried to prevent myself from rolling, scrambling with my feet and digging my fingers in, and finished up spread-eagled, glued to the slope with my face in the gorse.

Gingerly, I rolled over until I was sitting. It seemed I was stuck there. How could I continue if the surface was ridged and pitted, with rock breaking through the ground and the soil washed away beneath it? I had no way of being certain that all the sudden drops were of no more than a foot. The only thing I could think to do was to use my torch.

But this slope, I recalled, had risen almost from Renfrew Coombe's terrace, though slightly to one side. A light could not possibly go unobserved. I looked back. The peak was outlined dimly above me against the lighter sky. I could just detect the nose of the car. The temptation was to begin the climb back to it; this was something very much removed from my normal experience.

I decided to give it a little more time. There was a possibility of being able to back down, feeling with my feet and with my hands trailing in the gorse. This I managed for perhaps a hundred feet, by which time my face was becoming scratched and my hands sore. I tried it seated, edging down in tentative jerks. Nobody's behind can stand this for long.

Wearily and desperately I got to my feet, realizing I'd have to take it blind and risk the falls. Or go back. No, to hell with that! Aleric would laugh me out of existence.

I put one foot in front of the other, repeated it, and was moving again, and discovered I could reach down with each foot with more confidence if I progressed with bent knees, in a semi-crouch. My knees began to ache. Pain shot up behind my thighs. But I progressed.

Twice more I fell, the second time over a drop of three feet, which flung me in a tangle of pain on to a bed of small rocks. Something moved beside me. More skilful feet than mine clattered away. Hill sheep. I groaned, and rolled over, staggering to my feet before blissful inertia could capture me.

Now, I realized, I was in sight of the house. I could see lights, at windows too extensive to belong to any of the cottages. I had time, all the time I needed, I told myself. I stepped forward.

Some minutes passed without incident, and I realized I was now walking on a different surface. Lower down, grass took over from the gorse. Hence the sheep, I suppose. Also, when I could raise my head from the concentration of stepping forward, I noticed I could no longer see the lights of the house. For a moment this baffled me. Then I realized I had reached the tree line.

Now that my eyes had become accustomed to the darkness, I could see the dimly separated shapes of the trees. In assistance, the moon was rising. Not a full moon, but better than nothing. I wondered whether, once inside the tree cover, I might dare to use my torch.

I had covered no more than ten feet when I discovered I would have to.

My confident assumption that I needed only to move downhill now became a bad joke. Bruised and scratched and aching, I wanted only to sit down, lean back against the bole of a tree, and wait for daylight. But this I dared not do.

I moved onwards but the trees, their roots massed, had tossed up the ground unevenly. There was no down or up. It was all up and down combined. Besides which, I realized, I did not require to move downhill, because there I'd find the village. The big house should now be somewhere on my right. And possibly higher, I supposed.

Two hours later, still stumbling over root boles, I was using my torch unsparingly, in despair and frustration. In this way, having fumbled up a rise, I suddenly noticed I was walking on smooth and level grass. It could be nothing else but the croquet lawn, the only level surface for miles. I cut the torch, promptly hooked my foot in a croquet hoop, and fell flat on my face.

When I lifted my head, I saw first a reflection of the moon in glass, then, below it, three winks of light. A torch. I groped for mine and flicked back. Three times. Aleric was there.

I clambered to my feet. Clear now of trees, I discovered that the moonlight revealed the lawn and its hoops. I loped across, up on to the terrace, and directly to the plate-glass window. It opened. Aleric, a monkey on his shoulder, was standing there. I could have thrown my arms around him, but the monkey might well have objected.

The reason I could see him was because a faint green light filtered through the shrubbery around us. An all-night light, apparently. It showed me a chair. I collapsed into it.

'Never again,' I said, keeping my head down. 'Never.'

'I thought you'd got lost.'

'I did.'

'We'll have to move. He might come round soon.'

'He? Round?'

He prodded a shape on the floor with his foot. 'The guard. They leave one sitting in here all night. He's doped.'

I had forgotten guards, burglar alarms, all the protection Coombe would have laid on. 'The alarms!'

200

'Difficult to rig a glass door without the wires showing,' Aleric said briskly. 'I found 'em in two minutes.'

I was in no mood to move, but my breathing was steadying. 'The guards? Doped, you say?'

'Pa, I ain't been lounging around doing nothin'. Been making myself useful. Made out I was hopin' to be taken on the strength. They let me take round the coffee. I put barbiturates in, for tonight's guards.'

'Where the devil—'

'I carry 'em. Bennies and barbies.'

'You're on drugs?' I was appalled.

'Nar! But you gotta carry 'em. Uppers and downers at least. Or you're out, Pop, way outa the stream.'

'Ye gods.'

'We gotta move. You all right? You're not as young . . .'

'I'm fine. Lead on.'

He took me up a rear staircase and confidently along corridors. We dared show no lights, but the moon through the high windows helped. Aleric had certainly looked around. He knew every step of the way.

We rounded a corner. I stopped. At the end of a short corridor a light shone. There was a door, and beside it a chair, on which a man was seated.

'It's fine,' Aleric told me in a confident voice. 'He's asleep.'

As he was. A mug stood beside him on the floor, and his chin was down on his chest. Beside him was a tall container of sand, used as an ashtray. The door showed a steel surface, with a single round keyhole, beneath it a knob not intended to turn.

'That does it,' I said. 'It's a high-security lock.'

'Dad, now ask yourself. You've got this door, with a special key. Are you going to carry it around with you? No . . . you'd be scared of losing it. Maybe there's a duplicate, but you'd be afraid of losing that one too. So where do you keep it, handy for the door but concealed? Think, Pop.'

I thought, but nothing came. He was running his fingers through the sand in the ashtray bin. They came up holding a peculiar cylindrical key with tiny protrusions around it. He had to turn it in the lock three times, then there was a faint click, and the door swung open.

It was an impenetrable black inside. Aleric eased the door shut, pocketing the key, and pressed a switch. He raised his voice to normal.

'Reckon we're all right in here, Pa. Nobody'll hear. But make it quick, huh?'

Now that we were no longer whispering, I could confirm what I thought I'd already detected. Gone was the slurred and lazy clipping of words, the vernacular of whatever was in at that time. Inside this bulky slough, who was my son, there was a normal human being. A competent one, too, judging by the calm and matter-of-fact way he'd managed this.

'Two minutes,' I promised. 'Once I've found what I want.'

I said that because the gallery was confusing. What I'd expected was a large room with paintings hung on the walls, but that would have been too conventional for Renfrew Coombe. What he had was alcoves and corners and bits tucked away. He also had mirrors. For such a physically unattractive man, he had a strange addiction to mirrors, though perhaps he considered himself an example of *homo perfectus*. Whatever the reason, mirrors he had, and the impression was that he owned twice as many paintings as in fact he did.

'Cor strike!' said Aleric, wandering around.

It was no use asking for his help, because it was I who knew what the Frederick Ashe paintings looked like. Fervently, I hoped Coombe had them hung in one batch. I walked through quickly, my eyes darting around. There was a sense of urgency.

The collection appeared to be all Impressionist and later. Some I wouldn't have given hanging space to. The mirrors confused me. Walking round what I took to be a corner, I banged straight into one.

Aleric said: 'Did they get paid for this? I could do better myself.'

'They usually starved,' I told him absently. 'The people who make the money are the investors. I'm looking for . . . ah, there they are!'

They were, as I'd hoped, all in one line, six of them with the familiar overlapped A and F, and conveniently at my eye level. There were some more paintings farther along, and also in an alcove behind my shoulder, but I hadn't time for browsing. Behind me was a wall of mirrors, in which the six were reflected reversed, and there were more mirrors each side of them.

'Come and give me a hand,' I said. 'I'll want you to hold the flashgun. Point it at each painting from a spot just above my left shoulder. Get it?'

'Gotcha.'

I plugged in the lead, switched on the flashgun, and told him to watch for the little red light after each flash, and tell me when it came on. 'That's when it's charged.'

I got a near-full frame at a metre, and they were all the same size: twenty by sixteen. It meant I'd have to use f16 and guess distance, as there was no rangefinder or focusing screen on the little Ricoh. But I'm used to guessing distance. I steadied the picture in the viewfinder and the flash operated.

'Little red light,' he said. I took the next.

The charging time was around ten seconds. We had all six on film in three minutes, so I did them again for luck. Or rather, I started to do them again, but at the second one Aleric suddenly said, 'Psst!' just as I was taking the shot.

My nerves were so stretched that I jerked the camera as the flash operated. 'What the hell!'

'I thought I heard something. Just a sec.' He ran softly back to the door.

Ten seconds later he was back. 'He's stirring. Making groaning noises.'

'I'll finish this.'

'Then hurry it, Pop, for Chrissake.'

I completed the second run, dismantled the flash, and slid it all into my anorak pocket. 'Let's go.'

We stood at the door and extinguished the lights, then opened it and peered out. The guard was grumbling to himself and trying to lift his head. We slipped out and stood beside him as Aleric quietly closed the door, giving the key its three turns, then buried it in the sand again.

We ran, our feet silent because they barely had time to brush the floor. Aleric's memory was immaculate. We burst into the sun room, and stopped. This guard was groaning, too, but the light was to dim for us to see him.

'Quick!' said Aleric.

'You're coming—'

'No, Pa. No. The guards'll keep quiet, even if they guess they were doped, and nobody'll spot the alarm wire's cut. Unless somebody breaks in, I'm in the clear.'

'I don't like it.'

'Y' know I've gotta stay with Ma, now don'tcher! Get going, Dad, please.'

He had the plate-glass door open. Behind him, a shadow stirred in the dimness. A voice said: 'You're going nowhere.'

The green light was ghastly, but as he stepped forward I could see enough to recognize Paul Mace. There was also sufficient light to catch a glint of green from something he held in his hand. Surely, I thought in panic, that couldn't be a pistol!

Aleric took a step towards him. Somewhere beyond Mace, from the direction of the great hall, I heard shouts.

'Go, Dad, go!' Aleric shouted.

I hesitated. The pistol moved, and one of the monkeys jumped down on to Mace's shoulders. Aleric seemed to skip, his foot shot out and upwards, and Mace cried out. The pistol cracked sharply, but more weakly than I would have expected, and a pane of glass shattered in the roof, shards tinkling down.

'Get going!' howled Aleric as the door burst open behind Mace and white light thrust in blindingly. He seized the doubled Mace and hurled him at the group pushing their way in. 'I'll hold 'em!'

206

I turned and ran, across the terrace and the croquet lawn, my torch on because of the hoops, and plunged over the end, rolling down the slope and into the trees.

I stood, caught a glimpse of the moon just before I entered the trees, and placed it in my mind. Upwards, I had to move upwards, but I would find the slope only if I could hold a line. There was now no chance of using the torch. I prodded it into my pocket and stumbled forward, hands outstretched and with every nerve standing out, reaching for clues as to my surroundings.

There were shouts behind me. I heard a booming voice call: 'Spread out. Don't let him get away.' Distantly, somebody was screaming. I had to assume it was Evelyn.

They could use torches. I saw them flickering through the trees behind and to the sides. Only the boles of the trees hid me from their sight, but my guardian angel, the moon, was hidden behind the massed young growth of the leaves above.

From time to time I stopped, panting, my legs shaking. By moving my head sideways I could catch an occasional glimpse of the moon. It indicated that I could not simply run away from the torches. They were trying to head me off, and must have realized where I wanted to go. But I had to be true to the moon. A clear night—was it a clear night? I wondered—and I might survive. If it clouded over, I was done. They would be carrying not only torches but weapons.

The flickering torches now arced widely to my right. My intention was to head left, but in that direction they were closer together. I forced myself to trust the moon, caught one more weak gleam from it, and staggered in the indicated direction. Surely, I prayed, I would feel the slope under my feet soon. But the torches were closer. They were even closing in on me from both sides.

Branches lashed my face and I tasted blood on my lips. I tripped constantly, recovering from reaction, my reasoning now becoming confused. There were no more shouts. The torches seemed to be one blurred mass. For a moment I paused, my shoulders against the bole of what must have been an oak, my head back, gulping in great lungfuls of air. A man walked through a brake of shrubs thirty feet from me. I backed round the tree, my heart leaping about wildly.

In the split-second I'd seen him, his torch searching, I had noticed we were on opposite sides of a clearing. He entered it, and stood, his head turning, cocked, listening. Somebody shouted: 'Over here.' He moved to his left, which was towards me. I flattened myself against the tree. He walked past me, his torch and his attention focused ahead. Then he broke into a trot and crashed his way towards the shout.

I walked out into the clearing, because there was a chance that here the trees didn't meet overhead. It was a correct guess. I got a good look at the moon just before the clouds rolled in front of it, and forced myself to stand and calculate. Keep it over my right shoulder, I told myself, and go straight ahead. The difficulty was that most of the torchlight was in that direction. But it was, I realized, slightly at a higher level.

They had reached the slope.

Resolutely, I marched towards the lighter area. Then I had an idea. I drew out my torch, switched it on, and left it on. I yelled: 'Over on the right!'

And then I ran. I had become one of the hunters. They thinned. What had seemed a solid mass of torches, closer to was scattered. I came to within a hundred yards of the nearest, then I put off my torch, and found I could steer my way between the individual lights. But it was slower going. I tripped more often, now more from exhaustion than obstructions. Yet I detected a rise, and in the direction I wanted to go. As the searchers progressed farther, they had of necessity to spread out. I slipped and scrambled between two of them, and the trees were thinning ahead of me, the slope was becoming more pronounced, and abruptly, before I could calculate the danger, I was standing on the steepening grass slope.

209

But now I was in the open, and it needed only the swept beam of a torch to locate me. On that slope, I would be an open target. Yet the moon, my saviour, had now hidden itself away behind a heavy bank of cloud, otherwise I would have been as visible as a fly crawling up a wall.

I moved stealthily, my eyes turning over each shoulder in turn to see whether torches were coming my way. Occasionally light shone through the upper bank of trees, but nobody shone in my direction. Perhaps they thought they'd cut me off. I moved stealthily because I could barely move at all. I ached all over and my chest seemed to be congested. All I knew was that I was progressing slowly upwards, my arms and hands doing most of the work now. Eventually I would come out on the upper road, hopefully in sight of the car.

But hopefully would not do, I realized. If I could not see my car, and didn't dare to use the torch, I would not know in which direction to walk. In one of the clefts the sheep had been using, I sat and thought about it. Far below me in the valley there was now no visible activity. The possibility was that I'd been spotted, and they were advancing silently, no longer needing their torches. Definitely, I would need to head directly to the Fiesta. I stood, and stared upwards. The moon, behind cloud that was now breaking up, supplied a slightly lighter backdrop for the brow of the hill. It seemed smooth, apart from one indefinite shape, far over to one side. I had to risk it, and struck out on a diagonal line, rising and to my right.

Almost at once I was in gorse again. At least it meant I was progressing. But the drag on my ankles, which had been only a nuisance on my way down, now became close to disabling. I moved slower and slower. The shape on the horizon grew in size and took on form. It was the protruding nose of the car. I was now below it, with only two hundred yards to go. Straight up. My brain, robbed of oxygen, was swimming. I wanted to lie down. With my eyes firmly on the objective, the Fiesta. I felt it was growing larger than my progress justified. I stopped, waiting for my eyes to clear.

I discovered that although I was now still, the nose and bonnet were still growing larger. It was moving towards the edge, towards me. Then the front wheels were over the edge, and the acceleration became definite. The nose tilted, and it was charging down the hillside towards me.

There was nowhere I could go. I was directly in its path. For one moment I forced myself to my feet, and stood swaying, and watched it coming, rustling the undergrowth, bucking and bouncing. Then I threw myself face down in the gorse. Yet still I could not

211

cover my face with my arms. It fascinated me, robbed me of all conscious thought. There was nothing but terror. The bouncing increased. The nose dug in. Its tail came up, and the whole car left the surface, plunged down again, nose in, pitched right over, and the terrible crashing sound preceded it as the hammered metal protested. It bounced on its roof. A door flew clear. It leapt again, and it was on me. I wrapped my arms round my head. I think I was screaming, but I could not have been heard.

The bonnet pitched in only ten feet from me. The din flattened me. It arched over my back and as it landed behind me a wheel flew off, and the tailgate hung by one hinge.

I twisted, and watched it down into the darkness of the trees, the noise decreasing as its bulk grew less and as it distanced itself from me, until eventually it was taken by the trees and cushioned by them into silence.

There was no fire, because the ignition wasn't switched on.

I lay, panting and gasping, lay for a full five minutes before I could force myself to my feet again. It didn't matter any more at what point I reached the road. All that I could think about was that I'd have quite a difficulty with my report to the hire firm. I couldn't get my mind from that, but when I did I realized that, inside the car, there had been my set of prints of the eighty-one loft pictures.

I crawled up to the road and began to plod along it.

CHAPTER TWELVE

I reached the coast road about equidistant betwen Lynmouth and Porlock just as dawn was breaking. On the bank of tight moor grass at the verge I sat and tried to recover. There were decisions to be made and plans to be drafted, but my brain would not operate. There was a light emptiness to me. I saw clearly, but could not associate image with fact.

When I'd recovered my breathing, I lit my pipe. Usually it helps. This time it made my head swim. Which way should I go? That was the first decision to be made. Porlock was nearer home, if there was a home to go to, but in Lynmouth or Lynton I'd be more likely to find a car-hire firm. But would my credit card now carry any financial weight? Unlikely. Worry about that later. Worry right now about the fact that Coombe's men might come looking for me, and there was nowhere I could hide.

On this open road, high above the Bristol Channel, there was very little cover. The naked moors spread in both directions, steeply downhill inland. I could only sit and wait, and pray that they were still searching for my body on the slope. They would assume I had reached the Fiesta, and stupidly engaged forward gear instead of reverse. Or would they? Perhaps not. The car hadn't pushed itself over the edge. No, they would probably know I had not reached the car. In any event, they would need to locate what was left of me.

Pleased, now, that my brain was working again, I tested out my other senses. Sight and hearing. Out there in the open, engine and tyre sounds give prior warning. I heard a vehicle coming from the Porlock direction, and prepared to scramble over the meagre bank behind me. But the multiple curves revealed it long before the driver could have seen me. It was a white van.

I stood in the roadway, too weary to raise a thumb. He stopped. It was a newspaper delivery van. The driver got out.

'You all right?' he asked. 'You look terrible.'

'Car accident,' I told him. 'Can you get me into Lynton? I'm about done.'

'Sure. Hope in. Hey, you look awful!'

Hopping in was out of the question. He helped me up. It was seven o'clock. He asked no questions, but I thought he deserved answers.

'The inland roads are tricky at night. I missed a turn.'

'Nasty. You ought to see a doctor.'

'It's only,' I lied, 'superficial.'

He took me into Lynmouth, where I sat in the cab as he dumped his parcels of papers. Emptily, I watched him. He drove me up to Lynton, told me where I might hire a car, and dropped me outside an early-opening café. It was just after eight. I thanked him.

'I can't tell you how much—'

'Do the same for me some day,' he said cheerfully. 'Drive the next one more careful, like.'

I used the men's room while they prepared me a pot of tea and bacon and eggs and chips. Truly, I did look terrible, my face black and my hair tangled, bits of gorse stuck in it and all over me, my clothes torn and slimy with green, the left knee out of my jeans. I was bang in fashion. I tidied up as best I could, but it would be a fool who'd let me step inside a hire car.

I ate voraciously, and downed two pots of tea. The pipe tasted better, and my head remained where it was. I was ready for the next step.

The car-hire firm was dubious, but computers never lie, and this one confirmed that I had a balance sufficient to pay for a week's hire plus insurance, in advance. Perhaps, this early in the morning, the computer was half asleep. I drove away in a blue Metro with a fault in its silencer.

Three and a half hours later it was making a loud noise in my home town. I had decided on a sequence of procedure. First: park, walk round to my photo-lab, and observe it to check whether it was under surveillance. I saw nothing suspicious. Second: nip inside quickly and dial Margaret's number. This I did. It rang and rang, but there was no reply. That meant two things: one, that I had nowhere to go, which in turn probably meant I'd have to sleep rough at the lab—dangerous because Coombe probably knew by then where it was located. And two, that I had comparison shots of Coombe's six paintings, and nothing to compare them with, my set of eighty-one prints having been in the crashed Fiesta. So . . . I would have to run off another set of the whole eighty-one, or at least go through them until I found six that would match.

But before that, I wanted to try out a slim chance. Aleric had been very subtle in suggesting how I could enter the Coombe residence, so there was a possibility he'd been doubly subtle. Wanting to try this out, I deferred the photographic work, and was just pulling shut the outside door when I heard the phone ring.

I dashed back inside and grabbed it up. It was Margaret.

'Tony! Where have you *been*?'

'You know damn well. Coombe's place.'

She didn't ask if I'd had any luck. 'Listen, I've got some news. Not good, I'm afraid.' Her voice was brisk and businesslike.

'I'm getting used to that. Say on.'

'I didn't take them to Sotheby's—'

'Didn't?'

'I took them to a friend of mine, who's got a gallery just off Bond Street.'

'I thought we agreed—'

'And he's a bit of an expert on the Impressionists.'

'I thought you were the expert.'

A slight tang entered her voice. 'There are others.'

'You said you didn't want a second opinion,' I insisted, a little needled that I'd expended so much effort in obtaining evidence, and all it had needed, for Margaret, was a consultation with a friend. Also a little needled, to tell you the truth, that there was a friend she could run to.

'I can change my mind, can't I?' she demanded.

'If you wish.'

'And he says—'

'An opinion.'

'He says he's certain the eighty-one are not Frederick Ashe works.'

I allowed a pause to build up, trying to recover my equanimity.

'Tony?'

'Margaret, I've got what we were after. Six

217

photographs of Coombe's set of Frederick Ashe. We can check the business of the right or left viewpoints, and at least—'

'You got *in* there? Inside the gallery?'

'Yes. How else would I do it?'

'And that's all you've got to say?'

I didn't understand what she meant. 'What else is there? Oh yes, I've got those six, but I've lost the set of photos of the eighty-one. So . . . to save reprinting the lot, wouldn't it be better to check against the original canvases?'

There was a slight pause, then: 'Do you think that would be a good idea, Tony?'

'It's the best one.'

'Correct me if I'm wrong, but you'll surely have had difficulty getting into Coombe's gallery.'

'You could say that.'

'And he's not pleased about it?'

'Not noticeably.'

'Then he'll certainly have you followed, and it wouldn't be sensible to lead him straight to the canvases.'

'I can't see that it matters, if you're so certain they're not by Frederick Ashe.'

There was a snap to her voice. 'Don't be foolish. They're worth *something* . . .'

'I was forgetting—school of Frederick Ashe. But what happened to the idea of selling them as genuine?'

'Now . . . I ask you! One expert, that's all

I've needed to go to, and he said, without a doubt, they're not by Frederick Ashe.'

'Quick on it, wasn't he? It took you days . . .'

She didn't like that, but I wasn't in any mood to be considerate of her sensibilities. 'Never mind that. It was only a suggestion.'

'Yes,' I said. 'I see,' I said. Which I did. It had been a suggestion that made it unnecessary for me to visit Coombe. But I'd done that, and I was safe. Nothing much had happened. 'Coombe would still be in the market for them,' I suggested.

'He wouldn't expect to pay, he'd just take them,' she said acidly. 'By force, or whatever was necessary.'

'Not if we can prove to him they're not Frederick Ashe.'

'Why are you being so difficult, Tony?' she asked, her voice wearily conversational. 'Everything I say is sensible, yet you do nothing but quibble.'

'Shall we say I'm tired.'

'Then do get some rest.'

I was about to ask where, but she didn't give me the chance. 'I'll be in touch. Goodbye for now.'

And she'd gone before I had time to ask for her number, her new address, anything. It was highly unsatisfactory, and it seemed clear to me that her interest had died the moment she decided the loft set were not by Frederick

219

Ashe. Her interest in the paintings and in me.

So now I was committed to another stint in the darkroom, to produce prints of the six Coombe shots and of the six they matched from the loft set. If I could locate them.

But first . . . I locked up, and went to the meter where I'd left the Metro. Then I drove home. By home, I mean Evelyn's house. I drove a roundabout route, using every device I'd ever read about to avoid being followed. Only when I was certain I was not did I head for Evelyn's.

I was playing a hunch on the way Aleric had said it. His meaning could have been taken at face value, that the house might be entered from the rear. This I had to test. I needed somewhere to lay my head.

The motorbike was in the drive, as Aleric had said. I went round the back and tried the french window into the living-room. She might well have changed the lock on this, too—though I had never carried a key to this door—but, as Aleric had claimed, it opened. The relief was immense.

I had brought along all my photographic equipment, the workplace being too vulnerable in my opinion. With this unloaded from the car I felt better. After that, the first thing was to get a bath and a change of clothing . . . and decide the next move.

The advantage of this place as a refuge from Coombe was that Evelyn would have told him she'd changed the locks, so it was the last place he would look for me. I would have to be careful not to show a light after dark, though.

Evelyn's departure had been so abrupt that she'd left the immersion heater switched on, controlled by its thermostat. So I enjoyed a glorious, blissful soak, and felt much better for it. And, unfortunately, sleepier. I'd lost a night's sleep, and the reaction was setting in. I went down and raided the deep-freeze and cooked a decent meal, by which time the thought of bed was so overwhelming that I went out into the garden hoping that fresh air would revive me. It had begun to rain. That helped. I turned my face up to it.

It was three o'clock in the afternoon. I decided I had wasted too much time; Coombe's men could be closing in from all directions. I went up to Aleric's room and searched the drawers in which he kept items I cared not to linger over, and found the spare keys to his bike. I discovered his leathers inside his wardrobe, and his boots and his crash-hat. A disguise. The bike would also be difficult to catch, if I needed to use evasion. And if I could handle it.

I unloaded the film casette from the Ricoh and put it in my pocket, shut the french window, and clumped round to the front.

It had been nigh on twenty years since I'd ridden a motorcycle, and that had been a

250cc BSA. They had changed. This thing was a 1000cc V-twin, with a self starter, and shaft-drive instead of a chain, and a whole seat of control buttons on the handlebar console that I had to sort out. It was heavy, but Aleric and I are about the same size, so the seat height seemed correct and, straddling it, my feet were firmly on the ground, and the weight disappeared.

I did what I thought to be the right things, and the engine thrummed into life with a strangely off-beat pulse. I engaged gear. We were moving.

It felt like a dream, and at once became part of me. All the old joy of being on a bike flowed back. The acceleration took my breath away.

One advantage of a motorcycle is that you can park it almost anywhere. I left it in the yard behind a nearby pub and walked to my photo-lab, looking, I hoped, very unlike Tony Hine. I went in as though I were a customer, though having to use the key spoiled the image a little. Once inside the darkroom, I shut the door and wasted no time. Off with the leathers and into the tank with the film, and while that was proceeding, in the intervals between solution changes, I got out the loft canvas negatives, and tried to discover, from memory, which ones might duplicate the six from the Coombe gallery. I was working in white light at this stage, but the task was near impossible.

I now had the negatives cut into lengths of six frames, but for colour it's not just the black and white that're reversed, but also the colours. This makes identification difficult. I put aside the strips that had possibles on them, completed development of the film, and hung it in the drier. You can't rush these things. I needed prints of the Coombe gallery six before I could proceed further.

In practice there were twelve Coombe gallery prints, as I'd run through them twice, thirteen if you counted the spoiled one. This one I printed, too, before I realized what I was doing, which is an indication of how tired I was. My concentration was failing. What with having to work now in near darkness, and the lack of ventilation, my head was throbbing and my eyes were going out of focus. Aware that I was rushing it, not taking my usual care on colour control and density, I knew it was probably a botched job.

While they dried and glazed, I opened the door for a breath of air, but I didn't dare to go as far as the street.

With the six best Coombe shots to go on, I managed to find the matching six from my original photos of the loft set. That there were six that matched was an advance in my knowledge of the situation. It confirmed there had been two sets of eighty-one canvases, and that out of one of the sets, only seven now existed.

I slapped the six loft-set prints into the glazer, switched everything off, and lit my pipe. Home—Evelyn's—and bed, that was the next thing on the programme. Comparison of the prints could wait until later.

At first I thought it was my pipe burning rank. It couldn't have been the enlarger overheating, because I'd turned it off. It was burning I could smell. Of necessity, a darkroom door has to have a good seal but, now in white light again, I saw that smoke was seeping from under and round the edges of the door.

Without thinking—I was long past considered thought—I opened the door . . . and slammed it again. Outside there, where my tiny reception office had been, there was an inferno.

Coughing already from the smoke, sweat streaking my face, I switched off the glazer, peeled off the prints, and crammed the day's production into my pocket. I scrambled, falling twice as I raised one leg from the floor, into Aleric's leathers, put on his crash hat and his driving gloves, and slammed down the visor.

Then I opened the door again. Even through the helmet I could hear the roar, through the visor I could feel the heat striking my face, and already there was the smell of

224

scorching riding kit, before it became overwhelmed by the choking smoke. There was no other way but through it. I tried to avoid the counter, not simply because it was beneath it that the fire seemed to be centred. Coughing and choking, and rapidly losing my sense of direction, I fumbled towards where the door should have been. There was no light from the windows, which were blocked by my show prints. I came up against something solid. Flames ran up it, so that the chance was that it was a wooden door. Heat pounded at my back, and I thought the overtrousers were alight. I grabbed for the latch and turned it, and pulled. The door would not move. The heat—or something else—had wedged it.

Inside the helmet there were whimpering noises. I could see nothing, as the smoke was in there with me. Forcing myself to the effort, and against the pain of retreating towards the centre of the heat, I took a pace backwards and kicked out with my foot, flat on. Futile, of course. The door opened inwards. Then, with fury and panic, and a reserve of energy I didn't realize I possessed, I attacked the door, kick after kick. Pain racked me. My breath caught, and I drew in fumes and smoke. I kicked, and a panel gave way. Air rushed in. I fell to my knees, reaching for it.

It was what the fire had craved. Air. It

sucked it in, and what had been a roar became an explosion, and with my face to the gap, aware that through it was coming not just air but the wail of sirens, I lost consciousness as a rush of water flung me on to my back.

CHAPTER THIRTEEN

It is a good way to catch up on your sleep, but not one I would necessarily recommend. I regained consciousness in a hospital bed, remained awake long enough to discover I was suffering from an intake of smoke and fumes, and minor burns, then apparently slept for twelve hours under an oxygen tent. With a little help from a needle, no doubt.

A policewoman was waiting for me. She smiled. The nurse smiled. My face was stiff and sore, so I didn't. A doctor came and checked various things and said I was doing fine, and that the policewoman had a few things to ask, if I was up to it. I had things to ask, myself, but kept them for later.

It appeared that the fire had not been accidental. How could it have been, with nothing to start it in the reception area? Did I know anything that would help the police? Had I enemies? Had I offended anyone recently?

Oh yes, and yes, and yes, but I wasn't going to say so. Would they send a local bobby to arrest Renfrew Coombe? I could just see it. I shook my head only once, a painful process, and afterwards said no, sorry, to every question.

The young policewoman, who had started off all smiles, finished with annoyance on her face and a shake of the head that indicated sadness for me. Enemies who projected such fear in their victims were just the ones the police wanted to interview.

I was alone. Carefully, I assessed the damage. The visor had not given full protection. The lower half of my face was stiff, and burned even now. My calves were bound and padded. I touched one, and even through the padding it hurt. My hands were fine. My chest ached when I breathed in too heavily.

That was me, physically.

But the damage in other directions would not mend. My darkroom, its equipment, my records and my filed negatives, had all been destroyed. That meant a large hole in my career. It meant I no longer had the negatives for the eighty-one loft paintings. Nor—until I became active—could I reach the paintings themselves. Not even then, come to think about it, because I could not reach Margaret, and the only phone number she had for me was now extinct.

All I did have, and these had been placed on the bedside cabinet for me, was the set of photos from the Coombe gallery, and the matching six from the loft set. As there was nothing else to do, I sorted them out.

I chose the best six of the Coombe shots, and laid them beside the other six. It was easy to tell which were which, because Coombe's paintings had been framed, and this was just visible round the edges of the prints.

The position was at once clear. The Coombe paintings, as in the case of my own original one, were in all cases right-biased viewpoints. It told me that mine and his had been painted by the same hand. No, I'll qualify that. The odds were that they had been painted by the same hand. And, if Margaret's search of the archives had to be considered valid, Maurice Bellarmé's painting of Frederick Ashe indicated that he was left-handed. Therefore, he had most likely sat to the right of grandma Angelina.

So I'd progressed not one iota. It simply confirmed what Margaret had said, that the eighty-one loft paintings had been done by my grandmother, and the other seven by Ashe.

I put them aside, and lay a long while trying to recapture my enthusiasm for the truth. Proof positive. That was what it had been. A kind of crusade. But even the crusaders must have felt a similar lack of enthusiasm when they'd had the stuffing knocked out of them.

It was true that the paintings had already brought about too many deaths. Arthur Hine, Angelina, Grace Fielding. But all I was doing was keeping the legend alive by trying to add my own to the list.

Then I thought of Coombe, the acquisitive Renfrew Coombe, who had obtained most of his paintings by theft, and was prepared to maintain their inviolability by murder. He could not afford even the suggestion that his might not be genuine Frederick Ashes, and needed to destroy anything that might be used as a questionable comparison.

I thought of Coombe, and a spark of anger grew. He was unassailable. His arrogant assumption of this was infuriating. He assumed, now, that I would surrender the paintings gladly. Gladly? I'd see him in hell first. Angelina Footes or Frederick Ashes, to me that no longer seemed relevant. Their possible value was an issue not even under consideration. They were mine, to do with as I pleased, and if what I did in some way annoyed him, then I would do it twice, and twice as vigorously.

Thus musing, I fell asleep, and awoke to find Detective Sergeant Dolan at my bedside.

'They're going to let you out tomorrow,' he said, shaking my hand as though I was an old friend long lost. 'We'll probably be taking you in.'

'Protective custody?'

He didn't think that was amusing. 'That'd be a good idea. It'd save a lot of argument.'

'Who's arguing?'

He drew up a chair, and took the question seriously. 'The Super and the Chief Inspector. The CI's all for charging you on what we've got.' He stared at my flaming chin. 'You feeling all right?'

'I was. Keep to the subject. Charging me with what?'

'Murder. Your grandmother and Grace Fielding.'

He made the whole issue sound a bore. If there was something better he could be doing, he would be elsewhere.

'And you?' I asked. 'What do you think, Sergeant?'

'Me?' He shrugged. 'Who cares what I think?'

'I care.'

'Well, if you must know—and if it matters—I think you're a prize idiot, but not a murderer.'

'And nobody cares what you think?'

'Not at the office, where it counts.'

I wondered where that left me, and wondered why he'd come. He seemed to read my mind. 'But that isn't why I'm here,' he admitted.

I waited, but he wasn't ready, seemed

distrait and wouldn't meet my eyes.

'Why am I a prize idiot?' I asked quietly.

In answer, he reached over to the bedside cabinet and picked up the pack of photographs I'd been looking at. He flipped through them as though they were holiday snaps.

'The car in your drive,' he said, 'was hired in Lynton. That's a hundred and eighty miles from here. A long way to go in order to hire a car, especially when you already had one on hire.'

'I lost it.'

It seemed not to register. 'But Lynton is only a few miles from the home of Renfrew Coombe, art collector and well-known anonymous philanthropist, one of our richest and dirtiest crooks, and the owner of two Frederick Ashe paintings.' He jutted his lower lip and tilted his head, examining the quality of my photography. 'At least two,' he amended.

'I've heard about him.'

He flapped the pack of prints against his other palm. 'And it's Frederick Ashe paintings you're interested in, Mr Hine, if I'm not mistaken, so the coincidence gets a bit too much to take.'

'That's an opinion, Sergeant.'

'Mine.' He nodded. 'Not the Super's, nor the DI's. Just an idea of mine.' He switched topics again. 'Had a word with the doc on the way in. He says there're contusions and bruises and scratches not involved with any fire. This is your body we're talking about.'

'It sounded like me.'

'So I've got this feeling you've been tangling with our friend Coombe. Just a feeling. And that's not healthy, Mr Hine. We want him. Want him badly. Got anything to say to that?'

He tossed the prints on my lap, or rather, on to the bedcover beneath which my lap was hidden. It was a challenge, or an offer, or a veiled suggestion of alliance.

'You've looked at these?' I took them up and shuffled them, then put together the six from the Coombe gallery, the ones showing the canvases as being framed.

'Before I woke you up.'

'Right. Then I'll tell you something. Not officially, Sergeant. Just you and me.'

He inclined his head. Maybe it was agreement.

I went on: 'The paintings from the loft, which my grandmother gave me, may or may not be Frederick Ashe works. Equally, the ones Coombe has may or may not be what he thinks they are—Frederick Ashes. Both can't be right. So I took photographs of the ones Coombe has. These six here, the ones showing the frames. Six, you'll notice, when he's only supposed to have two. The other four have been stolen from national galleries in the past two years. Are you interested?'

He looked up at me, directly in the eyes, probably for the first time since he'd entered my tiny personal ward. 'Possibly.' But his eyes were bright.

'So . . . in his gallery are four paintings that can be shown to have been stolen. Right?'

He picked up the theme. 'So I take those photographs to the Super, and we get a search warrant. For years we've been looking for evidence that'll get us inside there.'

I shoved them under my pillow, just before his questing hand reached them. 'No you don't. I've lost the negatives in that fire, so these are all I've got.'

'I'll have them officially copied for you.'

'I'm not letting 'em out of my hands.'

'I'll legally impound them as evidence, if I have to.'

I grinned at him. 'Evidence of what? That they're photographs, and that means nothing. You'd need an affidavit from me, to provide the proof that I took six specific photos of paintings on the wall of his gallery. No, let me say it, Sergeant. You see . . . whereas you could subpoena me to a trial, and get me on oath, there's nothing you can do to force me into swearing an affidavit. My wife's a lawyer, Sergeant. Details rub off over the years.'

His brows had lowered. He wasn't certain what to say. 'Why're you telling me this, if it isn't going to do me any good?'

'I owe him, Sergeant. He tried to kill me, or have me killed. I owe him a lot. But I need you to give me time. It's a *quid*, as my wife would say, *pro quo*. Give me time, and you'll have your evidence. But there's another point. I now think that I can prove to him that the paintings he has are not by Frederick Ashe.' I tried to sound convincing about this, though all the evidence was to the contrary.

'I don't like the sound of this. You're thinking in terms of revenge.'

'Partly. But you see the snag? No? Well, if I succeed, and convince him that he owns copies, what good would it do you to get a search warrant? He'd claim they weren't stolen, because they're only copies. And it'd be Coombe, and not the prosecution, who would subpoena me as a witness, to prove in court that they're copies. You get my point?'

He levered himself to his feet. His face was flushed and his voice was a growl. 'Oh, I get it, don't you worry. You offer with one hand and take away with the other! You're too bloody clever by half, strikes me.'

'I need time.' I was fighting for it.

'You might get all you need in gaol.'

'Now don't be niggly.'

He took a deep breath. 'You're talking about going to see him again?'

I nodded solemnly.

'Then it'll be protective custody for you.'

234

'If I'm around when you come next time.'

He leered. 'You'd better be.' He paused with his hand on the door. 'And now, you see, you've put it right out of my mind. Why I came. Your son—Aleric is it?—he's been found in a ditch in Wiltshire.'

'Wh . . . wh . . . *what?*'

'Oh, he's alive. A broken bone here and there, cuts and bruises, but he'll live. They've got him in Salisbury General, if that's any use to you.' He shook his head. 'I shouldn't be telling you this,' he admitted sadly. 'It'll only make you more stubborn.'

He had the door open, and again paused. 'Oh . . . something else. There's a lady to see you.'

At last he got through it.

They had propped me against a couple of pillows, an awkward position, neither sitting nor recumbent. I tried to lever myself upright, wished I could have been shaved—though my chin was too sore—worried about my hair. Evelyn? Evelyn! How could it be?

Margaret put her head round the door tentatively, eased the rest of herself inside, then stood with her palms to her face. She seemed nervous of what she would find.

'Tonee-ee-ee! What have you been doing to yourself?'

'I was done to. Come in and sit down. It's good to see you, but how—'

235

'Are you all right? Let me look at you.'

Grinning, I discovered, hurt. I was not pleased to be stared at like a barbecued burger. She sat. I thought she was about to burst into tears. Of course, I had to remember that her life was spent in the company of painters usually long dead, and thus out of harm's way.

'How did you manage to trace me here?'

'I kept getting the unobtainable signal when I phoned your photo place, so in the end I drove down . . . and found the place gutted. Oh, Tony! I stood and looked at it, and my mind . . . I just couldn't make it work.' Her face puckered. I had never seen her so attractive. 'Then in the end I went round to the police, and they told me you were here.'

She drew in her lower lip, nodding, seeming nervous about my possible response.

'Out tomorrow,' I assured her. 'It's not as bad as it looks.'

'You *say* that . . .'

'Because it's so.'

'I *told* you not to go there again. That man's powerful and vicious . . . and . . . you *did* go there?'

'I've told you this. I didn't just visit, I managed to get into his gallery.'

'I didn't believe you. You actually got in?'

'I did. But not with his permission.'

'Oh, you idiot. You've annoyed him.'

'Hopefully. And worried him too, with a bit of luck.'

'You got a look round? You'd be the first one—'

'There wasn't time for that. It was a matter of a quick in and out.'

'Oh.'

She looked past me, her eyes vague. I couldn't decide whether she was disappointed or not. Possibly, and because she hadn't been with me. There was a pause. We had been batting question and answer at each other, and seemed to have run out of both.

At last: 'But it's not serious?' she tried again, eyeing me discouragingly.

'As long as you don't kiss me.'

Her little laugh was awkward. She got to her feet and leaned over me and kissed me gently on the lips. It was like an electric shock.

'There,' she said, nodding as though she'd given me an injection, and she sat down again. 'Now tell me all about it.'

I told her, the whole thing. Not for one moment did her eyes leave my face. She searched it. There was agony in her eyes. It took a long while, and when it was over she produced a tiny handkerchief and wiped the palms of her hands.

'You're lucky to be alive,' she said huskily.

'Yes.'

'And you didn't—no, I can see you

wouldn't have had time to look round his gallery.' It was the third time she'd asked that.

'Why should I trouble? I headed straight for the six so-called Frederick Ashes.'

'But there must be some wonderful things . . . I'd give anything . . .'

'I'm sure you would.'

'But you've got your photos?'

'I've got 'em and they're printed. It's about all I've rescued from the fire, those and the six new prints they match from the loft set.' I gestured. 'There they are,' I said negligently.

If she'd noticed them before, there had been no sign. Now her hand pounced on them. I gave her a couple of minutes.

'The ones showing frames—'

'I realized,' she said sharply.

'You'll notice his are painted from the right-biased viewpoint. The same as my original one.'

'I'd noticed that.'

'Which seems to show—'

'What's this one?' she demanded.

She was waving the spoiled shot, me having jumped when Aleric said, 'Psst!'

'I jumped just as the shutter went off. Better throw it away.'

She looked at me doubtfully, glanced at the waste-basket, and asked me: 'Have you *looked* at it?'

I took it from her. There wasn't much to

238

see. It was just a shot involving two paintings, angled in the frame of the photo and painfully out of focus.

'I'd got the focus at a metre or so,' I explained. 'These paintings were farther away, so they're blurred. The flash has got a bounce response, so the exposure's all right . . . ah, I see what you mean. You told me the two by Maurice Bellarmé were in a private collection. His private collection. Well, well!'

'Those are Bellarmé's paintings, the ones he called *Frederick Ashe* and *Angel*. I recognized them.'

I peered closer. 'You can see that Frederick Ashe is painting. And look at this . . . you can just detect that he's got the brush in his left hand.'

She sighed. 'So it's most likely he'd sit to the right of her when they worked together. So yours and Coombe's, painted from the right viewpoint position, must almost certainly be Ashe's, and the loft set are therefore your grandmother's.'

'Angel,' I said softly.

'As Bellarmé called her.'

I handed it back to her. 'So you were right first time. One look at mine, and you said: Frederick Ashe. And you must be right about the loft set.' I looked directly at her and tried not to grin. 'With a little help from your friend.'

She grimaced. 'They're not exactly worthless, you know.'

'Can you see what she's doing?' I asked, pointing at the print in her hand.

'You're not listening, Tony.'

'I can't make it out. She's not painting, is she?'

'Something domestic,' she said impatiently. 'In those days, women were expected to be motherly and domestic. Will you listen to what I'm saying!'

'Say on.'

'The loft set. I can lay on an exhibition—'

'Not yet,' I cut in.

'I don't understand.'

'I owe Coombe a favour, and I intend to get something out of him. I can't kill him, though I'd like to. But I can squeeze *something* out of him. Money. I'm going to sell him the six canvases that match the six he's already got.'

She jerked to her feet. 'You're crazy.'

'I think not.'

'You're not to go near him.'

'Not alone, I agree. I'm not going alone. I'll need you with me, Margaret.'

'Me?' Her eyes were wild.

'The art expert. To back me up. To help me persuade him that he has to have those six.'

'I will do no such thing.'

'Then I'll do it alone.'

240

Furiously, she moved to the door, flung herself back, stood over the bed, and almost stamped her foot. 'You'd never get out alive!'

'Yes I would. I'd persuade him that he has to have them, but I wouldn't be able to tell him where they are. No—don't tell me. The need to know, they call it in the trade. The secret service trade. What you don't know they can't extract from you with their nail-pullers and things. No, come to think of it, you'd better not be there, because you *do* know. Forget what I said. I'll phone you when I get back—you'd better give me a number to call . . .'

'Damn you, what're you trying to do?'

'Get back at Coombe.'

She was almost in tears. 'How can I let you go alone?'

'I said forget that bit.'

'Forget it! Forget! I'd have it on my conscience.'

'I forbid you—'

'Forbid! Who the hell're you to forbid? I go where I like.'

'But this you wouldn't like.'

'If you insist on going, then I'm going with you. But what you hope to get out of it . . .' She shook her head miserably. 'You frighten me, Tony. I don't . . . can't understand you.'

To tell you the truth, neither could I, and I was frightening myself. But then, I've always been easy to frighten. Offer me violence, and

241

I would go to pieces. Always have. It's something to do with imagination, I think. I never had any difficulty in imagining the pain about to be inflicted on me. So I would back off. But now . . . oh yes, frightened I was, though for some reason I wasn't feeling like backing off. You take so much, experience enough pain, and there comes a time when anger overrides the fear. The anger I was feeling wasn't a transient thing. With every minute it was gaining strength. Mind you, I wasn't any happier about the anger than I was about the fear, but there was an outlet for the anger. The same outlet, hopefully, would also blanket the fear.

'I didn't mean to frighten you,' I said gently. 'You can walk out of here—I'd never know where to find you—and I wouldn't blame you—'

'I'm staying at the Metropole in town here.'

'A bit of a dump, that.'

'And I'll be there. When you're ready, Tony.'

'You're leaving? We haven't really talked . . .' I meant in any way personal.

'There'll be time. Other times.'

'The Metropole,' I said. 'I'll be in touch.'

She kissed her palm and blew me a kiss. I watched the door close behind her, and wondered why she'd registered at a hotel, when she'd driven from London for no more than an exploratory visit.

242

Then I realized she had not yet registered. She had noticed the hotel as she drove past, and had now deliberately severed her one escape route by deciding to stay there. The thought warmed me.

I gave it ten minutes, then I pressed the buzzer for my nurse, and when she came asked how I could make a phone call. She went and fetched a trolley, complete with pay phone, and plugged it in. I called my friend Terry Bascombe, the only other pro photographer in town, by which I mean the only one who did his own processing.

'Tony!' he said. 'I heard. Jesus, I'm sorry mate. What can I do for you?'

Good old Terry. 'Can I borrow your darkroom for a couple of hours?'

'Any time, old son. What for?'

'I'll need a copying stand—six prints, that's all I want to copy. Six by four—'

'Where are you?'

'In hospital, you idiot.'

'Then how can you . . . have you got 'em with you?'

'Well, yes.'

'I'll come straight there. Get 'em done, and back with you tonight. That do?'

I was silent.

'You know I can do a good job, Tony,' he said.

'It's not that. How are you at picture framing?'

'Lousy. I thought you said six prints.'

'It's a masking job. Tricky.'

'Ah!' he said. 'Sounds interesting. I'll be right round.'

He hung up. I lay back, relaxed. It would leave me a clear day I hadn't counted on, and could use.

The idea was beginning to clarify.

CHAPTER FOURTEEN

At ten the next morning I limped out of the hospital in shirt and jeans and Aleric's boots, but carrying his leathers in two plastic bags. My legs were painful, my face felt stiff, and I became short of breath very easily. But as long as I didn't break into a run I was fine.

There was no reason to run, no sign of Dolan's protective custody, no lurking shapes behind the hospital trees. I strolled to the bus stop, collected Aleric's motorbike from behind the pub in town, and rode to Salisbury.

This was quite a long trip, though it gave me plenty of miles in which to become used to the bike. By the time I reached the other hospital I was pulling and kicking the correct things by instinct. Nothing else on the road had a chance to keep in touch with me.

I took off the leathers again, intending to

look respectable on this visit, and not wanting Aleric to see how I'd mistreated his riding kit. They weren't leathers, they were a wax-treated black fabric, which was why they'd burned through around my legs. The holes had provided a cooling draught of air to my burns, and the limp was now much smoother.

He was not in intensive care, but looked as though he ought to be. There were fractures not apparent, but a tent inside the foot of the bed indicated trouble with his legs. He did not at once see me there, so I had time to study the damage to his face. What I could see of it. He was extensively bandaged, but minor damage such as the purple and black bruises had been left showing. His right eye was almost closed, the left brow swollen. In his right hand, which had a stiff-fingered cast on it, he was gripping a pad of paper, in his left a black felt-tipped pen. Aleric is ambidextrous.

I cleared my throat. He looked up. For a moment his eyes went blank, then he said:

'Hi, Pa! They told me you'd had it.' Not one to display emotion, my son.

'Not so far wrong, at that.'

'Get yerself a chair. Hey, this is great.'

I reached a chair over and sat down. He wasn't moving his jaw much. 'When did they tell you that—me being dead?'

'Just before they dumped me in the ditch.'

I gestured. 'What happened?'

'Oh . . . this? Yeh. Well . . . a couple of 'em held me and that ponce Mace worked me over with his gun.'

'I see.'

We stared at each other. Conversation was difficult. I cleared my throat.

'I suppose you're lucky, on the whole. They tell me there's nothing serious.'

'More'n they told me. Feels serious from where I am.'

'I bet. What've you got there?'

'What? This?' he turned it round. He'd been sketching on his pad of paper. He seemed ashamed of it. 'Gotta do something. The nurse over there got me this. It's her. See the likeness?'

And I did. I grinned at him. A mistake. I winced.

'You ain't too good yourself, Pop,' he observed, cocking his head to favour his better eye.

'My continuing existence is not wanted. A bit of a fire, that's all.'

'All?'

'I got out of it.'

'Sure you did.'

'I'll have to buy you a new riding kit. I was wearing it at the time. I've borrowed your bike as well. Hope you don't mind.'

'Help yourself. Hey, I'd like to see this. You'll kill yourself.'

246

I raised my fist to give him a friendly punch, then thought better of it. 'I was riding motorbikes before you were born.'

'A tip, then. Don't accelerate on right-hand bends. It pulls. Something to do with the shaft-drive transmission.'

'I'll remember that.'

There was another pause. Awkward. Apart from the motorbike, we had little in common.

'I'm gonna do the Sister next,' he told me at last, gesturing with the pen.

'I don't think they use that word now. It's sexist.'

'The boss-lady, then. Don't see her much, though. Got nice eyes.'

'I hadn't noticed. Look, I'll see you again, Al. I've got to get away now. Things to be prepared, sort of.' I put back the chair. 'When I see him—any message?'

'See who?'

'Paul Mace.'

'You ain't goin' back there!'

'It isn't finished.'

'When?'

'Tomorrow.'

'Can't you put it off? Give me a couple of days—'

'No, Al. Thanks, but no. I've got to get your mother out of there. I'll give him your best wishes. That do?'

He looked at me without expression, then away. 'I can't wait to try colours,' he said.

'Look out for yourself, Pop.'

'I'll do that.' I turned abruptly and went out.

As I'd told Aleric, I'd ridden motorcycles before he was born. But that had been more than twenty years earlier, and 320 miles in a day was now more than I could take. By the time I reached home I was hanging on to the bike rather than controlling it, and my head was swimming from concentration. It was an effort to lift my leg over it and lower it on to its stand, and for a moment I had to steady myself before stumbling round to the back to get into the house. It was only when I had coffee filtering and was cutting a cheese sandwich that I remembered I hadn't checked for miles about being followed.

It was eight o'clock by the time I was feeling as though I would live. The skin over my shins felt tight and hot. My pipe tasted fine again and didn't affect my breathing, so I went to the phone in the hall, taking a chair with me. Directory enquiries gave me the number. It rang a long while before it was snatched up. I sensed the snatch from the tone of voice.

'Yes?'

'Paul Mace, please.'

'Speaking. Who the hell—'

'It's Tony Hine.'

A pause. I heard him take a deep breath. Then: 'Where are you?'

'Let's not be funny, eh?'

'We thought you were . . .' He stopped.

'Dead? Yes, I'm sure you did. But I'm not.'

'You'll wish you were. Don't waste my time, Hine. We were eating.'

'Too bad.'

'D'you know where your damned car finished?'

'Tell me.'

'On top of the pub.'

'Oh dear. Then you'll have found the photos in the glove compartment?'

'I've got 'em. Now get off the bloody line.'

I gave it five seconds, but he didn't hang up. I had him. Curiosity, and perhaps fear, held him.

'I was hoping you had those pictures,' I told him. In fact, everything depended on it. 'You'll realize, of course that they're photos of the eighty-one I hold.'

'Copies!' he snarled.

'So what I want you to do—'

'You *want*!'

'What Coombe wants you to do, though he doesn't know it, is sort out the six that match with the ones in the gallery. You'll remember which those are, I'm sure.'

'Will you get on with it!' His voice was cracking with tension. He had sensed my confidence.

'Plenty of time. Don't panic.' I paused

again. Let him panic. 'Now what you're going to do is take those six to the gallery, and compare them with the six on the wall.'

'Don't you give me orders,' he snapped.

'You'll be glad I am. Listen. Are you listening?'

He was breathing hard. He said nothing.

'Are you listening?'

'Yes.' It came through like a whiplash.

'Right. I know you believe my lot are only copies of the ones your boss has. So you'll take those six and compare them with the others, then you'll come back and tell me what you've seen.'

'I'll see you in hell—'

'No. You'll come back and sit by the phone, and I'll call you back in fifteen minutes. Oh . . . one thing. I take it that Coombe has relied on you completely when it comes to authenticity? Yes? Then you'll sit by that phone, friend, because you're in for a shock.'

I hung up. I was trembling. I felt great.

Then I went and poured another mug of coffee, took my time over it, and exactly seventeen minutes after I'd hung up I dialled the number again.

He gave it one ring, then I heard him breathing. 'Well?' I asked.

'I see what you mean.'

This was a different Paul Mace, chastened and scared.

250

'They're painted from different view-points—correct?'

'So . . . it seems.'

'Two people, sitting side by side, sharing a palette between them on a table. Eighty-one were done like that. Eighty-one pairs, Mace. Seven left of one set. Guess which set your boss's come from!'

'You can't pull that one.' He was trying to sound more forceful. 'I know a Frederick Ashe when I see one. Ours are his.'

'Ha!' I said. 'I know another expert who thinks the same. But you're both wrong, and I can prove it. Prove, Mace. Not persuade or argue. Prove. And to back it up, I'm coming there tomorrow, about three, say, to do the proving.'

'You're out of your mind.'

'No. You'll see. You'll tell Coombe what I've said, and to save any waste of time you'll tell him to have a certified bank cheque ready, made payable to me to the sum of three hundred thousand pounds—'

'What!'

'Which he'll be willing to part with by the time I've finished, pleased to. For *my* six. Get it?'

More heavy breathing. Then he laughed thinly. 'By all means come. Welcome! I wouldn't miss this for the world. Somebody trying to con Renfrew Coombe out of three hundred thousand . . .'

'I'll see you, then.'

'You'll see me.'

'Good. I didn't want to miss you. Until tomorrow . . .'

I hung up. Though it hurt, I laughed.

Then I went to bed early, resting up for the big day tomorrow, though I didn't sleep well. Mace had been correct. I couldn't actually prove anything. It was, after all, going to be a con trick, and by the very nature of it I was unable to rehearse the participants. But I had a good idea of their reactions. On these I had to rely.

In the morning, after a large breakfast and a bath, a tentative one because I wasn't sure about the legs, I rang the Metropole. I asked for Margaret Dennis, and they paged her. Knowing the Metropole, I guessed it would be a shout from the desk. In a couple of minutes she came on.

'You were quite correct, Tony,' she said.

'About what?'

'It is a crummy place.'

'Yes. We'll have to meet up for lunch.'

'Not here, I hope.'

'No. There's a service station just this side of junction 19 on the motorway . . . the M5.'

'Aren't we travelling together?' she cut in.

'I didn't think it'd be a good idea. Assuming you still want to be in on it.'

'You know I do. But I've got the Volvo here—'

'I've got a hired Metro, but—'

'And we could talk about it on the way down.'

There was a pause. We'd been interrupting each other so briskly that we were both out of breath. In the end, it was I who broke the silence.

'I thought we'd discuss it at the service station. Eat there, then tail each other to Renfrew Coombe's place.'

'Well yes, but—'

'No buts. I'm likely to be followed, and I don't want you involved if there's trouble. I'll start early, and go by minor roads to shake anybody off. Then we meet at this service place . . .'

'I hate eating on motorways.'

'Yes. It's a pity. It ought really to be a good meal, if it turns out to be our last.'

'You're trying to put me off,' she said sharply, not at all amused.

'Exactly. I can manage on my own.'

'No you can't, and you know it. You need an expert. You said that.'

'All right. Shall we say one-thirty at the service station? There'll still be time to back out.'

'I have not the slightest intention of backing out,' she said with chill dignity. 'Yes, I'll see you there. Goodbye for now.'

'Be seeing you. And drive carefully.' But I didn't think she heard the last words, the line had gone dead.

I was inside Evelyn's private little office when the doorbell rang. It set my nerves jangling. Nobody was supposed to know I was there. But that was optimistic, based on the theory of being where I was least likely to be. I peeped round Evelyn's curtains, from where I could see the front door. It was Detective Sergeant Dolan. Of course, he knew, because of the hired Metro in the drive.

Sighing, I went to open the door.

'It's just the wrong time for protective custody,' I said.

He was dangling from his fingers a set of car keys. 'You left these in the Metro.'

'I lost a set of keys once, and it caused me a hell of a lot of trouble. Now, when I've only got one set, I leave 'em in the car.'

'Dangerous.'

'Toss 'em on the seat as you leave.'

'You're using it?'

'Not today. Keep 'em yourself, if you like, then you'll know where I am.'

He laughed. 'You're a tricky bugger, Hine.' I noticed he kept them in his hand. 'I came to see you about that affidavit you mentioned.'

I didn't turn away because I didn't want him in the house. 'I bet you've promised something to your Super.'

He shook his head, the hat wobbling, and

254

tossed the keys in his palm. 'Haven't mentioned it. This is just you and me . . . you said.'

'So I did. Well, don't worry, you'll get it.'

'When?'

'Heavens, Sergeant, don't push. Tomorrow, if I'm still around.'

He grinned. 'You'd better be. They're getting a warrant, and tomorrow's when we're taking you in.'

I stared into his eyes. They didn't flicker. He turned away and walked off cockily, tossing the keys through the Metro's open side window as he passed. It was a gesture that indicated he didn't care where I went, because he would know.

Having watched him drive away, I went back to Evelyn's room. I couldn't find what I wanted in her desk drawers, so had to try her briefcase, which had combination locks on the latches. Before going to the length of breaking it open, I tried an idea. It was a three-digit lock and her birthday was 17 March. I tried that—173—and it worked. It didn't for the other latch, so I tried mine. 23 May: 235. It worked. I found this strangely moving.

I was wearing slacks and my old tweed jacket, because it had large inside pockets. From the briefcase I took a sheet of her law stationery, folded it in four, and put it in my left-hand inside pocket. I banged her little rubber stamp on its little inked pad, and slipped that into an outside pocket, to pick up fluff. In my outside breast pocket I clipped her Sheaffer fountain pen, and I was ready.

I had the photographs waiting on the kitchen table. There were two sets, six in each, one of the photos of Coombe's paintings, and one of the matching ones from the loft collection. These I put behind my wallet in the right-hand inside pocket.

The set of six copies, which Terry Bascombe had printed for me, I carefully placed in my left-hand inside pocket, next to the blank sheet of law stationery.

It was vitally important that I didn't get them mixed up.

I was ready. It was an early start, as I intended to take a meandering cross-country route by way of Bridgnorth and Ludlow, then across to pick up the M50 the other side of Hereford, and thus to the M5 at junction 8.

There was no intention of using the Metro, never had been. I climbed into the motorcycling suit and went out to Aleric's Yamaha.

The road to Bridgnorth is fast. Along it, I saw no sign of being followed, though the rearview mirrors on the handlebars had a tendency to vibrate and shatter the reflection. Once I'd taken the new by-pass around Bridgnorth, and was on the Ludlow road, the hills and the winding turns gave me little time to watch my tail. I poured the bike into the corners, having mastered the trick of using power to lean me into left-handers, and easing off for right. I was riding as I'd always done, rolling the twistgrip with my right thumb, my fingers resting on the front brake lever.

Ten miles short of Ludlow, I became aware that a car was on my tail. There'd been little traffic, and I wasn't pushing it, merely trying to hold a steady 50. There had been opportunity to pass me, but it hadn't been taken. I raised the speed. Fifty-five, then 60. I could still hear it behind me, but the bends were so close together that I had no chance to turn my head. The road surface was poor. The mirror images were jumping all over the place.

As I said, I had heard it, and the implication of this took some time to sink in. Inside a crash-hat, and on a 1000 cc twin, you don't expect to hear anything. I heard it because its silencer was blown. I saw it as it edged up at my right elbow, along one of the rare straight stretches. It was my hired Metro. The cheek of it; they were using my own car with the intention of pushing me off the road.

Then it was not an intention, but a fact. The car eased across my nose. There is a technique in this. The nearside tail of the car has to touch the bike's front wheel. No more than the tail, at 60, or the car might itself be ditched. It was during the two seconds when the calculation was being made that I had time for evasion. Fingers already on the front brake, ease it on. Not too hard, it would raise the weight off the rear wheel enough for it to break away if I stood on the brake pedal. I felt the speed drop, rolled the throttle off, and the tail of the car skimmed my front wheel by two inches.

It accelerated away, its broken exhaust blatting back in defiance. I could have chased it, but I didn't know who was driving it—hadn't had time for a glance—and pistols might be brought into play. The Metro was doing about 70 when it disappeared around the corner ahead.

I stopped, a little shaken. The ditch that side of the road was deep. I propped the bike up and got off and had a smoke, waiting for my nerves to settle. Clearly, it was optimistic to expect that I'd seen the last of the Metro, unless I could once more get ahead of it. I would have to keep an eye open for side roads, in which it might be lurking.

Getting going again, I settled into a steady 50 but, as these things usually do, the speed crept up to sixty as I gradually relaxed, seeing nothing of the car. There was always a chance I'd already got in front of it. With this thought in mind I began to put on the pressure, forcing the bike round the bends.

I had expected it to wait down a side,

minor road. In practice, the driver had chosen an open farm gate on the right-hand side of the road, catching me by surprise. It was a nice bit of straight. The speedo was on 70, and suddenly it was pulling out, right across my nose.

The driver was taking a big risk, because over 350 lbs of metal, moving at my speed, would make a nasty hole in the side of a Metro. I was fifty yards short when my reactions snapped in. They were as sharp as they'd ever been. I rolled off the throttle and eased on the front brake, feeling it in, judging by the bite and the dip of the nose. Short, sharp dabs of the footbrake; I didn't dare to allow either tyre to break away. The over-run on the shaft drive applied its torque, and it wanted to turn right. I let it. The Metro had gone a yard too far, assuming I would try to squeeze through under his nose. I aimed for the tail. It moved forward another six inches. I leaned into the right turn until I was opposite the gap, then I rolled back the throttle and gave it the lot, felt the tail kick, and the torque helped me throw the nose round the Metro's tail.

I was right over, my left shoulder dipping. I felt the wind-fluttered sleeve of the suit brush a corner of the tailgate, then I hauled the bike upright, stuck my head down, and fed in the power until I was up to eighty and too near the next corner, scrambled round that, and settled down to put miles under the wheels in as short a time as possible.

I didn't relax until Hereford forced me to, but by that time I was satisfied I'd lost the Metro. I picked up the M50 and drove east, picked up the M5, and settled into the middle lane, heading south.

Because of all this, and in spite of the fact that I'd taken a roundabout route, I was much too early for Margaret. It was barely one o'clock when I rode into the service area. I stripped off the suit and locked it in the panniers, locked Aleric's crash-hat to the bracket, locked the steering—so many damned keys on his ring—then went to have a coffee. Afterwards, I strolled, placidly smoking, around the car park until Margaret's Volvo turned in. By that time I was relaxed, and, indeed, more than a little pleased with my performance on the bike.

I opened the door for her. 'Had a good journey?'

She stood beside me. 'Very easy. And you?'

'No difficulties.'

We stood and looked at each other. I grinned, and she threw herself into my arms, her lips at first firm and cool, but then melting. Not, this time, an electric shock, but a warm bath of intimacy.

For a moment she held herself away from me, her eyes moist and her hair wild, then she put her head on my shoulder and clutched me close.

'Oh, Tony! Tony! Why did you have to do it like this? Every minute I've been worried.'

'And all for nothing,' I said softly. 'Come and eat. I've seen the menu. You'll love it.'

There comes a time when a tone of levity needs to be introduced.

CHAPTER FIFTEEN

Worried or not, ten minutes in the ladies restored her to normal, and in practice she had been a few minutes late arriving, the worry not bringing about any panic speeding, so that we didn't have much time to spend on eating. I had said three o'clock to Paul Mace, and I'm the sort of person who likes to be prompt. I didn't want them worrying too.

Over the meal I explained, roughly, what I had in mind. As I'd expected, there were objections.

'If you expect me to lie for you Tony . . .'

Her professional integrity was creeping back. 'Only to back me up.'

'But if *you're* lying—'

'With a bit of luck, I shan't have to.'

I followed the Volvo down the motorway to Bridgwater. From there we were on ordinary roads. Margaret showed no inclination to linger. I managed to keep her in sight. Put it like that.

One behind the other we rolled smoothly into the courtyard of Coombe's stately home. The front door opened before I'd got all my riding equipment off. I let him wait. Margaret lit one of her rare cigarettes. I realized she would probably be meeting Evelyn, which could well be as unnerving as meeting Coombe.

The gaunt retainer led us through the hall, through the sun room, and out on to the terrace. There, a tableau was being played out. It held all the gruesome viciousness of a medieval ritual, and for several moments I had difficulty in reminding myself it was real.

Evelyn was standing to one side. When I had last seen her there'd been evidence of joyful self-indulgence, even if hysteria hadn't been far away. But now, I saw, she was quiet and withdrawn, her face pale and her clothing untidy. She had had no chance to change for several days. Her face had encountered soap, but with no make-up her complexion was sallow. Her hair, usually so flamingly flamboyant, now seemed lustreless.

She saw me and took a pace forward, then, seeing Margaret, she stopped. Her mouth formed the word: 'Aleric?'

I nodded, smiled. 'He'll be fine.' But it was said absent-mindedly, my attention being captured by the scene on the terrace.

Previously, apart from the episode in the

woods, I hadn't seen much evidence of Coombe's armed back-up. Now they were all there, lined up with their backs to the balustrade. They, I thought, hadn't even noticed my arrival, their attention being concentrated on the tableau, as though they might have been witnessing a keel-hauling with Captain Bligh in charge.

I reminded myself that I had been expected at three o'clock. It was three minutes past, so the whole thing could have been staged to impress. Or perhaps not.

Coombe was standing, in a dark blue tracksuit he'd have had to get tailored, with his fists on his hips. Paul Mace, shrunken and grey, was swaying in front of him, legs apart to prevent himself from falling over, holding in his right hand a three-inch paintbrush, and in his left, by its handle, a half gallon can of white emulsion paint, its lid off. He seemed unable to move.

Coombe made a pretence of having just seen me. He waved, all friendly and jovial.

'Come on over. You can help him.'

Not sure I wanted to, I nevertheless strolled over. 'Anything to oblige. What's going on?'

'It's a courtesy I extend to my employees when they're about to leave us. He puts a cross where he'd like to be buried. We simply lift a couple of the flagstones. Come on, Mace, we can't take all day on it.'

263

Mace's grey lips opened, but nothing came out.

'*Pour encourager les autres*,' I suggested.

'Eh?' said Coombe.

'Bonaparte,' I told him. 'When he—'

Evelyn cut in. 'Voltaire.' She always likes things to be correct.

'What?'

'Voltaire wrote it. A sly dig at the British when they shot Admiral Bing. To encourage the others, he said.'

I stared at her. Everybody stared at her. She fidgeted with her fingers, and blushed. I turned, and grinned at the line of men against the balustrade. Stiff, vicious faces stared back.

'Funny!' said Coombe, aiming it at me. 'Perhaps you'd like a go. Give him the paint, Paul. And the brush.'

Paul Mace sagged. In his eyes, tears appeared. His employer had called him Paul. Limply, he offered me the brush, but he had difficulty lifting the paint can enough to offer that.

I took them. The brush was in my left hand. I put down the can in order to change over, and straightened.

'Well?' I demanded.

'A cross. Where you'd like to lie in peace.'

I considered him with fascination. It was impossible, with this man, to decide where a joke finished and serious conversation began.

'I get a choice?'

He waved an arm. 'Feel free. Where you'd like to lie.'

I lifted the can and dipped in the brush, giving myself time. When I had it well loaded I lifted it out, and painted a cross on his chest.

'On top of you, Coombe.'

He was late reacting. Suddenly his face suffused with blood and his fingers tightened into huge fists. I think he would have lashed out, in spite of a disinclination towards doing his own dirty work, but somebody giggled. He turned ponderously; he couldn't whirl. The row of faces went stiff, and Evelyn belatedly screamed.

I had been right about the scream, the night I raided the gallery. I recognized it now. Never before had I heard her do that. Somehow, one never expects screams from a solicitor.

I turned to her and laughed. Not at her, not at Coombe's discomfiture, but at the fact that in painting that cross I had seen where my absolute proof lay. Relief and elation prompted that laugh, and when I turned back to Coombe I found that he too was laughing. Or at least, had recovered his good humour enough to smile and making a whickering noise.

It was then I realized that Coombe had astonishing reserves of character. How else could he have risen to the position he now held, a multi-millionaire in command of a group who feared his very glance? He had a great control over his emotions. When he needed calm and considered thought, he achieved it. Now, he needed every iota of his subtlety, because he had recognized my laugh for what it was.

'I hope,' I said, 'that you've got that cheque prepared.'

His eyes narrowed. 'A piece of paper can be torn to shreds.'

So he had been sufficiently influenced by my continuing persistence to feel uncertain about his own position. Which meant he was already tentative about the authenticity of his six paintings, which in turn would explain the predicament in which Mace had found himself. And this in spite of the fact that four of them had been stolen from accredited sources, national art collections.

It wouldn't be the first time that experts have been wrong, including Mace and Margaret.

'Let me see it,' I said.

For one moment the anger returned. Then he snapped: 'Paul!' and at the same time gestured behind his back. Released at last, his consort of hooligans dispersed rapidly for cover.

Paul Mace, recovering rapidly now that the attention had drifted from him, reached into his inside pocket and produced a wallet. From it, he took a cheque. He held it up before my eyes, not letting me reach it. It was a certified cheque.

I put down the paint can, carefully placed the brush across it, then smiled at Coombe. 'A hundred thousand?'

'At the most, they're fetching twenty thousand each.'

'They?'

'Frederick Ashes.'

'Good. So, if you're agreeing that mine *are* Frederick Ashe—'

'I'm agreeing nothing.' Coombe's face was dark again.

'Then I propose to prove that they are, and yours are not, and when I've finished doing that I think you'll be pleased to produce the second cheque you've got ready, for the other two hundred thousand.'

'Tony!' moaned Evelyn feebly. She now knew enough about Coombe to know he was not be taunted.

'Pff!' said Coombe in disgust. 'All this talk about proof, and you're arguing with two experts.' He nodded, his lower lip vibrating. 'That's right, I've checked on our Dr Dennis. Her reputation is world-wide. Mace was quite jealous. Weren't you?' he jerked out, not looking at Mace.

Mace, disconcerted at becoming Mace again, mumbled something.

'Weren't you?' Coombe snapped.

'In comparison, my experience is limited,' Mace admitted.

'So let's hear from the lady.' Coombe beamed at her, like a malevolent laser. 'What do you think of my set of Frederick Ashe?'

Margaret was caught unprepared. 'Well, I don't . . . I haven't seen them, of course.'

'The photographs,' I prompted.

'Well yes, I've seen those, but the actual canvases are a different proposition. Ask me again when I've seen them.'

'Ah!' said Coombe. 'That, I'm afraid, is impossible.'

Margaret shrugged. She managed to get into it an element of contempt for Coombe's cageyness. 'I'd hoped to be shown round. Your collection's legendary.'

Coombe lifted his head. 'We're wasting time. Hine, you'd better get on with it. Let's hear about this proof of yours.'

I tried to repeat Margaret's shrug, but it hadn't her impact. 'I'll need to go with you into the gallery, and I'll need Mace with me, and Dr Dennis to confirm a few points. Otherwise, there is no proof.'

Coombe stood before me like a rock. He made a movement as though to cross his arms, then realized the paint on his chest was still wet. His face darkened at the thought. 'Paul,' he said, 'you might as well tear up that cheque.'

I smiled at him. 'Then we'll be off, though I did hope for a cup of your Darjeeling before we leave.'

Evelyn took a step forward. I glanced at her. She became motionless. I added: 'Over the tea, we can discuss the basis of my proof.'

Coombe considered it for a few moments, then a couple of teeth appeared, one at each corner of his mouth. He was smiling. It was terrifying.

'Paul,' he snapped. 'A minute.'

Then he turned away, and he and Mace walked away along the terrace, conferring animatedly. I was left with Evelyn and Margaret, my predicament no less fraught.

'Evelyn,' I said, 'you ought to meet Margaret Dennis. My wife, Margaret.'

Margaret had moved no farther than a yard from the plate-glass door. She made no move now. Evelyn inclined her head coldly and with reserve. She was not at her best, in dirty jeans and a crumpled shirt, and was facing a woman who could always look smart and poised whatever the circumstances. Nevertheless, Evelyn managed to convey a contained dignity. She turned to me.

'You haven't told me about Aleric, Tony,' she said. The voice had a beckoning quality. It was a quiet request. I moved towards her, to face her so that I could watch Coombe and Mace beyond.

'He's a bit knocked about. They've got him

269

in Salisbury General. Nothing that won't repair. He's more disturbed, I think, at finding that two of his great grandparents were artists.'

'What? You're being clever again.'

'My grandmother, and Frederick Ashe.'

She absorbed that in a flash. 'I didn't like her,' she said definitely.

'Never mind that, now,' I told her firmly, and to my surprise she didn't snap straight back at me. 'We haven't got much time. You heard what I said to Coombe. I need you in that gallery. So play along with it, please.'

Her eyes searched my face. 'You're different, Tony. You've changed. What are you up to? And what's all this talk about three hundred thousand pounds? That's nonsense, of course. Isn't it?'

I shook my head. 'I've seen Aleric. Coombe's going to pay for that. Call it compensation, if you like.'

She bit her lip. 'I can't make you out. Tangling with a man like *that*.' Her head jerked towards him. 'There's a basic precept in law: don't take on a case until you know the strength of the opposition.'

'This isn't law. There's nothing legal about it. He's going to pay.'

'But you're such a simpleton!'

'They're coming back. Will you help me?'

'For Aleric, yes.'

'Not for me?'

Her lips flickered. 'You'd be lost on your own.'

Coombe was coming back, but not Mace, who had disappeared inside the house.

'We'll have tea,' Coombe grumbled. 'You can talk. Then we'll decide.'

'Has Mace gone to get the strawberries and cream?'

He sneered at my humour. 'He's making preparations. In case.'

He didn't say in case of what, but I guessed that Mace was heading for the gallery. A man appeared, sent no doubt by Mace. He arranged four chairs around one of the tables. We sat, Coombe and I facing each other, the two women disconcertingly facing each other. Coombe lifted his head. The tea-tray appeared. No delay this time; Coombe's rumbling mood of near explosion had upset everyone.

As the man leaned over the table I caught a glimpse of the butt of a gun under his left armpit. I watched him leave, and had the impression he went no farther than just inside the door.

'Now,' said Coombe. 'Talk.'

'There's a story behind it,' I said, and watched his fist clench on the table surface. 'Frederick Ashe met my grandmother, who was Angelina Foote at the time, and she was just about seventeen. Quite apart from a natural affinity for each other, they had other

271

things that linked them, such as the fact that one of them was left-handed, and they had the same initials, only reversed. And the fact that they were both painters. She learned to work in his style, and went away with him to Paris in 1910. They used to paint side by side, with their palette on a table between them, and they invented the same signature for their paintings, an A and an F, overlapped. All this I got from my grandmother, very recently. Margaret was there. She can confirm it.'

I glanced at her. She was sitting with her fingers interlocked on the table in front of her, her eyes on them, saying nothing. Evelyn sat the same. I nodded to Coombe.

'Looks like you'll have to be mother.'

His bushy eyebrows lifted. He frowned. He reached for the pot.

'So,' I went on, 'there were two sets of paintings completed, each of eighty-one canvases. Out of one set six were sold in Paris, and these are the ones now in your gallery, Coombe, and one went to my father, and on to me. The other complete set I now have. The whole point is: which set was painted by who?'

'Sugar?' said Coombe, looking at Margaret.

'Pardon? Oh, I'll help myself, thank you.'

Having attracted her attention he asked: 'Is he making this up?'

'Not one word. It's all true.'

'And it doesn't get us anywhere,' he

decided.

'Oh, but it does.' I reached inside my right inside jacket pocket and produced the two sets of six prints each. 'One of these sets is of your own six, Coombe, and the other set is of the six matching ones out of the complete batch of eighty-one.' I spread them out in front of him. 'Check 'em. Go on. Tell me what you see.'

Coombe had a reluctance even to look down at them. For too long now he had paid people to do things for him. He wouldn't, for instance, do his own killing. Paul Mace was the person he paid to look at photographs for him, and probably to arrange the theft of paintings that Mace had decided Coombe should own. It was now beneath Coombe's dignity to do anything for himself. He probably had someone whose sole duty it was to go to the toilet for him.

Crooking his finger like a fractured banana, he sipped his tea, then growled: 'Mace has told me.'

'Told you what?'

'That they're painted from slightly different viewpoints. If it matters.'

'Oh it does. It does. Two people, sitting side by side and separated by a table on which they have their palette—and one of them is left-handed. Now ask yourself, wouldn't it be more convenient if the left-handed painter sat at the right of the table? It would save either

273

of them reaching across with the brush. You agree?'

He grunted. Evenlyn had not touched her tea, but her eyes were fixed on me. There was a light in them I hadn't seen for years. Encouraged, and because Coombe hadn't answered, I demanded: 'Don't you agree?'

Margaret stirred uneasily.

'Margaret?' I asked.

'You know I agree. We've already discussed this.' For one moment she glanced at me. There was bewilderment in her expression. She believed that this presentation would get me nowhere, in fact would play right into Coombe's hands. Perhaps Coombe recognized this. Mace would have briefed him fully, in so far as Mace himself understood the implications. But Coombe's face had set into an expressionless front. His poker face, this was, though no doubt he had someone to play poker for him.

'Do *you* agree?' I insisted to him, determined to provoke a response.

'You're pushing it, Hine,' he said, his voice grumbling at my presumption. 'Don't press your luck.'

'I'm only asking you to agree that it would've been more convenient for them to paint in that relative position, the left-handed one to the right of the table. Not that it proves anything.'

274

Margaret made a sound in her throat. Evelyn's cup clattered in her saucer. Nobody had looked at the strawberries and cream.

Coombe said nothing.

'How in God's name does anybody do business with you!' I cried.

'Nobody does business with me. I do business with them.'

'Then *do* something.'

He poured himself another cup of tea. I had disturbed him, or he'd have poured three others, too.

'Or I take my eighty-one to Christie's, and they sell them as Frederick Ashes, whether they are or not, and your six'll be worth nothing. Damn it all, Coombe, are you stupid or something? I'm offering you a business proposition, not robbing you of something.'

'Three hundred thousand,' he barked. 'That's robbery.'

'I'll prove to you it's not. If you'll just agree. The left-handed painter would most likely sit to the right. Yes?'

'Much more of this . . . I agree. Yes. Paul explained that. So what?'

'So look at the photographs,' I shouted. A man appeared at the end of the terrace, another in the open doorway. I grabbed up one print from each batch, and waggled them in front of Coombe's face. 'That's one of yours. This is one out of the eighty-one set. Which one is painted from a right-hand point of view? Look, damn it. They're not going to bite.'

He stared at me through the space between them. I registered the fact that I was destined to place my cross on the flagstones.

'Look, or I'm leaving.'

A corner of his lips twitched into a sneer. His eyes re-focused. He actually looked at the photographs.

'Mine,' he growled, 'is painted from the right-hand side, yours from the left.'

'Fine. Good. That's something.' I put them down on the table surface, then collected them all up, patted them into neatness, and slid them back inside my jacket. 'For your information, my original painting, the one that came to me from my father, is the same as yours. It's painted by the left-handed artist.'

He lost his temper. It had to come some time. His huge fist slammed down on the metal surface of the table and a dent appeared. The tray danced.

'I've had enough of this!' He put back his head and raised his voice, and in the woodland the rooks rose in droves. 'Mace! Where are you? Carter! Phillips! Green!'

The two men I'd noted came running, and a third appeared from behind me. Mace walked from inside the sun room, so appositely that he must have been lurking there.

276

'You wanted me, sir?'

Coombe was on his feet. 'What the hell's the idea of letting this madman come here? It was your idea. Yours, Mace . . .'

'With respect, sir—'

'I want no blood on the terrace,' Coombe cried. 'It soaks in. But I want him silent.'

It was not the remark of someone out of control. His fury had been measured. Evelyn didn't realize this and flew at him, hammering as far up his chest as she could reach. Coombe picked her off and handed her to one of his men, who steered her back to her chair. Margaret seized on the diversion to whisper to me: 'What are you *doing*, Tony?'

'Getting somewhere,' I murmured. Aloud, I said: 'Let's get along to the gallery and confirm it, shall we!'

'I think it would be best, sir,' Mace suggested.

'It's ready?' said Coombe.

'As you said.'

'Then we'll go there, and let this idiot dig his own grave.'

I realized then that this had been his intention all along. Mace had expressed an uncertainty Coombe couldn't live with. I was the only one who could return his continuing existence to its former complacency.

'Come along, Evelyn,' I said. 'You mustn't miss this.'

'I'd prefer to.'

I took her arm. 'I need you desperately.'

'You won't need me, Tony,' said Margaret in a distant voice.

'Oh but I do.'

'You know it all.'

'This is your reputation we're talking about. Your expertise. Your integrity. You're surely not going to allow me to say what I like?'

She managed a smile, but still hesitated.

'Besides,' I went on, 'you said you'd give anything to get inside that gallery.'

'Not my life. As it'd be, if I saw too much.'

'Then don't look.'

Coombe raised his voice. 'Aren't you coming?'

'Be with you.'

With one woman on each arm I followed Coombe and Mace through the sun room.

CHAPTER SIXTEEN

We used a different route from the one by which Aleric had initiated me to the gallery, up the main staircase, with one of the gunmen leading, then Coombe, tailed closely by Mace, myself following with a lady each side, and two more gunmen behind us. The pace was steady and measured, like mounting a tumbril.

Margaret hissed in my ear: 'I don't need you to hold my arm.'

'I got the impression you were about to turn and run.'

'I don't see why you need me.'

'You will.'

We marched on.

Evelyn hissed in my other ear: 'Let go my arm. I think you're out of your mind.'

'I can't do it without you.'

'Well, that's an admission.'

The gunman turned to the right at the top. It was like a conducted tour, though Coombe blocked most of the view. We turned a corner, and we were in a corridor I recognized, if only because it needed artificial light in the day time. At the end sat the guard alert and prepared, watching our approach nervously.

Mace already had the key. He held it up for all to see, like an illusionist. The guard stood to one side. The door swung open, and Mace reached through a hand and put on the lights. We entered. Mace closed the door behind him, locked it, and dropped the key in his side pocket. It clinked against something else metallic. He set his shoulders against the door, plunged his hand into the same pocket, and smiled thinly.

I could barely detect the smile, because when I said lights, the plural was hardly applicable. There was a small one above the door, trapped in a wire cage, and farther into the darkness of the gallery, six strip-lights above paintings.

Mace had performed well. He had switched off all but the appropriate lights, and as they were hooded the illumination extended for no more than a yard in any direction. Quite efficiently, the other secrets of the gallery were kept.

The one guard ahead, and the two guards behind, were still in their relative positions, but the one in front had disappeared into the darkness, and the ones behind had slipped into deep shadows. Nevertheless, I was aware of them.

We stood facing the paintings. Coombe turned massively.

'There they are. Tell me what you can see that isn't in your damned photographs.'

'Not me,' I said. 'But Dr Dennis hasn't seen the actual paintings before. Perhaps she can tell us something.'

Smiling, I turned to her. The light, angled deliberately on the canvases, offered a very poor reflected glow at face level. Margaret seemed to be confused. Her shrug and her gesture of resignation told me more than her expression. Her voice was empty of emotion. 'What d'you expect me to say?'

'Well,' I said encouragingly, 'we know these are by the same hand as my original one, because all seven are duplicated in the

280

eighty-one set. Mine, you were sure, is a Frederick Ashe.'

'Mmm, mmm,' she said, when I paused.

'And you seem to be sure that the eighty-one are all by my grandmother. So look at these. Go on, Margaret, touch 'em and smell 'em, whatever the technique involves. Would you say they are genuine Frederick Ashe works?'

Still she hesitated—I was introducing nothing new—then she went to them, and we waited. I took out my pipe. 'No smoking in here,' Coombe grated. I shrugged. Something to play with, that's all it was, something to occupy my shaking fingers.

She did all I'd suggested, plus a few other things, making it look good. She produced from her shoulder bag a contrivance I hadn't seen before, a magnifier with an open-work wire frame, for placing over the surface. She used it mainly to study the signatures. Whatever the canvases told her, they took a long time to yield their secrets.

At last she turned. Back-lit, her face was cut into hollows. I could see her lips move, but she was whispering.

'I'm sorry,' I said. 'I didn't hear that.'

She spoke too loudly. 'My opinion hasn't changed. These are by Frederick Ashe. I'm sorry, Tony.'

'Just what I said,' Mace called out from the door. He sounded jubilant and relieved.

'So that's the end of that,' Coombe decided. 'Let's go.'

'Wait.' I still held Evelyn's arm and I could feel it shaking. 'Margaret, do you agree that these were painted from a right viewpoint, so probably by a left-handed painter? Would you like to see the photos again?'

She frowned. I was becoming pedantic, flogging the same point over and over. She said: 'I don't need to, thank you. These are right-hand viewpoints, compared with the six that match them.'

'Good,' I said.

'Good?' Evelyn jerked my arm. 'What's good about it?'

'It was what I expected. They're by the same hand as my own original one, from the house.'

She groaned. 'So all right. So you own a genuine Frederick Ashe. That was what this lady expert told you in the first place. Nothing's changed. Why can't you let it lie, Tony? Why can't you?'

'You're wasting my time,' Coombe said harshly. 'I've had about enough of you—'

'But you agreed.'

'I agreed what, damn it?'

'That the person who painted your six, and my own, which are painted from a right viewpoint, must have been left-handed.'

'No!' he roared. That sound in the labyrinth of his gallery bounced around and

282

back, returning in a mirror image, but still as no. 'Most likely! Most likely!'

'Very well.'

'So let's get out of here.'

'In a minute. There's more.'

'More what?'

'Evidence. Dr Dennis found a reproduction of a painting in a biography. It showed Frederick Ashe to be painting left-handed.'

'Well that *proves* it!' Coombe bellowed. 'You stupid or something?'

'Sometimes pictures get printed backwards in books.'

'And sometimes people get carried out backwards, and feet first.'

Mace permitted himself a soft snigger, and Coombe beamed at him in approval.

'There's another photograph I want to show you.'

Coombe clamped his hand on my shoulder, nearly bearing me to the floor. 'No more pictures. I've had enough.'

'Then I'll describe it.' The grip on my shoulder increased, but I managed to speak through the pain. 'When I was here—as you know I was in here—there was one shot I spoiled. I jerked. When I printed it, it showed two blurred pictures of paintings, one of them actually *of* Frederick Ashe. The same painting as was reproduced in the biography. You've got the painting here, Coombe. The biography was of another painter, Maurice Bellarmé.'

The fist was removed. I straightened. He made a hissing noise through his teeth.

'The camera swung to the right,' I said. 'There must be an alcove or something just there.'

Coombe made no move. Evelyn whispered: 'He's hurt you!' I touched her fingers. Margaret turned away in disgust at my foolishness.

Coombe said carefully: 'There is no alcove there.'

'My photograph showed Ashe, as far as I can tell, painting left-handed,' I said softly, offering it, praying he would react. 'What is there, Coombe, if not an alcove?'

'A mirror.'

I laughed. 'It's as I guessed. I got mirror images. So the Bellarmé paintings . . .'

I turned, my eyes searching the shadows behind me.

'Stay where you are!' Coombe rasped.

There was movement along the aisle. Two pairs of feet appeared inside the edge of the illumination. I was very still.

'What're you afraid of?' I asked quietly.

Coombe grumbled deep in his chest, then he moved past me, his hand swooped down, and a switch snapped on. I stared into the alcove that had been behind my right shoulder, as the two tubes flickered, then steadied.

Coombe could not have owned what he thought to be a complete collection of Frederick Ashe, and not also have owned a portrait of the artist. The two portraits went together, Ashe and his angel. My grandmother. Still they were not separated. There they were, side by side.

Bellarmé had been their friend. He had painted Frederick Ashe as though he was working on a portrait of his angel who, as Margaret had said, was performing a domestic chore in her painting. She was darning one of his socks. Ashe would not, of course, have been actually painting. Hadn't they always painted side by side? But Angelina Foote seemed actually to be darning. The concentration was there, and her beauty, the transparency of her complexion, and in her expression her devotion to such a minor item relating to her Freddie—his sock. Bellarmé must have had a sense of humour, because his picture of Ashe, seated on a hard-backed chair at his easel, showed him to have one foot bare.

'It's her!' cried out Evelyn involuntarily. 'Your grandmother, Tony!'

She had last seen Angelina twenty years before, when she was younger than my most recent memory. I felt choked, unable to speak. I wanted to meet these people, as they were then, and meet Bellarmé. And shake his

285

hand in congratulation. The two works were superb.

Frederick Ashe was holding the brush in his right hand, Angelina Foote had the sock on her right hand, and the needle was poised in her left.

I cleared my throat. 'You didn't tell me this, Margaret.'

She was behind my left shoulder. I turned. She was shaking her head, in bewilderment or in rejection. I couldn't be certain.

'Or perhaps they were both printed in the biography backwards,' I offered.

'I don't . . . remember.'

'Never mind. It doesn't matter now. The point is, we've got our proof at last. My painting, and the six in here, being painted from a right viewpoint, were done by my left-handed grandmother, Angelina Foote. *Now* what d'you say, Margaret?'

She gestured. She turned and stared at the six on the other wall. 'I don't know. I don't *know*, damn it!'

'Anybody can make a mistake,' I said comfortingly.

'But not me!' she cried out.

'You're insisting you didn't?'

'No. Yes. I don't know. Leave me alone. Please.'

She looked round frantically, as though seeking a chair for her shaking legs.

'We need chairs, Coombe,' I said briskly.

286

'Three chairs and a table.'

'Will somebody please tell me what the hell's going on!' he appealed, and the two guards moved closer.

'What is going on,' I told him, 'is exactly what I promised. I said I'd prove that you own six paintings which are not by Ashe. I've just done that. With Ashe shown to be right-handed, and Angelina Foote left-handed, it's inconceivable that they would paint in any other arrangement than he on the left and she on the right.'

'Then what d'you want with a table, goddamn it!'

'Because we now have to complete our financial arrangement.'

'I'm not sitting in here to discuss—'

'I'm not asking you to either sit or discuss. The sitting part is for my wife and myself, and there's nothing to discuss. I'm going to legalize the situation. My wife's a solicitor. Doesn't that make sense?'

'In here?'

'I thought you'd prefer that,' I said innocently. 'Then, if you don't agree with what I'm going to do, there'll be no chance of me getting away before you can tear things up. Get it?'

He stared at me broodingly, then he wobbled the upper stack of his chins and barked: 'Mace!'

Paul Mace came running. He was

revitalized. 'Sir?'

'You been listening to this?'

'Every word.'

'Well?'

'My assessment of the paintings was perhaps a little—'

'Never mind that. What's he up to? That's the point.'

'What I'm up to,' I put in, 'is the tying up of the loose ends. What you'll see and hear is going to be enough to justify fifty thousand pounds for each of my six genuine Frederick Ashes, to replace yours. So we need a table. And chairs.'

'Mace!' snapped Coombe. 'A table and chairs. This, I've got to hear.' He put back his head and laughed. 'Fifty thousand!'

Mace turned to the two guards. 'Get 'em.'

They went into the back of the gallery to search, each carrying a torch. There would be places to sit, and tables on which to place ashtrays that dared not to be used. We waited. Coombe stood in massive menace, Mace moved restlessly, and Margaret went to stand looking at the six paintings, perhaps not even seeing them. Evelyn leaned against my shoulder, her lips close to my ear.

'What've you got in mind, Tony?'

'An affidavit. A water-tight uncontestable affidavit. I'll pay your fee later.'

'You can have my advice free.'

'I know what it would be. Give him what

he wants—six paintings. Give him, Evelyn? Never. I'm going to hand him a rattlesnake with fangs at both ends.'

'You're an idiot!'

Then why did she squeeze my arm supportingly?

They came back with the chairs and the table. Margaret seemed to have recovered, and waved hers away impatiently. The table was placed in the centre of the aisle, where it received only a spill of the light from each side. I put the chairs facing each other across it, and held one for Evelyn. Normally, she would have frowned at my impertinence. This time she threw me a quick smile, and sat. I walked round and took the seat opposite.

'Can we get on with it?' Coombe demanded.

I smiled up at him. 'Can you see all right?' I asked Evelyn.

'Yes, thank you.'

'Right.' I plunged my hand into my left-hand inside jacket pocket and produced the folded sheet of law stationery, opened it up, folded it back the other way, and put it in front of her reasonably flat. I plunged again, and brought out six photographs.

Mace, who'd been watching me very closely and with suspicion, pounced in, and whipped them from my fingers. 'Wait a minute,' he said. 'What's this?'

They were the wrong set, the prints of the six from the loft set.

'Whoops!' I said. 'My mistake.' I grinned at him, and produced another set. Held them up. 'All right? You can tell these are the ones . . .' I gestured towards the wall. 'The frames. They show.'

He frowned at my prints, then nodded, stepping back. I reached inside my side pocket and found Evelyn's rubber stamp.

'Breathe on it and it'll work,' I told her. 'Is that all you need?'

She flicked me a look under her eyebrows. She has never plucked them. They caught the light redly. 'I'd prefer the atmosphere of my office, otherwise . . . yes, I can manage. What is it you want me to say?' She looked round. 'If I'd got something to write with.'

'Forgot.' I produced her Sheaffer.

She laughed. 'Tell me.'

'I want to swear something to the effect that the six photographs herewith referred to—I suppose we'll have to mark them in some way . . .'

'I'll put something on the back of each one. I hope the stamp'll hold out.'

'Yes. Herewith referred to . . . are of canvases to be seen on the premises of Renfrew Coombe, at Renfrew Coombe, Somerset . . .'

'So that's where we are!'

'Where they are hanging—'

Coombe's hand slapped down on the law stationery, confirming his contempt for anything relating to the law. 'What the hell *is* this?'

'An affidavit.'

'Paul!' he shouted.

Mace, at his shoulder, stepped forward.

'What's he playing at?'

'I don't know, sir.'

Evelyn looked up at Coombe. 'I'm notarizing an affidavit.'

'And what,' he rasped at me, 'do you intend to do with it?'

'Take it to the police. I promised Detective Sergeant Dolan—'

'He's insane!' bellowed Coombe.

'If you'll just listen . . .'

'Perhaps, sir—' Mace began.

I cut in. 'I'm just about to tell you why my six paintings are worth fifty thousand pounds each. If you'll only listen.'

I stared into Coombe's face. Slowly, his hand lifted. 'Say it.'

'I will take this affidavit, and the photographs of the six paintings, to the police. They will go to a magistrate—'

'A Justice of the Peace,' corrected Evelyn.

'Thank you. A JP then. And they will get a search warrant.'

Coombe was rumbling, close to an eruption. I held up my hand.

'I happen to know they've been trying for

years to get something, anything, that they can use to get into here. They'll pounce on this. And I can guess you've been expecting something or other from the police. But you'll notice that the affidavit will read premises. Not gallery. By the time the police arrive, you'll be expecting them. These six paintings here will then be displayed in your hall or your study, or whatever you call it, and if you've got any sense the two Bellarmés will be there too. Because you'll be able to show that the six paintings covered by the affidavit are *not* by Frederick Ashe, but are copies, so that none of them could have been stolen from the galleries who've unfortunately lost them. And because that covers the information in my affidavit, they can't look any further. You can even let them take them away, because by that time you'll have the six genuine versions of the same paintings, which I shall bring to you, displayed here in the gallery. And you can laugh them out of the house, knowing that they'll never be able to try a search warrant again.' I took a deep breath. 'There. Isn't that worth fifty thousand each to you?'

Coombe was wheezing, his huge chest shaking, and the cross on it vibrating. I realized what was happening. He was laughing. Then he raised his mauler, and I thought for one appalling moment he was going to slap me on the back. But it descended on Mace's shoulder.

'What d'you think, Paul?'

'I like it, sir. I like it.'

'Then do it,' he boomed at me.

So we did it. All through my exposition, Evelyn had been drafting the affidavit and annotating the backs of the six photographs. All I had to do was sign, watch her bang on her rubber stamp (with seven breaths it just managed to work seven times) and add her signature. I picked it all up, folded the affidavit round the certified photos, and slipped the package inside my jacket. I got to my feet.

'No!' said Margaret.

Nobody had been taking any notice of her. She had been silent in the background. Thinking, no doubt.

'No?' I asked.

'It isn't valid,' she plunged in, almost breathless with it, her hair flying about with the emphasis. 'It won't work.'

'And why not?'

'Because it is *not* valid. Not enough to support legal action, or anything else based on authenticity. Tony, I'm sorry. But I can't let you walk out of here, and have the whole thing crumble away . . .'

She stopped, biting her lip. I'll swear she was close to tears. Because of this, I spoke quite gently.

'Tell us why it isn't valid.'

293

'Because you can't—positively—argue that two people, right- and left-handed, would sit the way you've described. It isn't *proof.* They might not have done that. They might have both leaned across to use the palette. It's possible, Tony, and you know it. Just possible.'

I sighed. 'Oh, Margaret! I did hope you wouldn't say that. You see, there's another proof. I was keeping it in reserve.' I smiled at her. 'Just in case you did say it.'

She gave me a long, considered look, then pressed thumb and fingers to her forehead, and said dismissively: 'Let's hope it's better than your last load of proof.' Her tone sharpened. She was unable to control her tension. 'It wasn't proof, and you know it. Ask her—ask your wife. She's the solicitor. Everything's black and white with that lot.'

I turned to Evelyn. She gave me a crumpled smile. 'Evelyn?'

She shook her head. 'It wasn't proof, Tony. Not what you could take to court.' She said it sadly.

'Then we'll have to give this other thing a try.'

'A try! Do you mean to tell me it's something you haven't tested? Tony . . .' She could think of nothing to add.

I ran my fingers through my hair, and tried to grin. 'It was only half an hour ago that I got the idea.'

'Can we get on!' shouted Coombe.

'Right.' I stood face on to him, my eyes level with the cross. 'The idea came to me when I did that cross. One of the strokes has to come after the other, and crosses it. You can see. Even though it's dry, you can see which came second.'

He tried to peer down at his chest, but one of his chins got in the way, so he went and stood in front of the nearest mirror.

'He's right, Paul. Come and have a look at this.'

Paul Mace did. He prodded the chest. 'Yes. But I don't see . . .'

'It's like this.' I looked round for something to draw on, but there was only the affidavit. I took it out of my pocket and used the back, borrowing Evelyn's pen.

'These two people,' I said, 'Frederick Ashe and Angelina Foote, were so intrigued by the fact that they had the same initials, only reversed, that they both used the same combined form of initials. They used the F and the A overlapping, to sign their paintings. So they look the same. But they wouldn't be the same, would they? Ashe would naturally do the F first, then add a down stroke to complete the A. And Angelina would do the A first, and add a cross stroke at the top to make the F. Like this.'

I did it quickly, and found it quite difficult, but managed a reasonable representation.

295

'Frederick Ashe,' I said. 'F.A.' And I drew:

'But this would be Angelina Foote. A.F.'

'You can see the difference is mainly in the top left-hand corner. It all depends on which stroke does the overlapping.'

I looked round. Margaret, distancing herself from my antics, had withdrawn into the shadows.

'Margaret, may I borrow your magnifier?'

She came forward, plunging into her shoulder bag. 'If you must. But I've got no faith in this.'

'We'll see.'

Mace and Coombe were almost in my back pocket as I bent to the paintings on the wall. The magnifier was a superb instrument, bringing the image up very clearly. There was absolute silence behind me. I moved slowly along the line of six, stopping from time to time to wipe the lens, as sweat was dripping from my forehead. It was not easy. The texture of the paint beneath the initials obscured the result, and the clarity of the overlap depended on the fluidity of the paint that'd been used to inscribe it.

I straightened. Margaret was now pacing. Evelyn watching me with strain in her eyes.

'Give me side-lighting and a camera with a macro lens and I could blow the initials up to ten by eight, and there'd be no doubt. I'm certain of two, not so certain of the other four. Mace, you want to take a look? It's the top left-hand corner, remember.'

He took the magnifier. I stood and watched, playing with my pipe to stop myself from screaming. He straightened, and nodded to Coombe.

'Numbers one and four?' I asked.

'Yes. Those for certain.'

'And what did they indicate?'

'The cross bar at the top of the F came last.'

'Which is a definite and unarguable proof that they were painted by Angelina Foote?'

Mace stuck out his lower lip. It cost him a lot to say it, but he managed to get the words out. 'They're Angelina Footes.'

My legs went weak. I leaned a cheek on the table. 'Right then. Fine.' I picked up the affidavit and waved it. 'So what I've got here's not just evidence that'll bring the police rushing round, but on the back there's absolute proof that what they've come to see are only copies, not genuine Frederick Ashe paintings.'

I could tell that Coombe was delighted at the outcome. He was shortly to acquire the genuine Ashes, and the evidence to make complete fools of the police. He would perhaps invite the TV newsmen to bring their cameras along. His delight was expressed in the fact that he unzipped the top six inches of his tracksuit and a quarter of an inch of a smile.

'My cheques then, please,' I said.

'When you bring your six.'

'Oh, come on, Coombe. If I brought six paintings, I'd leave with no cheques and no paintings. If I take the cheques and don't bring the paintings, d'you think I'd expect to live long enough to spend any?'

He contemplated this. Then he said: 'Paul.' Mace produced two cheques. The total was three hundred thousand pounds. I folded them, my fingers uncertain, and tucked them in with the affidavit.

'Your wife stays,' said Mace flatly.

'Oh . . . Tony!' she wailed.

'It's all right, love,' I assured her. 'It's only another day. Back tomorrow with Coombe's paintings—'

'And how d'you intend to do that, Tony?' Margaret demanded from the shadows. 'You don't know where they are.'

'Oh my God,' said Coombe. 'The clown doesn't know where to put his hands on them.'

CHAPTER SEVENTEEN

She advanced into the light. The starkness of the tubes drained her face of colour, its shadows hid her eyes. There was a tense authority about her. She had made a decision.

'But Margaret,' I said quietly, 'you know where they are.'

'And why should I tell you? I've listened to all this, to you calmly proving that you own eighty-one genuine Frederick Ashe works—his complete collection—then you happily promise to let this ape here have six of them!'

'For good money, Margaret. Your commission—'

'To hell with my commission. What do I care for that! It was a find! The complete set, and a way to authenticate them. And you'd rob me of that!' Her voice was brittle. It crackled round the gallery. Nobody said a word. 'You'd break up the collection, just so that this thieving swine, who hasn't got one atom of feeling for any of his collection . . . so that he can get one over on the police, and go on with his rotten, underhanded pirating of art treasures . . .'

'Be quiet, woman,' put in Mace.

'Quiet! Oh, you can easily silence me. And don't think I would care. Tony, I just don't understand you. You prove you own all that beauty and perfection, and before I can begin to take it in you start to split it up!' Her voice was breaking with the emotion of it.

I took a pace towards her. 'But, Margaret, you've known all along that the loft set are the genuine Frederick Ashes.'

'What?'

'You used your magnifier just now. D'you think I didn't notice? I did, because I'd only just thought of the idea. And the first thing you examined was the initials. Now be sensible, Margaret. You're an expert. You know all about signatures. It's one thing you'd think about, that overlapping business of the initials.'

'I don't know what—'

'But you do. Your first sight of my painting . . . and you said: Frederick Ashe. But at that time you knew nothing about the story of the two sets. When you *did* know, you couldn't wait to get your hands on the loft set. And in that loft you had no magnifier, and not enough light. You had to know! Had to. So you said you would wake my grandmother and ask her. Then you came back and told me she'd shouted for Grace. As I suppose she would, because she'd found herself looking at a genuine Frederick Ashe, when Grace had told her they'd been destroyed. Of *course* she would shout for Grace, and of course you would want to know why. And my grandmother would have told you why. There

300

was no reason for her to keep it from you.'

'Conjecture.' But Margaret barely parted her teeth.

'Perhaps. But it sounds right, and when you consider what followed . . . You knew, in that second, that this was a wonderful discovery, and it was *your* find, *your* glory, *your* rung right to the top. As long as it *was* your find, and they didn't belong to that fool, Tony Hine. So . . . I must not be allowed to know what I had. Who knew what I'd do with them? Give them away, or some damn fool thing like that. But my grandmother would have told me, if you gave her the chance. So you covered her mouth and nose with your hand, Margaret . . . no, don't talk about what you intended. Don't say you only wanted to stop her from shouting out for Grace. Because I wouldn't believe you.'

'Who cares what you believe? Anybody can say anything. It's all lies. You're making it up!' She spoke in frantic appeal, as though I might be persuaded to stop doing it.

'I'm afraid I've got into the habit of trying to prove things. What I've just said can be proved. The dust on your hand also had bits of brown paint in it. They—the forensic people—can analyse the paint specks that were found in my grandmother's lungs, and analyse the brown that Ashe used—'

'You could have done it.'

I shook my head. 'Dusty I was, but it was

301

from the crates. It was you who wiped a hand over the surface of one of the canvases.'

'I'm getting out of here. Tell your stupid ideas to the police.'

'The door's locked.'

Her chin lifted. I caught a glint in her eyes. 'Then tell it to somebody else.' Then she turned her back on me and tucked her hands beneath her arms against a chill that wasn't there.

It wasn't difficult to understand her. In the formative years there had been her frustration that she could not become an artist. Then the cold, ruthless determination to master something which she herself had called a science and not an art. She would have had no emotional feeling for it, so that she'd succeeded in something to which she had had to drive herself. And somewhere in the intervening years all emotion had died, until she was no more than an unfeeling machine, one that wouldn't balk when the ultimate opportunity presented itself.

'I could forgive you almost anything, Margaret,' I said quietly, 'except the cold-blooded murder of an old lady in her bed. I could even forgive you the three attempts on my life . . .'

'Tony?' Evelyn whispered.

I reached back and touched her hand, and went on: 'I know I was supposed to accept that they were the work of Coombe's

302

men . . .'

'Now hold it right there!' Coombe snapped.

I didn't glance round. 'But how could they have been? The first one, on the hill above here—Coombe couldn't have known I'd come from up there. His men didn't even chase me up the hill. So I must have been followed, and you knew, Margaret, that I was coming here. The second: you were the one who knew I'd be working in my darkroom. The third: you knew my hired Metro was in the drive at my home. So you see, by that time I knew it was you who was trying to kill me.'

She whirled round, and stared at me with challenge. 'Knew! Knew!' she snapped in contempt.

I continued as though she hadn't spoken. I had to get it all out, before it choked me.

'I didn't understand why you wanted me dead. I thought your idea was to pass off a lot of Angelina Foote paintings as Ashes, and that I might object. But it was better than that, because you knew by that time exactly what you had. And only I knew you had them, and Grace Fielding, she knew. But she died. Suicide, they thought, though there are doubts. I haven't got any doubt at all. Grace not only knew about the paintings, she was also threatening legal action, because she knew that my grandmother was dead before we left that house.'

'Ye gods,' said Coombe. 'What have we got here!' He spoke in a voice of awe.

'You've got to admit she's got plenty of nerve,' Mace commented.

'More than you can know,' I told him. 'She had to get Grace Fielding into a loft—probably on the pretence of looking for crosses on the old crates—and strangle her there, then put a noose round her neck, and push her through the trapdoor opening.'

Evelyn made a high, shrill sound of disgusted protest.

'Exactly,' I agreed. 'And she would have had to climb down the ladder past her dangling body.'

Coombe whistled absently.

Margaret, apparently annoyed that the catalogue of her activities should have drawn admiration from such an uncouth oaf as Coombe, turned to face us again. She advanced on me with a determination that was quite admirable under the circumstances.

'This is pure imagination,' she said briskly. 'It wouldn't stand up for one moment.'

Evelyn tugged at my sleeve. 'She's right, you know. In law, you haven't produced anything that would convince a magistrate, let alone a jury.'

Encouraged by this apparent support from such a quarter, Margaret went on, her voice professionally crisp. 'One: Grace probably killed your grandmother, and committed suicide from remorse. Two: your accidents were the work of Coombe's men, though the police would never be able to prove that. Nor that I had a hand in them. And three,' she produced in triumph, 'I didn't know the loft set was all Frederick Ashe, until you proved it, just now.'

'No?'

'If I'd known, I wouldn't have come here.'

'It was because you knew, that you couldn't afford not to. But you did know, and this is one thing I can prove. And with it, your motive.'

'You can prove nothing,' she said in disgust.

'The biography of Maurice Bellarmé,' I reminded her. 'It's most unlikely that the reproductions were printed backwards. Not in a work like that. I think that book will show them printed as they were painted, and from seeing them you would have your proof, if you still needed any, that Frederick Ashe painted the loft set. You were vague about that biography. You didn't want me to come here, because you knew those two paintings were in the Renfrew Coombe collection. Probably it told you so in the biography.' I turned to Coombe. 'Ones you actually bought legally?' I asked him.

'Of course,' he said gravely.

I returned my attention to Margaret. 'And I'll make a bet that the biography you said

305

you hunted out in London is in fact in your own library, at what you modestly call your cottage.' I held out my hand. 'May I have the key, please.'

'You may not.'

'It'll save me breaking in to collect the six for Mr Coombe.'

'They're not there. I told you—'

'Of course they're there. You told me you'd moved them, and I was able to tell Mr Coombe, quite convincingly, that they were safe in London.' I turned to him again. 'Were you convinced?'

He lifted his eyebrows. 'Completely.'

'So . . . your cottage is the one place they'd be, Margaret.' I waggled my fingers. 'The key, please.'

'You're not having it.'

I sighed. 'I can ask Mace to pull on all the lights. I can ask Coombe to get two of his men to carry you, if necessary, round the gallery, so that you can't help seeing every painting he's got. And then, Margaret, he wouldn't *dare* to let you stay alive.'

Furiously, she reached her hand into her bag, fumbled, and produced a set of keys.

'Thank you.' I looked at them. 'I'll use the Volvo.' It was a statement. 'And all I'll ask Mr Coombe to do is hold you here in the house, until the police arrive. It's them you'll have to convince.'

Panic caught her. 'But you can't—'

'I know, Margaret. You've heard so much about the little trick he's going to play on the police that he might decide it's safer to remove you, anyway. I'm sorry. A little worry won't hurt you.' I grinned at Coombe. 'Perhaps you'll be careful to keep her healthy, if only to offer some little morsel of comfort to them by handing her over.'

He clapped his palms together. A hundred or more paintings shuddered. But he was only expressing pleasure. 'I can't wait for them.'

'Fine,' I said. 'So we're all agreed? Then you can open the door, Mace.'

We trooped out in much the same order as when we'd arrived. I had a little difficulty walking straight, but Evelyn took my arm. Margaret did not take the other, though she walked beside me, her head up, a small defiant smile on her lips. She was still fighting.

I said to Coombe: 'Tomorrow afternoon I'll be back with the six paintings. You'd better make room for them in the gallery and start hanging the others somewhere near the front door.'

He nodded. Mace was frowning. He was not happy with the arrangement, though he didn't know why. Evelyn came with me to the car. 'Is that Aleric's?' she asked, noticing the bike.

'I've been using it.'

'You're too old for that sort of thing.'

'I'll bet I've got more experience than him.'
We stared at each other. She smiled. 'You should have been a solicitor, Tony.' It was her ultimate in compliments. She capped it by leaning forward and kissing me briefly on the corner of the mouth.

'Tomorrow,' I said.

'Yes.'

I drove away in the Volvo. The trip was uneventful, apart from the fact that I had to stop at three service stations to use their toilets. It's free, now, you know.

When I got home I managed to contact Detective Sergeant Dolan. When I told him I had his affidavit ready he said he'd be over in the morning.

And so he was. He was waiting for me when I got back from the bank.

I had been their first customer. I had cherished an expectation that the size of the cheques would at least raise an eyebrow. I had imagined that the deputy manager would have me in, to discuss investment. Even, perhaps, the manager. But . . . nothing. Not even the bat of an eyelid from the cashier.

That sort of money safely in his account gives a man confidence. I felt solidly comfortable when I dealt with the sergeant. We were in the kitchen, disposing of a pot of tea. He made no comment on the fact that we'd had to go round the back to get in.

I explained the situation to him in detail,

showed him the proof sketches on the back of the affidavit, and gave him the relative photos with the affirmations on their backs. Inside, I was laughing.

'Make it tomorrow,' I said.

'The day after. We'll need to rake in an art expert and so on.'

'Right. Now we'll go and pick up the paintings.'

'We?'

'I want you as a witness.'

What Dolan was a witness to was the fact that the complete set of eighty-one loft canvases, plus my original one, were there. But more important, to the fact that the Maurice Bellarmé biography was in Margaret's library. As it was. The paintings were printed, side by side, exactly as they had been in the gallery.

'So you'll need another warrant,' I told him.

'So it seems. But we already had our suspicions.'

'Of me,' I reminded him.

'That too.'

I collected together the relative six paintings and packed them carefully. Margaret had all the correct materials for packing paintings. Dolan took along the biography of Maurice Bellarmé. It was in French, but it was the pictures that mattered.

'You'll need a magnifier,' I said. 'For the initials.'

'Have to buy one.'

'I thought all detectives carried a large magnifying glass.'

'Ha!' he commented.

After lunch, I drove to pick up my wife. This time I was not even allowed to enter the house. Coombe stood in the open doorway, watching, whilst Paul Mace came out and opened up the package in the back of the Volvo. Each canvas received a searching examination. He used Margaret's magnifier. In the end, he raised his head and nodded. They were genuine Frederick Ashe paintings.

Coombe gave a bleak smile.

'Is it all right if I take my wife now?' I called.

'She's here.'

Evelyn came from the front door. She stood there a moment as though this was a special brand of fresh air, then she smiled and walked towards me.

I had another package, especially for her, inside the Volvo.

'What's this?'

'I popped round to see Aleric's latest girlfriend. She's about your size. I've borrowed her riding kit for you.'

'I'm expected to—'

'Yes. You'll love it. I can't take the Volvo, now can I! It'd be theft.' I handed Mace the bunch of keys. 'Tell Dr Dennis that I'm keeping the key to her cottage, until I've taken away the rest of my paintings. It'll be under the flower pot by the front door.'

He said he would do that. Everything was calm and civilized.

'When?' he asked.

'The police? Oh, I couldn't say. They don't confide in me. Tomorrow, perhaps, or the day after. You'll be prepared?'

'We're ready now.'

While we'd been talking, Evelyn had been climbing into the overtrousers, and trying to master the snaps on the jacket.

'I feel an absolute fool,' she said.

I caught a glimpse of Margaret at one of the windows upstairs. If she found it amusing, there was nothing in her expression to confirm it. I was reminded of Evelyn at her window. There was the same complete lack of emotion.

'All you've got to remember,' I told Evelyn, 'is that you lean with me. Don't try to lean against the bike.'

I supported the bike as she climbed on. Then we were away.

One advantage a bike has over a car is that it limits conversation. From time to time she shouted something, but inside the helmet I could make nothing of it. I made one unbroken run of it. My technique was now as good as it had ever been. No incorrect decisions, no hesitations . . . straight through.

She climbed stiffly to the ground, removed the helmet, and said calmly: 'I really enjoyed that.'

I laughed.

Two days later, Dolan visited us and told us what had happened. The police had arrived at Renfrew Coombe in a large contingent, headed by a superintendent. The police were not armed, though there was a wagon full of men in camouflaged battle jackets and berets, but with no weapons visible. They were not called into action.

The Superintendent told Mace he had a warrant to search the premises for six paintings, four of which were believed to be stolen. The leading group was politely invited inside. The main group of police dispersed themselves in a surrounding move-ment.

Coombe's six paintings had been displayed in the hall. The Superintendent stood and stared at them. The art expert examined them. In his hand he had six photographs with my signature on the back of each.

'These,' he said at last, 'are not the relevant paintings. They do not correspond with the photographs attested to by a Mr . . . er . . .' He turned them over. 'A Mr Anthony Hine.'

At this point there was a certain amount of aggressive movement, some of it violent. Coombe's men had been out at the front to consider the implications of the camouflaged jackets, and surrendered their weapons without argument.

Coombe, restrained by four large policemen, shouted: 'These are the paintings. I watched him sign the damned photographs.'

But the photographs I had attested to, and quite correctly because the paintings were, now, on Coombe's premises, were the six Terry Bascome had copied for me, from the loft set. He'd done a grand job. What it entails, this masking, is exposing your six prints under the enlarger with part of the printing paper masked off, so that it only exposes the bit you want. Then you reverse the masking, covering the portion you've just exposed, and print the other part you want. For the first run he had printed six picture frames from the set of pictures in Coombe's gallery, and for the second part of the job he had printed my six matching canvases, from the loft set. So he'd framed them, and they looked, at a superficial glance, as though they were prints of Coombe's own paintings. Which they weren't.

Remember the name. Terry Bascombe. Any time you need a special job doing.

The Superintendent was able to point out that, as the paintings reproduced in the six photographs were not on show anywhere he could see, it would be necessary to search deeper. This of course now included the gallery, and quite legally. It was part of the premises mentioned in the affidavit.

It was in the gallery that the art expert really came into his own. With a free run of the display, he trotted in ecstasy from one canvas to the other, discovering, quite apart from the ones they had come for, twenty-seven major works that had been given up as lost, having been stolen over a period of twenty years.

Charges were made, arrests were made. Coombe quivered in dissolution in his special chair.

There was an unexpected bonus. I had told Dolan about the episode of the white cross, and he'd passed it on to his superiors. On an inspiration, prompted by a complete lack of any sense of humour, the Superintendent had tried an experiment. He ordered the slabs on the terrace to be lifted.

For two days his men worked at it, and uncovered three skeletons and one decomposing corpse. The corpse still contained the bullet that had brought about its death, and the forensic experts later matched it to Mace's gun.

The trials are expected to last several months. The Superintendent has made much of his triumph on television, but I have seen no mention of Detective Sergeant Dolan.

That was six months ago. Aleric is now at home. He is working at this time in acrylics. I tell him I can now afford to send him to any art school of his choice, but at the moment he seems to want to remain at home. I never could understand him.

Evelyn intends to continue with her practice. This, I expected. I intend to continue as a professional photographer. This, she didn't. I am having a proper photo-lab built, with a reception area, and already I've engaged a secretary/receptionist and a lab assistant, this as Evelyn had suggested. Both are young women. Evelyn disapproves, of the lab assistant particularly. She believes this is not a proper profession for a young lady. I don't think I'll ever understand Evelyn either.

The four paintings from the collection found in the gallery have now been returned to the art galleries from which the thefts were made. But now they have genuine Frederick Ashes, in place of the Angelina Footes they originally owned. I wonder whether any of their acclaimed art experts have noticed the difference. I wonder whether Ashe should now be described as school of Angelina Foote, and whether it matters.

Unfortunately, this now leaves Renfrew Coombe as the legitimate owner of two genuine Frederick Ashes. But it'll be a long while before he'll be able to gloat on the fact.

I have kept only two, my original painting of the cottage with the morning sun, which after all was painted by my grandmother, and its mate from the loft batch, painted by my grandfather. I have them displayed side by side on the sitting-room wall, in their relative positions, Grannie's on the right. After all, she was the one who was left-handed.

The remaining seventy-four I have donated to the National Gallery. After much thought. For after all, my grandmother *was* dead before we got the canvases out of the house, so that they were legally part of the legacy to Grace Fielding. So I have no right to them. So I've given them away.

No right or not, I nevertheless listened carefully to the gentleman who came from the Home Office, and I made no protest. In view of my gift, it is hinted, I shall see my name in the next honours list. A CBE, or perhaps an OBE. Who am I to argue?

And that about wraps it up.

Oh, I nearly forgot. The second warrant was not used, because Dr Margaret Dennis was not at Coombe's house. He claimed she had given his men the slip, and got away. Maybe that is so. But perhaps his nerve went, and he didn't dare to allow her to speak to the police.

Wherever she is, she will never be able to utilize the expertise and world-wide acclaim she fought so hard to acquire.